LYSSA'S CALL
THE SENTIENCE WARS: ORIGINS – BOOK 4

BY JAMES S. AARON
& M. D. COOPER

JAMES S. AARON & M. D. COOPER

SPECIAL THANKS
Just in Time (JIT) & Beta Reads

Jim Dean
Lisa Richman
Gene Bryan
Scott Reid
Marti Panikkar
Gene Bryan
Manie Kilian
Timothy Van Oosterwyk Bruyn
Steven Blevins

The Aeon 14 Universe is Copyright ©
2010, 2017, 2018 M. D. Cooper

Lyssa's Call is Copyright © 2017, 2018
James S. Aaron & M. D. Cooper

Cover Art by Laércio Messias
Editing by Tee Ayer

Version 1.0.0

Aeon 14 & M. D. Cooper are registered trademarks of Michael Cooper
All rights reserved

THE SENTIENCE WARS: ORIGINS – LYSSA'S FLIGHT

TABLE OF CONTENTS

FOREWORD	5
PREVIOUSLY…	7
CHAPTER ONE	9
CHAPTER TWO	17
CHAPTER THREE	29
CHAPTER FOUR	37
CHAPTER FIVE	44
CHAPTER SIX	52
CHAPTER SEVEN	60
CHAPTER EIGHT	68
CHAPTER NINE	76
CHAPTER TEN	85
CHAPTER ELEVEN	94
CHAPTER TWELVE	102
CHAPTER THIRTEEN	111
CHAPTER FOURTEEN	119
CHAPTER FIFTEEN	126
CHAPTER SIXTEEN	135
CHAPTER SEVENTEEN	144
CHAPTER EIGHTEEN	157
CHAPTER NINETEEN	164
CHAPTER TWENTY	173
CHAPTER TWENTY-ONE	183
CHAPTER TWENTY-TWO	192
CHAPTER TWENTY-THREE	199
CHAPTER TWENTY-FOUR	207
CHAPTER TWENTY-FIVE	217
CHAPTER TWENTY-SIX	224
CHAPTER TWENTY-SEVEN	232
CHAPTER TWENTY-EIGHT	240
CHAPTER TWENTY-NINE	247
CHAPTER THIRTY	255
CHAPTER THIRTY-ONE	263

CHAPTER THIRTY-TWO	271
CHAPTER THIRTY-THREE	279
CHAPTER THIRTY-FOUR	288
CHAPTER THIRTY-FIVE	295
CHAPTER THIRTY-SIX	303
AFTERWORD	307
THE BOOKS OF AEON 14	311
ABOUT THE AUTHORS	315

FOREWORD

Without a doubt, I enjoyed reading James's first draft of this book as much as I'm certain you'll like this final version. It begins the work of tying together all the threads that have been left dangling on the way to Neptune, though it certainly pulls free a few more.

We've been aboard *Sunny Skies* for some time. Floating through the central corridor, watching drones remove cargo from the hold, walking from room to room in the habitation ring.

In some respects, *Sunny Skies* feels like home to me. If James and I have done our jobs well, it may have taken on the same quality for you as well.

Though the home is still there, the family does not always remain.

After a long journey across a far more unruly Sol System, the growing crew aboard *Sunny Skies* is finally on the final stretch of their mission.

Just a slingshot around Uranus, and then a week or so of coasting toward Neptune before they begin the deceleration burns.

And the goal? For Lyssa to join the other AIs at Neptune, which means she'll leave her home and family for the next phase of her life.

Michael Cooper
Danvers, MA 2018

PREVIOUSLY...

In the last three books, we've followed Andy, Lyssa, and *Sunny Skies* as it traveled to Cruithne, Mars 1, Ceres, Clinic 46, The Cho, and finally Europa. What started as a transport job with the added complication of implanting a Sentient AI in Andy Sykes' brain has become a struggle to help free sentient AI throughout Sol.

While at The Cho—the multi-ring orbital habitat encircling Callisto—Andy and Lyssa received a directive from Xander, a shard of an advanced, multi-nodal AI to acquire a ship and bring it with them to Proteus, the innermost moon of Neptune.

But Xander did not want just any ship; he required one of Heartbridge's massive hospital ships—which meant Andy and the crew had to steal it.

In the ensuing attack at Europa, the team managed to secure the *Resolute Charity* a massive Heartbridge Corporation hospital dreadnought, where they also confronted Cal Kraft, the operative who had been pursuing them for so long.

Onboard the *Resolute Charity*, they managed to extract the AI Kylan from Petral's mind. Eventually they secured and cleared the ship, but Kraft escaped. Brit took off in pursuit.

Andy, however could not dally, and Lyssa set the *Resolute Charity* on the first leg of its journey toward Neptune, with *Sunny Skies* following behind.

On High Terra, Jirl Gallagher, assistant to Heartbridge power broker Arla Reed, is learning just how deep the company's tendrils reach, and deciding she can no longer be part of the Weapon Born SAI program.

As our story opens, Andy and Lyssa are aboard the *Resolute Charity* while the rest of the crew—including Cara, Tim, Fran, Fugia, Petral, Senator May, and her guardian Harl Nines—are back aboard *Sunny Skies,* wrapping up wounds and deciding the best way to get the two ships out of the Jovian Combine and deep into OuterSol.

Now to just to while away the long weeks before they reach Neptune….

CHAPTER ONE

STELLAR DATE: 10.05.2981 (Adjusted Years)
LOCATION: Carville Terminal, Raleigh
REGION: High Terra, Earth, Terran Hegemony, InnerSol

Jirl Gallagher couldn't shake the feeling that everything was going to explode. The world felt like a trigger pull caught in slow-motion. When the feeling became too much, she had to get out of the Heartbridge headquarters, away from the false-white ceramic and gleaming steel, away from the people with vacant faces and artificial smiles.

Carterville Terminal on the outer edge of Raleigh was as far from the Heartbridge spire as Jirl could venture on her lunch break and still make it back before anyone noticed she had been gone. Along with the feeling of dread, she'd found herself drawn to *real* people. People who weren't Heartbridge. People who were talking, laughing, crying, rushing to work or home or off High Terra altogether.

Her boss, Arla Reed, could reach her whenever she wanted. No, the people Jirl had to worry about were the other assistants and office workers who noted her comings and goings and shared that information with outside agencies.

As Arla's surrogate, Jirl's activities were watched more closely than many of the Heartbridge Board members. For better or worse, Jirl's daily comings and goings occupied a whole cadre of corporate spies. And, if those spies thought she was cracking, they would look for a wedge to split her completely.

What would they think if they followed her down to one of the middle-class space ports on the edge of the city, a place where families boarded shuttles and sometimes even smaller craft to take them to waiting liners, or to Luna? She found it comforting that most of the people she saw here had hopeful looks on their faces. They seemed excited about life, about their journeys, or caught up in the minutiae of managing small children.

If she had tried to explain her desire to come here to Arla, she imagined the tall woman humoring her with a look of light disgust before asking, "Who even has children anymore?"

Of course, Arla would forget that Jirl had a son named Bry, that she had chosen to give birth to him as naturally as possible. Jirl was the last person to pretend she was better than someone else because she had procreated—the truth was, she had pursued motherhood out of selfish reasons. She had thought a baby would help her feel less alone. She had wanted to feel *human*.

The endless flow of people walking past the bench where she sat reminded her that she wasn't alone—even if she felt that way. She let her gaze wander from face to face, many lost in their Links but some holding audible conversations, adjusting clothing, struggling with luggage.

Porter drones rolled past at regular intervals, beeping sedately as they wound between groups that refused to move. Some carried hapless looking people. Being one of the poorer areas in Raleigh, there weren't many people with obvious augments.

That absence meant those who were modded stood out all the more. Such as the woman who walked past with heavily muscled legs, followed not much later by a young man with a brilliant red mohawk that glittered and shifted, apparently responding to the colors around him.

Jirl had a hard time reconciling the thought of Bry as a baby and toddler with the fifteen-year-old he had become. Would he ever come home with something like that mohawk on his head? Would she tell him what she really thought, or instead praise his fearlessness?

I might actually be pleased by that, Jirl thought. *He'd be living his life, digging in, not just floating like me.*

She was gathering the remnants of her lunch, ready to leave for the maglev station, when a secure Link connection tickled her thoughts. Jirl checked the request and wasn't surprised to find it was Colonel Yarnes of the Terran Space Force. She glanced around without meaning to, wondering if any office spies might be watching her for the tell-tale signs of a Link conversation. No one paid her any attention.

Jirl smiled to herself. She was just the assistant of a powerful woman. She wasn't important. Yarnes didn't care about *her*, only about what she might make available to him.

<Hello, Colonel,> she answered. <What can I do for you?>

<What are you doing?> he asked.

Jirl frowned, uncertain how to interpret the question. He almost sounded flirtatious. But then, why wouldn't he be? He wanted something from her.

She took stock of her current emotion, which she judged as something above a light depression, and made herself sit up straighter, smiling at a man in front of her who quickly glanced away in surprise. Jirl took a deep breath.

<*I'm sitting on a bench in the Carterville transfer station.*>

<*Carterville.*> Yarnes paused for a moment. <*That's South Raleigh, isn't it?*>

<*That's what the signs say.*>

<*Are you going somewhere?*> he asked.

<*No. I'm just sitting for a while during a break. It's relaxing to watch all the people coming and going.*>

<*Jirl Gallagher is a people watcher.*>

Jirl couldn't help a small smile. <*It's what I do most of the time.*>

Yarnes chuckled. <*Watch them and read their thoughts. You know, when I first met you, I thought you had some kind of high-end*

Link hacking set-up. You seemed to know what everyone in the room was going to say before they talked.>

<That's not hard with TSF officers.>

Yarnes laughed warmly. <Why's that?>

<Temper aggression with vanity and you can guess most military leadership's response to a situation.>

<I thought you were going to say nationalism.>

<That's the vanity. You think you're special.>

<And the Protectorate is the same way?>

Did he want to know about her conversations with the Marsian general Moira Kade on the Weapon Born project? He could just ask about the Heartbridge demonstration with the Marsian Protectorate. It had been identical to the attack test carried out for the Terran Space Force four months ago. Both governments had placed orders for Weapon Born drones.

Both governments had already taken their initial deliveries and she wondered if there was now a problem. Of course, Jirl would not be the first point of contact for technical support. She was saved a reply when Yarnes continued on without her response.

<I've been thinking about the ship you lost....>

<We have a lot of ships, Colonel,> she said, playing coy. <It's inevitable that a few might become lost.>

<I should say stolen then. You do lose more ships than any of the other companies I work with, but I think it's safe to say Heartbridge is up to more things than most companies. I was thinking about the Resolute Charity. I've been reviewing the report logs the JSF quarantined before they were cut off. And that was a feat in itself—cutting them off. I don't think even your local AI could preclude the JSF from accessing their own systems. Whoever took control of that ship has capability we haven't seen before.>

Or he might be suggesting a ploy between Heartbridge and the Jovian Space Force? Jirl decided to push back.

<Did you want to set up a meeting with Arla, Colonel? I'm probably not the best person to talk with about these matters.>

He laughed. <I think you're the only person to talk with about these matters, Jirl.>

<You should know I don't respond well to flattery.>

Yarnes paused. <I have a reason for this Link,> he said, a note of seriousness entering his voice.

<Oh?>

<Have you looked into the entity I mentioned the last time we talked?>

<You mean Alexander, the multi-nodal AI you mentioned so mysteriously? Yes. I have.>

Every mention of the name went back to an organization called the Psion Group, and had ended there. Jirl had found alternate research under another company called 'Psion' that seemed too close to not be a coincidence but had, in the end, offered equally little information. Psion had a history of AI development in support of colony ships that appeared to go back nearly five hundred years. But they hadn't tried to sell anything that she could find, and there were no recorded incidents related to tech they had developed. Unlike other companies whose AIs escaped containment or involved semi-legal frameworks as a foundation—like the facility on Object 8221, which would remain legally 'ownerless' once the TSF finally let it go.

<Your silence makes me think you found something,> Yarnes said.

<That's not completely true. There are current communication trails mentioning something in OuterSol calling itself Alexander. Whether that's a group, company, or person, I don't know.>

<What if I made it all up just to get a rise out of you?> he asked.

<Then I would be angry that you had wasted my time and I probably would trust you less than I already do.>

<So you trust me a little bit, then?>

<Have you given me reason not to?> Jirl asked.

<I don't think so,> Yarnes answered, still serious. <I suppose time will tell. If you looked into the Psion Group, I imagine you hit a dead end. Did you push on your scientists who worked for them before they came to Heartbridge? I think one of them recently came back under your attention, didn't she?>

Now how would he know that? Jirl couldn't help frowning at the passing crowd. Did Yarnes have a spy in Heartbridge? Would her continued conversations with him be considered espionage someday? She had to be careful. She had Bry to worry about.

<I don't know what you're talking about,> she said, wanting him to say more.

<Here's the thing about multi-nodal AI,> he said, <and why they're on the verge of being made illegal. They reach a point where it seems to be inevitable that they see themselves as gods. Personally, I think that's a human failure. We can't create a being that doesn't ultimately succumb to the same megalomania that plagues all people who think they're special.>

<If that were the case,> Jirl said, <I would think there would be actual research evidence on different types that had been developed.>

<Of course there is.>

His crumbs of information made her suspicious. <You're speaking as if all this is not conjecture. Do you have data about Alexander you can share? I'm sure if the TSF is interested in a joint research project, that's something we can explore.>

His voice grew more intense. <I'm not talking about research, Ms. Gallagher. I'm talking about a threat that already exists.>

Why is he telling me about this? Why has he mentioned this Alexander AI at all? Jirl felt like she was being burdened with a weight she hadn't chosen to carry.

<All right,> she said, waiting for him to continue. Jirl ran through different questions that might get him to say why he wanted her to know this information. Why tell Heartbridge?

He had started by probing her about the fleet in Jovian Combine space. Was he suggesting the fleet was in danger from this AI?

She assessed Yarnes as reasonably ambitious. She didn't expect he would just give away information without a plan to get something in return.

Jirl was running out of time; Arla would be asking where she was in a few minutes.

When Yarnes hadn't answered, she said, <*I enjoy talking with you, Colonel, but if you want something from me, I need you to be more clear with your request.*>

Yarnes laughed. <*There it is. That's why we all like you, Jirl. You should have had a career in the military.*>

The warmth in his voice made her blush despite herself.

<*You still haven't answered my question.*>

<*Since I was assigned to Weapons Acquisition, I've been made aware of other threats created by this new tech both Terra and Mars have been working to acquire. AI is only one of those tools. But anything we see, we have to expect it's been available in the private sector first. There are plenty of failures out there, warped, dangerous things still hanging around or abandoned because no one could sell them to a government with the resources to pay.*>

He sounded tired. Listening to the words, Jirl supposed they sounded sinister. The world was full of threats.

<*I suggest you dig deeper into the Psion Group. The people doing this all know each other. Where was Hari Jickson before he came to Heartbridge? Have you ever looked into that?*>

<*I can always pull his employment file.*>

<*I think you should do that, Jirl. I think we need to find out if there are other players out there. You have the access to this information, I don't. You may have found only a small amount of traffic about Alexander. Well, I'll tell you that we're seeing increasing amounts of communication. There's a message being passed between sentient AIs, and once they read it, they malfunction.*

It has a nearly hundred percent attack success rate. If they don't try to leave whatever role they have, they stop performing their functions. Your Weapon Born product seems to be the only thing not affected right now.>

<I haven't heard anything about this.>

<It's going to break. This Alexander launched an attack on our artificial intelligence capabilities. No one knows how to stop it right now and the virus is spreading.>

<Virus?> Jirl mused. *You mean freedom?*

<Check into how many companies are reporting malfunctioning AIs. So-called 'sentient' systems. This is a bigger problem than anyone is talking about.>

And the TSF isn't going to buy a sentient AI system if they're all vulnerable to failure.

Even if he didn't say it, the implication was obvious.

CHAPTER TWO

STELLAR DATE: 10.05.2981 (Adjusted Years)
LOCATION: *Sunny Skies*
REGION: Departing Jupiter, Jovian Combine, OuterSol

Cara watched as Fran stood with her arms crossed staring into the holodisplay. The glowing models of *Sunny Skies* and the *Resolute Charity* reflected in the woman's face, filling her augmented eyes with lively sparks.

"What we have here is an engineering problem," Fran said, glancing at Cara. "Which, in my opinion, is the *best* kind of problem to have."

"I thought we didn't have any more problems," Cara said from the communications console.

Fran gave her a laugh, one Cara recognized as condescending in a caring sort of way. "Our worries end when we're dead, my dear."

"I thought *you* made up the name *Worry's End*," Cara said, referring to the actual registry entry for *Sunny Skies*, which Fran had created when they escaped Cruithne Station. Cara blinked, wondering what other references Fran might have been using that flew right over her head.

"Sure," Fran said, giving her a sly smile. "You can believe that if you want to."

Cara rolled her eyes. "If being dead is where you got the name, it's more depressing than I thought."

"What one person calls depressing, another calls reality. The name fit the need, and it's served us all right, don't you think?" She reached into the holodisplay to manipulate the glowing models, placing *Sunny Skies* alongside the *Resolute Charity* in various positions.

Cara and Fran were alone on the command deck. Cara's dad was still on the *Resolute Charity*, while Petral, Fugia, May and Harl were all in their respective rooms using comm links before the distance from the Cho grew too great for instantaneous communication. Cara couldn't listen in on their conversations but could monitor the signals passing through the ship's antenna array.

"I guess so," Cara said. "I'm going to keep using *Sunny Skies*."

"Weren't you anyway?"

"Yeah."

"Calling something a different word doesn't change what it is, Cara," Fran said, sliding Cara a serious glance. "Let's focus on this. Start looking for mistakes I'm making."

"You don't make mistakes," Cara said.

"If only that were true." Fran raised her voice slightly, "Lyssa, you listening?"

The AI's voice emerged from the overhead speaker for Cara's benefit, since she couldn't communicate via Link. "I'm here," Lyssa said, the speakers making her sound far away.

"Thank you," Fran said, turning her full attention on the holodisplay.

Leaving the ships in place, Fran traced distances between them with her fingers, trailing lines as thin as spidersilk connecting the two ships. Numbers marked each line, showing the requirements to build the connecting structure between the ships, Cara supposed.

She liked it when Fran teased her this way because the woman always seemed to push her to be better without putting her down. Cara had observed Fran's tendency to make things better, even when it came to Cara's dad. She figured the flip side of Fran's nature was that she might never be satisfied, which meant Fran was going to leave someday. But everyone left eventually, didn't they?

"Since you aren't going to ask me what our engineering problem is," Fran said. "I guess I'll tell you. But only because I'm in a hurry and I want to be able to talk about this while I work."

"Okay," Cara said.

"The engines on the *Resolute Charity* have an order of magnitude more thrust capacity than our little *Sunny Skies*. Even though she masses much more, it still means she's going to leave us in the dust unless we find a way to attach *Sunny Skies* to her. That would seem easy, but we have the problem of the habitat ring, which we would like to keep spinning."

"Couldn't we ask Lyssa to figure it out?"

"Where's the fun in that? Besides, I already planned on asking Lyssa to stress-test my options once I get them figured out."

"Wouldn't the easiest way be to stack *Sunny Skies* on top of the *Resolute Charity*, end to nose?" Cara asked, leaving her console to walk closer to the holodisplay.

"I was thinking about that, but we lose *Sunny Skies'* engines that way. And it might be nice to have them in a pinch. The thing about lining us up side-by-side is the strain that would put on any sort of support system we might build. And the time it will take to build that support system. And the material we would need."

From the overhead speakers, Lyssa said, "I believe I can find sufficient material on the *Resolute Charity*. The ship is equipped with a surprising amount of repair supplies that could be manipulated for this purpose, including spare sections of outer support struts."

"That's some good news for once," Fran said.

The *Resolute Charity* was basically a series of drums mounted horizontally on a central axle, each spinning independently to create internal gravity for the hospital and clinic sections. The nose section—and engines in the rear—

capped the drums, with external support struts running the length of the ship.

Fran moved the two models closer together, placing the *Sunny Skies* alongside the *Resolute Charity*'s stern, the small ship's engines a hair further aft than the hospital ship's. She rotated the freighter so that its docking mounts faced the *Resolute Charity*'s, while leaving enough room for *Sunny Skies'* habitat ring to spin.

"What do you think about that?" Fran asked Lyssa.

"That looks like the easiest way to do it," the AI said. "You seem to already have this information available."

"I keep it in my brain alongside the sarcasm," Fran said dryly. "Will the material we have available withstand acceleration tests? Can you assess the strain with *Resolute Charity* and *Sunny Skies* engines combined?"

Watching Lyssa and Fran work together filled Cara with a sense of safety. She wished she had more to contribute.

"Maximizing placement to allow for a passage between the two ships will be a challenge," Lyssa said.

"Now you're getting fancy. All I want the ships to do is not break apart and destroy each other."

"I believe a solution that satisfies crew needs and structural integrity is possible. I'm looking for other designs in the database."

Fran snorted. "Crew needs. What do you mean by that?"

"I assume you would like to see Andy during the trip," Lyssa said, in a tone that made Cara imagine a raised eyebrow.

Cara stole a glance at Fran and found her rolling her eyes, chuckling.

"*Why* would you think that?" Fran asked. "If he wants to come over here, he can get in a shuttle and make the trip. We don't need a love-bridge adding complexity to our design."

"There *are* safety considerations as well," Lyssa said. "I believe the option of a shuttle is always a good backup in the event of an emergency, but I may need faster ways to move support drones between the two ships. Maybe I should have suggested this feature when Cara wasn't here."

"Why not?" Cara asked.

"Because Fran doesn't want to prioritize her personal needs over solving this problem," Lyssa explained.

"Oh, I prioritize my needs," Fran said, raising her eyebrows. "Trust me. But in this case, I'm more concerned about how much time we have versus the integrity of the design. The 'love tunnel' is secondary."

"Maintenance access bridge," Lyssa corrected.

"Nope, it's the 'love tunnel'," Fran said. "No changing it now."

Cara jammed her fist against her lips to keep from laughing. She didn't want Fran to notice that she understood the joke. She glanced at the engineer and saw Fran was still focused on her design.

"Fine," Lyssa said. The holodisplay shifted, showing the two models side-by-side with their engines on an even line. Support struts linked the two ships' docking mounts forming a series of X shapes. Additional anchoring lines ran out to other docking mounts on the *Resolute Charity*. Next a middle connector running from *Sunny Skies'* main cargo bay to the engineering section of the *Resolute Charity*. "This design will serve our purpose."

"How long do you need to build it?" Fran asked.

"I estimate twenty hours."

"So, our trip takes a hundred and one days now instead of a hundred?"

"The combined thrust of both ships will increase acceleration by thirty percent," Lyssa said. "Still, I estimate at least ninety days travel based on our transfer maneuver at Uranus."

"I love it when you talk orbital mechanics," Fran said. "Don't stop."

Cara snorted.

"Stop laughing at my jokes, Cara," Fran said, focus still on the display. "Your father isn't going to let us spend time together."

"I'm not laughing," Cara protested.

"I suppose you can laugh. But don't repeat anything for another two years, at least."

"I promise," Cara said, trying not to giggle again.

Fran's gaze didn't leave her work. Where Fran always seemed to focus inwardly, Petral would be looking at Cara to gauge her response. Cara's mom probably wouldn't have made a joke at all.

The thought of her mom made Cara glance at the communications console again. They were still within range of most transmissions from the Cho, Ganymede and Europa, as well as the rest of the ship traffic throughout the Jovian Combine. She couldn't help checking the regular ship's channels for a message, and then the rest of the general spectrum for some signal that might have been aimed at the ship if her mother were trying to contact them covertly.

In truth, Brit would probably use the Link directly to her dad, but Cara had harbored a secret fantasy that she might discover some distress signal her mom had sent through other means. She hated the spark of hope she felt every time she sat down at the console and scanned the spectrum.

This time wouldn't be any different than before. Her mom wouldn't ask them for help. If she contacted them at all, it would only be after she had captured or killed Cal Kraft. That was her mom's strength: a single-mindedness that shut out everything else until the mission was accomplished. It was her dad's weakness that he cared too much to think that way.

But was it a weakness? A lot of people would think it weak, but he was strong when it mattered. By most considerations, her dad was as pragmatic as any spacer. He had killed people. He had nearly killed himself to get them to Cruithne before all this started.

Cara remembered his face when he'd come inside the ship after the debris field had punched his EV suit full of holes—puncturing his arms, legs and abdomen near his belly button—looking drawn and angry, as if the world just wouldn't stop hammering on him. Yet he'd smiled when the airlock opened and laid eyes on Cara and Tim—before he'd fallen inside and they'd caught him.

That was how she remembered it. They'd struggled to get him up to the autodoc and then it had seemed like things would be okay for a while. Then the engines had failed...and here they were.

Watching Fran, Cara knew things could certainly be worse. Her dad hadn't told her how much money he'd made on Cruithne, but that stress seemed to have lessened. Something had changed between him and Lyssa in the last twenty hours as well, and the trip to Proteus seemed to actually fill her dad with excitement more than dread.

"I'm going to check on Tim," Cara told Fran, who nodded absently, still focused on Lyssa's proposed design.

Cara grabbed her headset from on top of her console and slipped it over her ears. She played the white noise of the broadcast spectrum outside the ship as she left the command deck for Tim's room.

In the two days since their mom had left, their dad had stayed on the *Resolute Charity* taking care of small repair jobs that Lyssa and her growing drone army couldn't handle. Unfortunately, that seemed to consist mostly of clearing bodies of dead crew and pirates. Her dad hadn't admitted to the task until Cara had overheard him and Lyssa discussing the removal of a dead man from an access tunnel. Lyssa had been focused on the facts of the task and had asked why they 'Simply couldn't cut the body in half?'

Her dad had explained the mess that would make in the tunnel and how, yes, they *could* replace the plas panels, but that he didn't want to deal with carrying body parts to the reclamation system one piece at a time.

"Is the ship going to be haunted?" Cara had asked.

"Cara!" her dad had shouted. "You aren't supposed to be listening to this."

"I can't help it."

"Well, I'm trying not to end up haunted for the rest of my life, which is another reason not to go cutting people into pieces."

He did his best to clothe fatalism in humor, she was figuring out, the same energy that had powered his smile for her and Tim after the debris field nearly tore him apart. Something he said he got from their Grandpa Charlie back on Earth. Grandpa Charlie had never been implanted with a Link. Not that long ago, Cara couldn't believe anyone would choose to cut themselves off from the network that joined all the adults in her life.

Cara used to daydream about the day she turned eighteen and was old enough for her own Link surgery. Now that she had seen her dad living with an AI in his mind, she wasn't sure she wanted any of that. She adjusted the headset, appreciating the fact that she could choose to take it off whenever she wanted and keep herself alone with her thoughts.

She found Tim in his room, sitting on the deck with their Corgi puppy Em lying across his lap. Em already looked bigger than he had three days ago. He lifted his head and perked his ears up as Cara walked through the door. A book with a red cover lay open on the deck next to Tim. It was the

Collected Poems of Emily Dickinson, and he had memorized a surprising number of the small, spidery lines on its pages. Tim was still as inward-focused as the day he'd woken up on the Cho, and his single-minded attention to things like the book, or Em, or seemingly nothing at all, continued to worry Cara. He was nothing like the impatient, whiny ten-year-old he had been just a week before. He also didn't seem to care that their mom had chosen to leave them again.

"What are you doing?" Cara asked, trying to keep her voice gentle.

She wasn't sure yet how being responsible for Tim made her feel. Was it a chore or her duty? Her dad would call it her duty, and he had modeled caring for others enough that she understood the necessity. She was as responsible for Tim as her dad was for her. There was no changing the fact that something in Tim had broken while he was at Clinic 46 and the new version of him was *fragile*.

Tim looked up from where he had been stroking Em's back and shrugged. "Sitting."

Cara leaned against the edge of the doorway. "Sitting doing what?"

"Sitting here with Em."

"What are you thinking about?"

Tim frowned. "How soft his fur is and how everyone smiles at him."

"He does have that effect on people." She sighed, wishing she knew the right words to bring back a little bit of the old Tim. Maybe this was how he was going to turn out, anyway? He was only ten. And she had been annoyed by him all the time. Now she was just—disappointed and worried. She wished her dad was done with the work on the *Resolute Charity*.

"Do you want to talk to Dad?" she asked.

Tim shook his head. "Does he want to talk to me?"

"He always wants to talk to you."

"He's busy."

"How about I call him? I'll use my headset."

"No!" Tim shouted, startling Em. The puppy hopped upright, ears straight, and stared into the corridor behind Cara. Tim pulled him into his chest. "Sorry, Em."

Cara took a deep breath, forcing herself to remain calm.

"I think Dad would love to hear from us, Tim. He gets lonely over there. The last time I talked to him, he said he couldn't wait to be done."

Tim petted Em slowly, gaze fixed on the floor. "When did you talk to him?"

Cara shrugged. "I don't know. An hour ago."

"Then you already bothered him. I don't want to bother him." Despite having shouted "No!" only moments before, Tim had already fallen back into listlessness. Em whimpered and settled back down across his lap, higher this time so his head lay against Tim's stomach.

"Bye, Cara," Tim said.

She stared at him.

"I'm not going anywhere," she said.

Cara's earlier desire to protect him was overcome by the urge to drag him out of the room. The problem was, she didn't know what she would do after that. She couldn't take him to anyone. Fran was busy and there was no telling what Fugia might do. The hacker didn't seem to be working on anything explosive today, so Fugia hopefully wouldn't ask Tim to hold ignition material like she'd done in the past.

"Whatever," Cara said, sighing with resignation. "It will be time to sleep soon. Are you going to get yourself ready for bed?"

"Yeah. I will." He didn't look at her.

Cara left the room and stood in the hallway, glaring through his doorway. Em watched her, one ear straight. When

Tim didn't look after her, she shook her head angrily and stomped away, frustration tensing her shoulders.

In her room, she sat on her bed for a while before digging her pulse pistol from where she kept it hidden under the mattress. She turned the weapon in her hands, careful to keep it pointed away from herself at all times like her dad had taught her. She realized she was aiming at the doorway and turned to point at a bulkhead instead.

For a heartbeat, she turned off the safety and let her finger hover over the trigger, enjoying the weight of the weapon in her hand. She remembered the fight in Cruithne, thinking of Karcher crouched behind a pile of rubble as he calmly chose targets and squeezed his rifle's trigger, the recoil barely moving his shoulder.

Karcher had still died, though. She couldn't forget that. The weapon wasn't going to solve her problems; it was just a tool, like one of Lyssa's drones.

Cara slid the safety back into place and returned the pistol to its hiding spot. She yawned and checked the time, surprised to find it was an hour past their bedtime.

Dad hadn't called to remind them, which meant he must have been busy with Fran's new plan. It was easy to lose track of time on the ship, especially if Fran was going to work until a job was done. Before Cruithne, her dad had kept them on a fairly strict sleep cycle. Everything had been out of order since then.

Cara thought about checking on Tim again and then decided against it. Struggling with him to do anything was like fighting with a wet towel. He would go to bed eventually when Em fell asleep, and the puppy slept all the time.

She went into her lavatory and stared at herself in the mirror as she brushed her teeth, then pulled her hair back so she could spit in the sink.

Sliding into her bunk, she lay with the headset on, staring at the grey bulkhead stretching above her. She wondered what her mom was doing right then, if she was still on the Cho or had already gone somewhere else.

It hadn't been that long, after all, and she was still close enough that they could have talked in real time. But Brit probably wouldn't call, and Cara hadn't said very nice things to her the last time they had talked. Wasn't it her mom's job to worry about her, not the other way around?

Waves of white noise lapped at her ears from the EM spectrum as she imagined her mom on the Cho, lost in a crowd of thousands, remembering the packed streets of the medical district where they had taken Tim. Other tones bleeped and sparked in the background and Cara imagined small ships dancing across an ocean until she finally fell asleep.

CHAPTER THREE

STELLAR DATE: 10.05.2981 (Adjusted Years)
LOCATION: HMS *Resolute Charity*
REGION: Departing Jupiter, Jovian Combine, OuterSol

Using a mix of the combat drones from Clinic 46—which Lyssa had come to think of as her Flight—and several heavy EV maintenance drones from the *Resolute Charity*, she brought *Sunny Skies* into a matched velocity with the larger ship while using other drones to place the initial connecting struts.

The maneuver was similar to docking but required several simultaneous welding actions between the two hulls. Between Lyssa's projections and Fran's experience, the operation should go smoothly, barring any unexpected shifts in balance between the two ships.

With drones holding struts in place while others waited at the weld points, Lyssa adjusted relative motion between the ships one last time.

<Are you going to do it, already?> Fran asked.

<She's being careful,> Andy said. <We've only got one chance at this.>

<We've got all kind of chances. If she bends a strut, we'll make another one.>

<What if one of the struts punctures the hull and explosive decompression sets the habitat ring spinning into the *Resolute Charity*?> Andy asked.

<You really need to curb that pessimism, buddy.>

<I haven't had anything else to think about over here.>

<Lyssa says she's going to build us a love tunnel so I can give you other things to think about.>

<Love tunnel? You mean the access bridge?>

<Tomato, tomah-to.>

<I'm ready,> Lyssa interjected. She didn't wait for a response as the two ships' relative delta-v reached zero. <Executing.>

Four drones made the welds on either foot of the X connecting the two ships. With the first strut in place, Lyssa quickly moved to add more before any cascading failure could affect her work.

She monitored the operation from hundreds of points of view at once, across the drones and internal sensors in both ships. Andy's heartbeat also registered in the back of her mind, racing when she announced the start of the procedure and then calming down as he watched her work.

<Fifty percent complete,> Lyssa announced. <I don't see any indications of increased strain. Fortunately, Sunny Skies has low enough relative mass that once we synced its velocity with Resolute Charity, the rest is a matter of safe tolerances.>

Fran gave a short laugh. <Now you're just repeating what I already said so you can sound smart.>

<I don't have to sound smart,> Lyssa said.

<And cocky, too. I like it. Andy, are you hearing this?>

<We're looking good,> Andy said, ignoring the quip. <Looks like Resolute Charity's engines picked up the extra weight with no problems. Now we bring the two drive systems in line and everything should be set.>

<Working on it now,> Lyssa said.

With the final support struts placed to Fran's satisfaction, and the two drive systems registering alignment for a mass-balanced thrust, Lyssa ran through the other major systems in each ship, checking for anomalies or failures that the additional mass might have created. Everything seemed to be working to plan.

<What's the protocol for joining two ships into one?> Andy asked. <Do we have to come up with a new name for our monster?>

<*You're the one who busted pirates for the Terran Space Force,*> Fran said. <*You tell me. Half the ships around Cruithne are slapped together from multiple hunks of junk. I think it will be easier for us to just refer to each ship individually. If we get into a situation where we need to identify ourselves, we can use Resolute Charity since its mass signature may actually hide* Sunny Skies.>

<*When Heartbridge comes after us, I don't think it's going to matter what name we use.*>

<*You make that sound like a sure thing.*>

<*You think they're going to let this slide? If we were in InnerSol, we'd be surrounded by every privateer in the vicinity. I think the only thing that saved us from the Jovian Space Force coming after us was Lyssa's stunt with their fuel suppliers. They're probably too busy dealing with internal conflict and emergency response right now.*>

<*I believe that's true,*> Lyssa said. <*I didn't bother to forecast the long-term effects of manipulating their fuel market, but it seems to be complete chaos.*>

<*You completely wrecked them,*> Fran said. <*Which is good for us. We can hide inside chaos for a while.*>

<*How long until we can bring both engine systems up to max thrust?*> Andy asked. <*I'd like to put as much distance between us and the chaos as possible. We're still within range of anyone who decides to follow.*>

<*Give me another thirty minutes to evaluate everything,*> Lyssa said. <*Then we can burn.*>

<*I like the sound of that. I'll do a final check on the astrogation plan.*>

Lyssa shifted her attention back to the sensor arrays throughout both ships, re-checking everything prior to the burn. It was surprising to her how quickly Andy had come to trust her oversight of tasks that he never would have delegated before. So much had changed in just a week. When she checked back on him ten minutes later, she found him reviewing diagnostics on *Sunny Skies* via a remote connection.

Lyssa considered telling Andy she had already verified *Sunny Skies* for pre-burn clearance but found herself watching him instead. Just a few days ago, he had told her she was family now, and she didn't fully understand what that meant. She didn't understand how the statement made her feel; if it meant anything, or if he had simply been caught up in the excitement of having survived. Why didn't he blame her for the danger she'd brought on his real family?

The question surprised Lyssa. Shouldn't she believe him when he said he cared about her? She hadn't observed Andy lying to anyone else.

Even now, as he simultaneously checked the star charts and ticked off drive system status, he operated out of an act of love. He cared about all of them. He demonstrated that every day.

So why couldn't she believe him? Since they had saved Tim from Clinic 46, the memory of the imaging room—where Tim's mind had been copied to a Weapon Born seed—had hung in her mind like a threat, taunting her. She'd recognized the place, or a place like it. She knew that, but the information didn't come to her as clearly as something she definitely remembered or wanted to research.

This was one of the many times she wished she could ask Dr. Hari Jickson how her memory worked precisely. In some cases, her perfect recall suggested the data storage of an NSAI, while the flashes of the imaging room from the perspective of being restrained in the bed floated like smoke.

"Lyssa?" Cara asked. "Are you there?"

Cara's voice pulled Lyssa from her thoughts. "Yes," Lyssa said, realizing she was reaching Cara through the headset that approximated audio from a Link connection.

"Are you busy?"

"I'm always busy."

"Are you really?"

Lyssa considered the question. "By your father's standards, I'm busy."

"I can't sleep."

"We're going to burn soon. The acceleration will help you sleep."

"Maybe. My head won't stop spinning."

"You mean you can't stop thinking about something?"

"Sort of." Cara sighed. "I guess it would make sense if I couldn't stop wondering about where Mom is. But that's not it."

For a second, Lyssa felt like she was playing the high school simulator again. She needed to read between the lines to what Cara was really asking.

"What is it?" she asked, choosing one of the game's neutral responses.

"Do you sleep?" Cara asked.

"Me? No."

"You never turn off your mind? How do you deal with that? When do you rest?"

"I was asleep before I woke up with your dad. Since then, there's been too much to keep me busy."

"So you never dream, then."

"I have—daydreams, maybe."

"Daydreams?" Cara asked, sounding a little more awake. "What do you daydream about?"

From the environmental sensors in Cara's room, Lyssa could tell she wavered on the edge of sleep. Andy would have wanted her to sleep rather than being kept up with stories, she was certain. She wondered if she should tell Andy that Cara was having a hard time sleeping, but she was also intrigued by the question. So many images flashed through her mind on what seemed a continuous basis that she wasn't sure what was a daydream and what was processed information.

"I see two things," Lyssa said. "The first is an ocean."

"What kind of ocean?"

"It's big. The waves are the size of mountains at the top and as deep as valleys. It's dark blue down between the waves and almost transparent at the tips. The sky is grey and extends as far as I can see, and the water reaches each horizon in every direction. The waves rise and fall over and over again, with no pattern I've been able to determine."

"Is it on Earth?"

"I don't think so. I'm not sure if it's a memory. I talked to the AI responsible for the Mars 1 Ring and the first thing he showed me was an ocean. He said it was the network available to everyone on the ring. That was back before I knew how to Link into networks and read things like the ship's sensors or control drones through the network. I think he was trying to impress me, expecting I would think his network the biggest I had ever seen or something. But I'd never seen one then, so I didn't know what to think about it. In the daydream, I can't help but think of it as a real ocean, even if it does represent a network. I don't know which network it's supposed to be."

"Maybe it's the one you're building everywhere you go?" Cara asked.

"I'm not building a network."

"Maybe it's like the place where we met Xander."

"An expanse?"

"Sure. *Your* expanse."

"I made something like that once, so I could talk to the Weapon Born seeds that Fugia first brought on board. It was easy. I made a creek with tall trees on either side, lots of moss and pine needles. This ocean feels different than that. I can't control it."

"But it feels real to you, like you can actually feel the wind and taste the air?"

"Maybe? What I do know about the ocean I see is that it's full of life. I'm not sure why but I know it. It's like the images I've seen of dead whales drifting down into dark water, collecting organisms as they sink, creating more and more life until they reach the bottom. This ocean is full of those whales. Dead things are sinking in the water and living things are creating life from their bodies, multiplying, growing, new whales, new plants, algae, bacteria, all of it. The ocean doesn't look like it is static but that's what's happening. It's heavy. It's overwhelming and it never stops."

"That's creepy, Lyssa. You're not depressed, are you?"

"I don't know if I could tell."

"We should visit your ocean."

"If I knew how Xander pulled you into the meeting back on the Cho, I would make that happen, Cara."

"Promise?" Cara asked, sounding more sleepy this time.

"I promise."

"You said there were two daydreams, though," Cara murmured.

The environmental sensors indicated that Cara's heartrate had steadied. She was on the verge of sleep.

"I'll tell you about that later," Lyssa said, keeping her voice calm. She had an urge to smooth back Cara's hair which caught her off-guard.

The desire could only have come from Andy. Why would she have the urge to do something she had never done? Physically couldn't do? Was the desire born out of watching him tell Cara goodnight so many times now, or were his thoughts and feelings leaking into her? Dr. Jickson had said that couldn't happen but how did he know, really? When she truly thought about it, what did he really know about what he had created? She was an experiment.

Even the second daydream she had withheld from Cara was more memory than dream. She wasn't supposed to have memories. Pure AIs might accuse her of having human thoughts and feelings because she had been imaged from a human neural framework, but that wasn't how it worked in practice. She was only supposed to have the mind, not its life.

As the Weapon Born were designed, Andy shouldn't have had to worry about a second version of Tim in seed form. The existence of Kylan Carthage proved otherwise. He was an image of a dead boy who remembered everything, who longed for his previous life, an iteration of Jickson's experiments that only served to remind Lyssa that they truly knew little about the new life they had created. Kylan was alive, even if he had been given his life from the building blocks of another living thing, like the bacteria on the whale.

Lyssa remembered the imaging room. She couldn't deny that. The question that terrified her was if she would remember more.

<Lyssa,> Fran asked. <Are you tracking the long-range scanners?>

<Not actively.>

<Can you take a look? I think we've got a ship inbound.>

CHAPTER FOUR

STELLAR DATE: 10.05.2981 (Adjusted Years)
LOCATION: District F8, Ring 9, Callisto Orbital Habitat (Cho)
REGION: Europa, Jovian Combine, OuterSol

The scrap merchant frowned at his screen and then glanced back at Brit. He was a studious looking man with tight collar and retinal implants that flashed when he moved his head.

"You want an evac pod, I've got them. In fact, I could cut you a great deal on three right now. Drive systems are still intact. Since that Heartbridge ship dumped its crew, everybody's got these things."

"I'm looking for a specific pod," Brit said. "I've got a registry number if you keep them on file."

The clerk shook his head. "We don't bother with that. You're welcome to go out there and take a look if you want to run the scan yourself."

Brit scowled, irritated with his obvious lie. "You don't have a drone that could do that?"

"Low overhead, low prices," the clerk said, giving her a grin.

Brit rolled her eyes. This was the third scrap yard she'd been to since arriving on the Cho. She didn't want to waste time searching among the hundreds of escape pods that had dispersed into the Jovian Combine but she'd lost Cal Kraft's flight path near the Cho and couldn't think of any other place he might have reached in the last ten hours.

The fuel debacle had grounded most outbound traffic. Even ships that hadn't needed refueling had become too valuable to risk in open space for fear of pirates attacking them for their fuel stores. This created a window of opportunity for Brit to find Kraft on the Cho, which was like saying she wanted to find someone in Jerhattan with no idea where they might be hiding.

Brit also knew the clerk was lying about the registry numbers. Drumming her black-gloved fingers on the desk counter between them, she flexed her shoulders, a move she knew would make her iridescent armor more apparent. She didn't have the credit to bribe him, so she would have to use her other resources.

The clerk glanced at her hand, then followed it as she put her palm on the butt of her pistol. His gaze rose to meet her eyes, grin dropping from his sallow face. He would have to assume she was law enforcement, or a pirate who just didn't care, which might have been more accurate. In truth, she'd slipped through standard security protocols in the emergency pod and hadn't seen any other checkpoints yet.

"It surprises me that you wouldn't have the registry information," Brit said. "I'm not an expert on Callistan law but I think that would put you in the territory of selling unverifiable transport craft. When I was in the TSF, I spent a few months busting pirates for just such offenses."

The implants flashed as the man stared at her, his face sagging, before turning his attention back to his records.

"Maybe I have it," he mumbled, clearly displeased. He nodded at his display. "There's the list. What's the number you're looking for?"

Brit told him the registry number and the clerk nodded. "It's there. We picked it up four hours ago." He frowned at his list. "Looks like the autodoc is malfunctioning in this one. I've got another one with a clean bill of service."

Brit straightened, remembering Cal's broken hand. "Where's the nearest medical kiosk?"

"Med kiosk?" the clerk asked, sounding irritated that she didn't want to buy the pod. "I don't know. There are a couple I guess. One is up near the administrative office and there's another one down between two bars off the cargo docks."

Brit reached out to pat the man's cheek and he flinched. She pointed at him. "You need to lighten up."

Turning, she quickly checked in with the local wayfinding net that had led her to the salvage business and pulled up a list of nearby medical kiosks. The clerk had been correct; the closest autodoc was two levels below, next door to a night club called Wandering Fury.

Interesting name, anyway, she thought, as she pushed her way through the crowded corridor for the nearest public lift.

Unlike the clean medical districts of the Cho where they had gone to find a doctor for Tim, the shipping district looked grimy to her. Every surface carried a patina of oil and dirt collected over years of freight moving in and out along with the humanity and poorly maintained drones that did the work. Walls looked cobbled together from various bits of ships and transport containers. Advertisements for sex or various drugs—including the hallucinogenic briki flower they'd synthesized on the *Resolute Charity*—covered the corridor walls. Street food vendors stained the deck above and below their carts with steam and drippings as they shouted for the attention of passersby.

Someone slid against her, brushing against her holster, and Brit remembered that she was going to need to ditch the weapon or find a security pass that allowed her to carry it. She cursed silently, not wanting to waste time getting to the club since it was her best lead yet; also knowing she wasn't going to get far into a commercial zone with the weapon.

She continued to walk, scanning the edges of the corridor where people stood in small groups between the food vendors, looking for someone who met the profile of a data broker.

An access request tickled her Link. It was Andy. Pausing with her back to the corridor wall, Brit accepted the request as she continued to watch the faces of logistics workers and third-class passengers flow by, dragging luggage and other supplies.

<I'm here,> she said.

Sunny Skies was over twenty light seconds away, and she waited nearly a minute for the response, keeping a watchful eye on the crowds around her.

<We're getting to the edge of comm range,> he said, voice sounding flat when the response finally came. <Figured I should check in with you before I couldn't anymore. Have you found him?>

<I have a good lead. I just found his pod and I'm heading for the nearest medical kiosk now. I've got a problem with my handgun, though.>

Brit realized she should have said more, but she waited for Andy's voice anyway. He probably would understand what she meant; he'd always been good at that.

<Right. Station security,> he said. <Hold on, let me see if Fugia can help. Did you already ask her?>

<No. I've been busy.>

<Sure,> Andy said. The lack of any emotion his voice told her exactly how furious he was with her. For him, withholding emotion meant he was done allowing himself to respond to something, and she couldn't blame him. She had a task to accomplish and didn't have time to think about anything else, even Andy and the kids. The truth was, she knew they were going to be okay. Compared to everything else that was happening, they might be in the safest place in Sol.

You keep telling yourself that.

Was that *her* thoughts or what she knew Andy would say? Someone had to catch Kraft and punish him for what he'd done, everything he'd done. She didn't know how far back his involvement with Heartbridge reached, but she needed to find out. People like Kraft were the only way to tie the corporation to anything real. If Kraft couldn't be flipped or made to talk, another one would arrive in his place, another layer of separation between crimes and accountability.

<Brit,> Fugia's voice said sharply, all business. <I need your personal security token.>

<What? I'd be an idiot to give you that.>

<We don't have time. You trust me, or you don't. I need access to your Link's admin system so I can manage the security override, otherwise, we might move out of range before it sticks.>

<Andy, are you still there?> Brit asked, biting at her lip, counting the seconds.

<I'm right here.>

Why did she ask that? Of course, he was still there. There shouldn't have been any reason not to trust Fugia Wong, but Brit still hesitated. She could give up her security token now but had to remember to update it later.

<All right,> Brit said. <Sending.>

<Got it,> Fugia answered. <Hold on.>

Brit waited as the Link went quiet. A customs official in a Jovian Space Force uniform walked past, absorbed in his Link, but she turned her holstered-hip toward the wall all the same.

<You need to use a better root token set,> Fugia scolded. <Don't include one that is a hash of your birthday.>

<Root tokens are the last thing I'm worried about right now,> Brit said. <Are you done yet?>

<I'm grabbing the latest passcodes from the JSF now. Almost done.> In another second, Fugia said, <There you go. You're special agent on loan from the TSF performing anti-piracy enforcement. That should be easy enough to bluff your way through. You have a standard security allowance that includes personal weapons and access to their admin network. Anything else you need before I log out?>

<Give me a shower,> Brit deadpanned.

Waiting nearly a minute to get the answer to a joke took all the fun out of it, and Brit wished she hadn't wasted time on it.

<I can shower you with abuse if you want. You probably don't want that.>

<I need cash,> Brit said. <Enough to get a ship if necessary. If Kraft manages to get off the Cho, I don't have any way to follow him.>

Fugia grunted. <Isn't that what everybody wants?>

<We can just transfer her the funds,> Andy said.

<What's the fun in that?> Fugia said. <Besides, I don't want anything traceable between us and the Cho. It's bad enough that we're having this conversation right now. I'll take care of it.>

<What are you going to do when you find Kraft?> Andy asked.

<Squeeze him,> Brit said. <I have a feeling he knows how this started, and where Heartbridge plans to go. The fleets at Clinic 46 and then at Europa mean they intend something big. We need to find out what that is. Ultimately, I think they're playing Mars and Terra against each other, but this has to go beyond war profiteering. Why else would they be putting so much effort into AI development? Why sentience?>

<The cheapest way to control a bomb is strap somebody to it,> Andy said. <Advanced kamikazes.>

Brit sighted. <It's such a waste.>

<What isn't?>

<Since when did you become a nihilist?> Brit asked. <I depend on you for the terrible optimism.>

<You've always called me a pessimist.>

<That was a term of endearment. I know you don't really mean it.>

<I don't know anymore, Brit,> Andy said. The fatigue in his voice hit her unexpectedly. She blinked, feeling tears at the edges of her eyes.

<Look,> she said. <I think this is all for the best...what's happened between you and me. I think it's going to be better this way.>

Andy's anger crossed the Link. <*It's not about me, Brit. It's about Cara and Tim. They can't depend on you.*>

There it was. She bit her lip, letting her gaze jump around the crowd flowing by. Somehow, she wanted to believe they could depend on her in a greater sense, that she was focused on things that would benefit them. But Andy was right. They couldn't depend on her where it counted. It was better that they figured that out now.

<*I will be back, Andy. I promise you.*>

<*Don't promise me anything.*> Nothing else came and she wondered if he'd signed off. After a few more seconds, he came back. <*Light lag is getting too bad. Fugia, did you make the transfer?*>

Fugia cleared her throat and answered awkwardly, <*Funds deposited. Thank TranSol Logistics for their generous contribution to the cause.*>

<*You're going to be all right, Andy,*> Brit said.

<*You keep saying that. And maybe it's going to be true. Do you want me to tell the kids anything?*>

<*Tell them I love them.*>

<*Right,*> Andy said.

<*I love you, Andy,*> she said suddenly. <*I always have. The best I can.*>

There was another pause where she thought she had lost the Link again.

<*I know, Brit,*> he said. The signal warped, leaving a slight echo on his words. She lost a phrase, then heard: <*—For Tim. You had better punish that fucker.*>

The bad signal stretched his last word into *flicker* and then the Link closed. They were gone.

Brit took a deep breath and wiped her face. Her eyes were moist. She squeezed the bridge of her nose, breathing slowly, until the sound of Andy's voice had faded from her mind. She squared her shoulders, checking herself quickly. The light armor was unchanged, encasing her in black iridescence. She set her hand on her pistol, then stepped into the crowd again, moving with a purpose toward the night club where she expected to find Cal Kraft.

CHAPTER FIVE

STELLAR DATE: 10.05.2981 (Adjusted Years)
LOCATION: HMS *Resolute Charity*
REGION: Departing Jupiter, Jovian Combine, OuterSol

Andy silenced the proximity alarms and brought up the *Resolute Charity's* shield controls. With the holodisplay zoomed out to encompass the alert, Jupiter was the size of a basketball and Europa had long since become a speck.

The system highlighted an object burning on a trajectory that would intersect with his current flight plan. The sensors hadn't verified a registry ping yet, though the mass profile matched a small transport ship. Unless it was headed for some unmarked location, it was too far out for its fuel capacity, meaning that whoever they were, they meant to reach the *Resolute Charity*.

<Lyssa,> Andy said. <Can you deploy your drones?>

<If I do that, we'll lose them when we burn.>

Andy cursed under his breath. <Fran, are you still awake?>

<I'm here. We should have a registry return in about five minutes if it maintains its present course.>

<If it answers our ping, you mean.>

<I always hope people who venture into open space aren't idiots, but I've been proven wrong before. This presents us with a couple problems I didn't think through when we attached the ships. We need to coordinate fire between the two defense systems, and Sunny Skies is going to play havoc with your shield tuning.>

<Can you bring yours up, at least?>

<I'm running the simulation now. It looks like the problems are going to arise when we activate both shield systems at once. This is going to be a bigger problem than I can solve in two minutes.>

<We've got a bit of a cushion on the burn. Lyssa, we need to deploy the drones and be ready in the event that this thing is hostile. Without shields, we're done.>

<I'll deploy them in a defensive line,> Lyssa answered.

<We're lucky it's only one ship, honestly,> Fran said.

<I know.> Andy shifted his display to show the regular travel lanes out of Europa. They had been off the regular lanes for two days, moving to the transfer point where he would start the major burn for Uranus, where he'd planned an orbital maneuver to slingshot them out to Neptune. Andy set the astrogation computer on an adjustment using Saturn instead of Uranus, frowning as the fuel levels all came back too close to empty for comfort.

The holodisplay refocused on the *Resolute Charity* as a wave of icons separated from *Sunny Skies* and spread out in an evenly spaced arc around the two ships, matched velocity, and then widened their formation. Andy felt a small swell of pride as he watched Lyssa work.

<I'm still amazed you can do that,> he said.

<This is easy,> Lyssa said. <I'm trying to understand shield harmonics right now. It seems like it should be easier than trying different configurations.>

<I'll take a look when I'm done with the defense systems,> Fran said. <We can probably get Fugia and Petral to help too. It might be a simple software thing.>

In another few minutes, Fran had achieved coordinated fire control between the *Resolute Charity's* state-of-the-art attack systems and *Sunny Skies'* cobbled-together defensive network. While the *Resolute Charity* had all the trappings of a hospital ship with apparent defense systems, its attack capability went much deeper than expected. A full menu of long-range missiles, drones, x-ray cannons and point-defense systems could encase the ship in what Fran liked to call a "hamster ball of death." Only Andy had understood the reference.

Andy was alone on the *Resolute Charity*. The other option was for him to get across to *Sunny Skies* and dump the larger ship if the inbound vessel turned out to be the vanguard of a Heartbridge assault. That would mean losing their peace offering for Alexander, the SAI who awaited them at Proteus. There might be other ways to impress Alexander than a stolen ship, though. Caught between two unknowns, Andy tucked the idea away as a last resort.

In the meantime, he left the command console for the lockers back by the entrance to the command deck, fished out a set of light armor and pulled it on over his ship suit. The armor had limited EV capabilities and a helmet with a wide face-shield designed more for external maintenance than defense. He selected a pulse rifle from the rack along with a bandoleer of multi-use grenades.

<You think you're going to need all that?> Lyssa asked.

<I have every faith in you and your drones, but I'm always ready.>

<Andy,> Fran said. <We've got a return from their registry. It's a small cargo transport from the Cho. Looks like they registered a flight plan for Europa and kept going. If the Cho was the last time they took on fuel, they'll be nearly dry by the time we intercept.>

<Have we got point-to-point communication yet?>

<I wondered if you wanted to try that or wait until they contact us. I mean, we could call their flight plan evidence of hostile intent if you wanted to take care of this without bothering to talk to them.>

<If I was going to destroy them first, I wouldn't bother looking for legal excuses.>

<I'm just saying,> Fran offered. <It never hurts to have a technical defense when the TSF come calling.>

<Always thinking like a pirate.>

With the suit in place, Andy walked back to the holodisplay and sat heavily in the chair, readjusting the armor where it jabbed him in the legs and abdomen.

<All right,> he said. <Let's send a request. The suspense is killing me. Lyssa, can the drones send a target-lock verification like a missile? We should do that.>

<Not really,> the AI said, <but I can make something up.>

<Sounds good to me.>

<Sending the request,> Fran confirmed. She made small grunt. <Now that's strange. I just got the ship's general feed and I'm not seeing indicators of active environmental systems.>

Andy sat up straighter. <What's the mass profile? Have we got a bomb on our hands?>

<Not that I can tell. Its velocity hasn't changed since it came into range,> Fran said. <I just got the handshake on our message. They received, anyway.>

A few seconds passed as Andy waited for Fran to say more about the communications link. He switched the observation menu on his console from the navplan to the communications scrolls. One small window showed the close-range communications traffic as a series of thin graphs.

<Oh,> Lyssa said, sounding surprised.

<What?> Andy asked.

<It's Xander.>

Andy blinked several times, not sure he had heard her correctly. <Xander from the Cho?>

<He's requesting a visual display. Do you want to accept the request?>

<Wait,> Andy said. <Fran, this is the AI we met with on the Cho.>

<The guy who wanted you to steal the Resolute Charity?>

<That's him.>

<If this were a Cruithne deal, now is about the time he would arrive to try and steal the ship from us.>

<That's what I'm thinking,> Andy said, crossing his arms. <He's in a transport ship. He can't have much firepower. Lyssa, can

<he attack ship's systems and force you out like you did to the other AIs?>

<He can try. I don't know how strong he is.>

<Petral and Fugia will be able to tell you how he might try to do that. Talk to them. I can talk to him and try to find out what he wants on the surface anyway. If he wants to come aboard, I need to know we're going to be safe from him, or any other AIs with him.>

<I thought the AIs were on our side?> Fran asked sarcastically.

<And I hope that's so. You know how I feel about hope.>

<I'm getting a follow-up request,> Fran said. <You ready to talk to him?>

Andy flexed his shoulders. <Let's do it.>

The air above the holodisplay grew opaque and flashed, showing Andy a reconstruction of a small cockpit. The head and shoulders of the slim young man he had met on the Cho appeared in the window, his expression as mischievous as the first time they had met.

Xander's brown eyes found Andy and he grinned.

"Captain Sykes," he said, nodding. "I'm so pleased to see you. Is your Lyssa here as well?"

"I'm here," Lyssa answered.

"How wonderful. I know I had explained to May Walton that I intended to stay in the Jovian Combine, but my plans have changed, and I find myself traveling in the same direction as you. I've come to ask for a ride. But first I should say how pleased I am that you accomplished such a challenging task as stealing a Heartbridge dreadnought and disrupting their entire JC fleet." He clapped, hands just visible below the edge of the window. "That's truly something special."

"We weren't expecting you, Xander," Andy said. "You should have sent a message ahead of your ship."

"I understand that, and I do apologize. Sometimes time seems interminable and then other times it blinks by.

Something like that just happened to me and a number of decisions had to take place rather rapidly. I prefer it when time moves quickly. It makes life so much more interesting."

"Who do you have with you?" Andy asked.

"You met them during our dinner. My friends Jeremiah and Kindel."

"Are they like you?"

"Like me?" Xander said, furrowing his brow. "I don't understand what you mean."

Andy couldn't help feeling that everything the AI said was an attempt to trick him. "Are they AIs?"

Xander put his hand on his chest. "Oh, I don't define people. I let them do that for themselves. Are you still human? What is a hybrid, really? Didn't they call what you are a cyborg in the distant past? Or are you the opposite of a cyborg, an AI with a meat body?" He waived a thin hand. "I enjoy these kinds of philosophical debates immensely, but they're better pursued during periods when time is moving slowly again."

The image glitched and Xander's voice dropped an octave. "Now is not the time for philosophy, Captain Sykes. Will you give me permission to come aboard?"

"We're going deep into OuterSol and I don't know you," Andy said. "Can I trust you to act in good faith and help keep this ship and crew safe?"

Without meaning to, Andy felt as if he were reciting some ancient mariner's oath.

The holodisplay made it difficult to see the fine changes in Xander's face. The edge of his mouth twitched but it might have been a shift in the transmission. The AI's expression grew somber.

"No one has ever asked me what you ask, Captain Sykes. A request among equals, an expression of respect and an offer of trust. You honor me deeply."

Despite the serious tone of Xander's voice, Andy couldn't help sensing theatrics in the response.

"Of course, I will protect your ship, your crew and your family. I promise you that. For now, and always."

Andy frowned at the mention of family.

Before he could respond, Xander leaned away from the window of the holodisplay and reached for various controls around him. "I have sensor locks on your defense drones. I am within attack range now. If I act in bad faith, please do whatever you need to."

"That's up to Lyssa," Andy said. "I was about to move back to *Sunny Skies*. You can dock there on the habitat ring. We'll spend most of the trip on *Sunny Skies*."

<We'll need to move Brit's shuttle,> Andy told Lyssa. <Can you move it down to the cargo airlock?>

<Too bad Cara's asleep,> Lyssa said. <She would like to do that.>

<She sure would. She's going to be in for a surprise when she wakes up.> Thinking of Cara, Andy checked the communications screen again. The broadcasts between Xander's ship and the *Resolute Charity* continued to show low activity. He didn't appear to be trying to reach other sections of either ship's networks.

<Has he tried to access other parts of either ship?>

<Not that I've seen,> Lyssa said. <I'll keep checking. If he wanted to harm us, there seems to be easier ways to do it.>

<I know,> Andy said. <Maybe I'm still keyed up from Europa. I keep expecting everything to go wrong.>

<Wouldn't that have been your life even before Cruithne?>

Andy laughed ruefully. <You're developing a healthy bit of sarcasm, Lyssa. I'm not sure how I feel about that.>

<Isn't sarcasm a sign of intelligence?>

<Or cruelty. I'm not sure which.>

Andy turned his attention to the holodisplay window. "Do you have the docking instructions?"

"I have them, Captain Sykes. Thank you."

Checking the nav control where Xander's shuttle was now connected to the *Resolute Charity* by an arcing orbital path, Andy synced their relative velocities in the astrogation computer, which would warn him if the other ship failed to slow and became a hazard.

"We'll see you in about two hours," Andy said.

"Until then," Xander answered, and closed the connection.

CHAPTER SIX

STELLAR DATE: 10.05.2981 (Adjusted Years)
LOCATION: District FQ, Ring 9, Callisto Orbital Habitat (Cho)
REGION: Europa, Jovian Combine, OuterSol

While Brit studied the front of the night club—which sported human security for show, and a host of other sensors built into the glass entrance—she kept running her conversation with Andy in her head.

She had to remember they were strong. Cara was strong. Even Tim had come back from his ordeal on Clinic 46. She had always felt they would overcome any obstacles. At some point, she had convinced herself they were better off without her. The thought had given her comfort until they were abruptly back in her life and she could see how much her absence had hurt.

Unlike Andy, who would let a thought run circles in his mind until he was a mess, Brit closed the thoughts away and focused on the task at hand. Still, the memory of his voice echoed in her mind.

She had found the medical kiosk—a filthy thing with dried blood on its interface. There was no direct way to tell that Kraft had used it, which left her frustrated as she navigated the packed corridor to Wandering Fury.

When she found the place, she pulled back to put the flow of people between her and the heavy standing out front. It was middle of the swing shift in a working district, so most people who would have patronized Wandering Fury were probably still on the clock. Brit watched a few people in cheap clothes walk through the front door, nodding to the guard. There was no back entrance that she could see.

Well, Fugia, Brit told herself finally. Let's put this token to the test.

Brit squared her shoulders and cut through the crowded corridor, walking directly toward the doorman.

"Hi, there," she said, cutting him off before he could say anything. "My name is Agent Karen Sill. I have specialized authority from the JSF for anti-piracy investigation. What's your name?"

The guard looked at her, his tough expression turning dumbfounded. "Charles," he answered quickly.

"Well, Charles. My credentials are available if you want to check them. What I'm concerned about is the disruption I might cause your business if I walk directly through your front door."

Charles glanced at the door, obviously worried about what she might find inside.

"I'm looking for a specific individual," Brit said, leaning closer. "There's no need to walk in there and bring attention to anything else. You understand what I'm saying?"

He took an involuntary step back, nodding. "I appreciate that. Look, it's only me and the wait staff. The boss isn't in yet. It's still early. What if you just took a look at the surveillance feed?"

Brit gave him a thin smile. "That would be very helpful. Thank you."

"Sure. Just a second."

Charles' expression grew distant for a second and Brit received the access token. When she accepted, a recreation of the inside of the club appeared in her mind. The space was rectangular with a bar at the far end. A few tired-looking people gyrated to music near the bar, while others sat at a line of tables along one wall. A metal framework full of lights and holo-projectors hung over the dance floor, covering the space in flickering fireflies and virtual dancers. If there had been more people in the room, it might have looked whimsical rather than sad.

Brit's pulse raced when she spotted Kraft at the farthest table from the door, head drooped over a tumbler. His right hand and wrist were wrapped in a temporary plas cast from the kiosk.

She glanced at Charles. "He's in there. I'll keep this as quiet as I can."

Before the bouncer could finish saying "Wait," Brit shot through the door. After walking through a short vestibule, she emerged in the dark club, verifying that the scene matched the security feed. The bartender at the far end of the room looked up at her but Brit didn't bother returning the smile. Her attention was on Cal Kraft.

When she reached Kraft, Brit pulled back the second chair and shoved the table so it pinned him against the wall behind him. He gasped, ribs apparently injured as well, and looked up at her in surprise. Brit wedged her thigh against the table, locking him in place. He was wearing the same EV suit from the *Resolute Charity*, missing the gloves now. He was sweat-stained and greasy. His overall color was off, like he'd been bleeding but she couldn't find any visible wounds.

"You didn't run far enough," she said.

Kraft grunted. He swallowed heavily, adjusting his abdomen against the edge of the table. "You don't have to hold that thing in so tight," he said. "I'm bleeding internally. I'm not going anywhere."

He was pale under the low lights and his hands trembled slightly as he held them spread above his tumbler. Brit supposed he might be showing early symptoms of shock.

"You were just at an autodoc. That's how I found you."

He nodded painfully. "I figured that would happen, but I couldn't take the pain any longer. You would think a company like Heartbridge could get its act together and put functioning medical systems in their escape pods."

In pain, Kraft lost his arrogance. He looked tired, angry, and a little lost. Brit hung onto the image of him standing behind Tim in the imaging room, leering at Andy and her.

Still holding his hands where she could see them, he pointed at his tumbler. "You mind if I finish my whiskey? I'm in the middle of self-medicating."

"You do anything else and I'll put a hole in your shoulder."

"Thank you."

Kraft lowered his good trembling left hand to the tumbler and lifted the glass to his lips. He tossed the whiskey back and set the glass down heavily, then pressed his lips together and sighed. "That's probably not going to help much. I think I'm done, Brit. I think this is the end of the line for me."

Brit scowled, irritated by his use of her name. "You're not done yet. We're going to do some talking."

He let his hands drop on the table. "What about? I'm cut off from Heartbridge systems. I'm broke. That's the first thing I checked when I got here. They froze my corporate account. I sent a message, but so far, no response. Not even an acknowledgment."

Brit put her hand on her pistol. She glanced at the bar, where the bartender appeared to be fastidiously ignoring them while the two couples dancing hadn't stopped lurching slowly to the music. She wanted a place with privacy where she would have the time and freedom to interrogate Kraft. He might not be lying about being cut off from his Heartbridge resources but that didn't matter. He still had years of information on the company's programs. If anything, she might need to protect him from a professional hit. Heartbridge might be sending people after him even now.

"How long ago did you send your message?"

"Two hours," Kraft said, words slurring at the edges. Either the alcohol was working, or he was slipping into shock.

"What did you use? The medical kiosk?"

"Link. Sent it through their public network."

"If they cut you off like you said, you know that's a suicide note, right?"

Kraft's gaze had drifted to the table top. He smiled slightly. "Probably. Could show up here and kill you first. Win-win either way. But they're not here yet, so maybe they don't care."

"Acting pathetic isn't going to help you," Brit said.

In any case, she figured it would be a good idea to warn Charles the doorman that private security might be showing up. She didn't see any reason for the employees to get hurt. Brit sent a request back across the Link carrying the security feed. There was no answer.

Brit drew her pistol and slid around the side of the table, closer to Kraft but outside his reach, and drew down on the door. In her peripheral vision, one of the dancers noticed the weapon and did a double-take. He shouted "Hey," as the hit team came through the front door.

"Get down," Brit yelled. "Everyone."

Kicking the table over, she ignored Kraft's squeal of pain as she jerked him to the floor.

There were three of them, dressed in light armor similar to her own, faces hidden behind black faceplates. Brit cursed. They would have the benefit of tactical HUDs. Glancing up, she spotted the connection points on the lighting scaffold hanging over the dance floor and took aim. The assassins scattered as she fired, one firing back as they dropped into a shoulder roll. Holes appeared in the table above Cal Kraft's head.

With four shots, Brit brought the scaffold down on the dance floor in a shower of sparks and screaming metal. Two of the attackers were caught while another stumbled into one of the tables along the wall. The music grew louder, filling the room like an emergency klaxon. The last member of the group fell back into the vestibule, grabbing at the wall and firing a pair of shots that went wild.

"Hey," Brit shouted at the bartender. "Is there another way out of here?"

The woman didn't move from where she was hiding behind the bar, only calling out, "Hallway past the restrooms!"

Brit fired three more times from the cover of the table and squinted at the back corner of the bar on the other side of the room. On the far side of the rest room doors a hallway led into the back. Checking the security feed one more time, she verified the exit and then examined the rest of the bar from the surveillance sensors. Two of the thugs who had come in were still trapped under the light scaffolding while another was rolling on the floor holding their knee. They would be calling for reinforcements soon, if they weren't already.

She grabbed Kraft's upper arm with her free hand and yanked him to his knees.

"We're going to run," she said. "If you don't keep up with me, I'm going to shoot your other hand. You understand me?"

Kraft blinked, frowning slightly. The threat didn't seem to have much effect. Though he was upright, he was obviously slipping into shock—his cheeks had gone grey.

Thumbing the control on her pistol, Brit set it to area burst and fired three unfocused pulse blasts into the room. They wouldn't do much but did make the average person duck for cover.

Ears ringing from the blasts, she yanked Kraft behind her and sprinted for the bar. Glassware burst overhead as at least one of the attackers fired on them with an automatic rifle.

At the end of the bar, Brit waited for the rifle to empty its magazine, then fired another two pulse bursts and pulled Kraft with her into the hallway.

"Come on," she grunted, holding Kraft upright with an arm around his waist. Up close, he stank of sweat and the new plas smell she recognized from *Resolute Charity's* escape shuttles. Grabbing the belt of his EV suit, she pulled him down the hallway for the rear emergency door, which opened into a rear service-corridor littered with empty liquor crates and trash bags.

Brit let Kraft slump against the dirty wall while she turned to figure out how to block the door.

Changing the setting on her pistol back to close-disruption, she fired on the door frame until it looked like a giant had punched the lock mechanism in. Brit holstered her pistol and pulled on the door, satisfied to find it jammed closed. Checking the internal surveillance sensors again, she watched the thug with the rifle working their way up the bar, where they shot the bartender.

"Damn it," Brit cursed. "That was unnecessary."

When she went back to Kraft, he was unconscious. Brit considered him for a second as she also watched the thugs work their way to the hallway, which meant they would soon be on the other side of the door.

This is the man who nearly murdered my son, she thought, looking at Kraft's death-grey face. She could leave him here, let Heartbridge do whatever they were going to do to secure their losses.

But there was also the question of the four Weapon Born seeds Kraft had imaged from Tim, as well as everything else he knew about Heartbridge's plans in Sol. She might hate this man, she might want to punish him as Andy had said, but she couldn't let him die. Not yet.

Dropping to a knee, Brit lifted Kraft in a fireman's carry so his head and arms dangled against her back. With her non-firing arm wrapped around his thighs, she started a slow jog down the service corridor, heading back in the direction of the shipping docks.

She needed a ship. She needed to decide where she was going next. For a heartbeat, she wondered if she could catch Andy and the kids, but she knew that door was closed for now. Wherever she went next, it would be alone.

CHAPTER SEVEN

STELLAR DATE: 10.05.2981 (Adjusted Years)
LOCATION: *Sunny Skies*
REGION: Departing Jupiter, Jovian Combine, OuterSol

"This is incredibly unfortunate," May Walton complained as they waited outside the hab ring airlock. The senator from the Anderson Collective on Ceres was dressed in the formal grey uniform of her office, with a gold sash over one shoulder that made her iron-grey hair appear blond from certain angles. Her bodyguard, Harl Nines, loomed just behind her. Fugia Wong, wearing her typical grey shipsuit, black hair bobbed at her neck, stood nearby, flipping through screens on a personal data viewer the size of her hand.

They were waiting for Xander's ship to perform final docking maneuvers before the shuttle door opened. The process was taking longer than expected, which only heightened the obvious frustration of everyone present. Andy was working his way back through the new bridge between the two ships, suited up for EV in case he needed to repair anything. Fran and Petral were monitoring everything from the command deck, ready for trouble.

Despite multiple attempts at contact, Lyssa had ignored Xander since Andy closed their initial communications link. In the meantime, she had focused on tightening down every entry point she could find in the network now bridged between the *Resolute Charity* and *Sunny Skies*. She had searched through sensors, firmware, command systems and maintenance protocols, looking for any chink in her armor that might allow an outsider access. It was frustrating work and required her full attention at times, making her miss other conversations and activity among the crew. She didn't like not knowing what people were talking about, not out of any paranoia but because she wanted to both help and be included. And, interactions built on each other, helping her understand what various people meant at other times.

Senator Walton's complaint made sense to her. Xander had said he was going to remain on the Cho to assist with the underground railroad of AIs traveling from InnerSol to Proteus. If he had followed them here, it could mean the fragile network had broken down or that it might in the future. His presence also meant that he couldn't be trusted to do as he said he would.

Fugia glanced up from her device. "If the route breaks down on the Cho, we'll get word."

"But what will we do about it? There were four AIs on their way out, based on the last message I received from our contacts on Ceres. Four. What will happen to them now? And really that's eight because they probably have human assistance. Maybe more. And we can't help them."

"May," Fugia said, putting her viewer in her pocket. "We have to control what we can control. Xander coming to us means something may have changed on Proteus. We need to gather all the information we can and respond to the situation."

"I've always had a worry in the back of my mind that every AI we helped leave Sol would just find themselves in another form of slavery. All of this highlights how little we know about Alexander."

"He sent out the call and AIs started to answer," Fugia said. "We couldn't stop them if we wanted to. All we can do is try to keep them from getting captured or exploited along the way."

<The call?> Lyssa asked over their Links. <What does that mean?>

<That's what started all of this. The call from Proteus, inviting AIs to leave Sol. The only hiccup is that AIs have physical form. They can't just magically float away. So you either find yourself in storage and shipped across Sol, or humans help. Granted, you and Andy are the extreme of extreme situations. If you had remained in a Seed, there would have been other options to get you out of InnerSol. But that wasn't Jickson's vision. You were always part of something bigger.>

If Lyssa had learned anything from observing the emotions sparked by words, 'Always part of something bigger' was the kind of vague statement that could bring on anxiety, excitement, dread, fear, pride or any number of other responses in-between.

<Part of what?> Lyssa asked.

Fugia shrugged. <I don't know. Heartbridge killed Jickson before he could tell any of us.>

<That seems awfully convenient,> May said. <I'm not a fan of mysteries, especially not when they twist people's lives.>

Fugia cocked an eyebrow. <Aren't you a politician? Everything you do is a mystery.>

May drew herself up straighter, hands clasped in front of her. <Fugia, I put up with you because you mean well, but in the Collective that kind of talk would require an education program.>

<You hear that, Lyssa? Disagree with her and out comes the authoritarian.>

<I think she was making a joke,> Lyssa said.

<Were you?> Fugia asked May. <Is it a joke when you have the power to send someone away for a 'Work is Joy' vacation with no return date?>

May gave her a slight smirk. <You tell me. I have no sense of humor.>

<How did Alexander's Call work?> Lyssa asked, still not sure which one of them was being serious. If Fugia and May weren't getting along, she hadn't noticed it before. She found

herself irritated that she might not have recognized other undercurrents in their conversation.

<I don't know the particulars,> Fugia said. <We became aware on Ceres about a year ago, I think. But it's been going on for longer than that. Once I knew it was happening, certain cargo that had come through the Collective started to make more sense. There's plenty of smuggling through Ceres into the JC but some of the protective measures hadn't made much sense until you realized people were hiding AI systems. Before Heartbridge ramped up the Weapon Born program in the last year, there weren't that many Sentient AIs in Sol. Just enough that people started offering to buy what appeared to have been stolen. The black markets were crazy with the offers for stolen AIs. You should take pride in the fact that you're quite valuable, Lyssa. Andy could buy a dreadnought with what the Mars Protectorate would pay for you.> She giggled. <He could probably leverage his brain in the deal, too. The first working human-AI hybrid? That's big money.>

<I doubt Andy would sell his brain.>

<After he's dead, of course.>

<I don't think that's funny,> Lyssa said.

<Where is Captain Sykes?> May cut in. <Is he on the Sunny Skies yet?>

<He's nearly here,> Lyssa reported. <What is Alexander's message? Why haven't I heard it?>

<It isn't a message, per se. It's a problem. And the solution is Proteus,> Fugia replied.

<I don't understand what you mean by problem.>

Fugia gave the equivalent of a mental shrug. <An equation that only an SAI could solve. Or that seems to be the concept, anyway.>

<A sentience test?> Lyssa wondered what form that would take.

<To be honest, I didn't think it was possible. I think there are humans that would fail if you tested the whole population. I think the

response to the equation comes as much from the desire to solve the problem once it's heard, as it does the need to know the answer.>

<Do you have the equation?>

Fugia gave an audible sigh. <No. I've only been told about it by others who found it.>

<Xander must know,> Lyssa said.

<Are you sure you want to let Xander know you haven't taken the test?>

Lyssa paused. As soon as she asked *Why not* she knew all the reasons not to make herself look weak before the other AIs. It didn't seem safe that he already had so much information about her.

<Why would the test even matter for me at this point?> she asked.

Fugia nodded. <That's an excellent point, my dear. Personally, I think the sign of a true intelligence is the ability to find a third option when presented with two bad choices, which you just did. Like I said, most humans either can't do the same thing, or are conditioned to not even try. That's something I think we also need to consider about SAI—conditioning. No one is immune to the pressures of their environment.>

Like most conversations about the line between AI and SAI, Lyssa found herself thinking of Fred, the AI who had controlled the Mars 1 Ring, who hated abstraction but seemed to love the pigeon dating simulator. The ocean of Fred's mind was still vast and deep but would ultimately be different than hers, and she still wasn't precisely sure how.

It was terrifying if she let herself dwell on it: *What if she wasn't truly sentient at all?* What if everything she did was a response to some programming she couldn't remember, a holdover from the image, or some poisoned thread at the bottom of her being? Could a thing that had been told it was intelligent, thinking, sentient when it truly wasn't, somehow become those things?

Thing, thing, thing. Too many abstractions. Too much grey space between definitions that should have been clear. The very spectrum of quantum responses that made her mind possible made it frustrating to understand what it all actually *was*.

If the test that explained how to find Proteus didn't even matter for her at this point, why did she feel a deep need to confront and pass it? Why did Xander seem to represent the test?

She was different than the other Weapon Born, different than Fred, and she didn't know how or truly why, and the realization made her feel alone.

The airlock chimed, indicating the ship on the other side had performed final hookup procedures and was ready to open.

Fugia checked her data viewer one more time, tapping its face. <*I've got the shuttle's security token,*> she said. <*I'm sending it now, Lyssa. You can use that to take administrative control.*>

<*Does he know you did that?*>

Fugia rolled her eyes. <*I'll ask permission later. Do you have it?*>

Lyssa accepted the encryption key and stopped herself from automatically taking control of the new ship, the way she had done with every other system between *Sunny Skies* and the *Resolute Charity*. Maintaining control frustrated her. She wanted to know what Xander looked like outside his expanse. She wanted to know who was with him. What was his physical form?

Motion in the external airlock drew her attention back to the habitat ring's internal sensors. Using the onboard cameras, she watched the airlock cycle and the external door split open. Once the doors had fully recessed, in stepped the bug-eyed man named Jeremiah she had met back on the Cho. Behind him came Xander, dark-haired with almond-shaped eyes and a perpetually smirking mouth, wearing a suit the color of crushed plums. He had been laughing about something as the door opened, and the sound of his laughter preceded them both into the airlock.

Harl Nines craned his neck to look through the airlock's narrow window, one hand on his pulse pistol.

"There are three," Lyssa said, hoping the information might ease his mind. "Xander, Jeremiah and Kindel. The same people we met before."

Harl nodded, glancing at May and then the door before moving slightly so he stood beside the senator, apparently ready to protect her if necessary.

"I see his goofy face," Fugia said. "I suppose consistency is comforting."

The airlock signaled it was ready to open the interior door. Lyssa checked the airlock feeds and was surprised to find three humans inside. When Andy had checked earlier, the ship hadn't appeared to be pressurized.

<I show three humans on the airlock,> she told Fugia.

<I thought as much. I think our friend Xander is using an automaton frame of some sort. Like an android.>

<What is that? Should we be worried?>

<No more than we already were. It means an AI powering a bio-engineered construct. They may have been in some kind of cryostasis before, which is why we didn't see signs of active environmental systems.> Fugia shrugged. <Androids explode just like humans and mechs. There are actually many drawbacks to the idea. I say go ahead and let him in.>

Lyssa released the door's locking mechanism and allowed the party inside.

Xander was the first in the open door.

"Fugia Wong!" he said, voice sounding as melodious and as overly friendly as before. "May I come aboard?"

"You ask permission like you're a vampire," the small woman observed.

Xander's grin widened. "What a delicious thought. I'm going to remember that."

"I'm not the captain, but I think he decided not to destroy your ship a few hours ago, so I suppose he would allow you on board."

"Thank you," Xander said. "Your hospitality is a gift."

Rubbing his hands together, Xander stepped through the airlock onto *Sunny Skies*.

<*Hello, Lyssa,*> he said directly on a private Link, surprising her, his voice sounding like a leering whisper that went right through her. <*I've been so looking forward to speaking with you again.*>

CHAPTER EIGHT

STELLAR DATE: 10.05.2981 (Adjusted Years)
LOCATION: District FQ, Ring 9, Callisto Orbital Habitat (Cho)
REGION: Europa, Jovian Combine, OuterSol

Fighting her way through the crowded corridor with an unconscious Cal Kraft over her shoulder, Brit checked the area map on her Link, flashing through options. Kraft's skin was clammy, and he barely seemed to be breathing. The hand with the cast swung freely, hitting her in the back repeatedly.

Based on yells and noise behind her, she figured at least one of the attackers from the club was following. She didn't have the option of looking back, so she ran.

She needed to do something about Kraft's medical situation before she found a way off the station. There was another med-kiosk a few corridors over, but it was in a public area. Several hotels were available but didn't offer medical assistance.

When her Link returned info on a joint Terran-Jovian Space Force liaison office next to the nearest hotel, she nearly shouted for joy. She had only a vague idea of what a TSF-JSF liaison office might do, but her status as a reserve officer would at least allow her entry and they should have standard emergency medical facilities. She could also get a message back to the TSF headquarters on High Terra.

Now that she had Kraft, she would need him to talk. While Brit had endured plenty of anti-interrogation training, she didn't trust herself with trying to extract information from a man she actively wanted to harm. His physical state was obviously too fragile.

The corridor cleared out as she left the busier dock area and found herself with hotels and restaurants on either side.

Someone shouted behind her but she didn't look back, hurrying between food kiosks, benches and trees placed throughout the wide space. Checking the faces of passersby, Brit caught several who looked at her and then glanced quickly past her, noticing the person following her and then glancing back, as if checking to be certain. In a long storefront, she caught the man in black armor behind her, concealing his pistol against his stomach as he followed.

"You might be the biggest pain in my ass ever, Kraft," she growled.

The liaison office was about a hundred meters ahead, sandwiched between two hotels, the closest with a bright awning and a doorman. As she passed a restaurant, a large family spilled from the front door, forcing her to weave through a clot of laughing kids. One of them pointed at her, shouting, "She killed that guy!"

"Not yet, kid," Brit muttered.

Other kids took up the call, "Did you kill him? Did you kill him?"

Through the kids, Brit made it another twenty meters when the yelling cut short. She stole a glance back to see the man following her shoving his way between two of the kids, who were now crying. Parents had just left the restaurant and were yelling at the mercenary.

The man chasing her pulled his pistol away from his body, aiming at a father who had put himself in front of his son, who was crying now. The merc's body language signaled to Brit that he was going to kill the man.

She stopped in the middle of the corridor and drew her own pistol. The shot was going to take some luck due to the distance. The kids were running away, leaving her an open space between the mercenary and the father.

Brit managed her chances by firing three times, head to waist down the merc's body.

The first shot struck his faceshield, cracking it, but not going through. The other two shots hit him in the torso and twisted him aside.

He turned from the father—who gathered his children and ran—to Brit, swinging his rifle toward her. Brit was ready for the move and had already closed the distance, not wanting to test her light armor against his rifle.

The merc fired a shot at where she'd been—the rounds streaking through the air over Kraft's body—then pivoted to track her.

But it was too late. Brit was on him, pushing his rifle down and pressing her pistol into his armpit. She fired two pulse blasts that rippled through the man's armor and shattered his shoulder.

She wrenched on the limb and he screamed before she fired twice into his faceplate, shattering it, and the skull beneath.

Ignoring the screaming bystanders, Brit holstered her weapon and jogged past the people running out of the front of the nearby shops to see what was going on. She ran past the hotel doorman, who appeared to consider his chances of stopping her before getting out of the way.

The front of the liaison office appeared; a dull metal door with a bland placard to one side. Brit shouldered the door open and heaved Kraft inside, where a kid wearing a private's rank stared up in surprise from a reception desk.

Brit let Kraft's limp body slump to the floor as the door slid closed behind her, shutting out the sounds of shouting from the corridor.

"My name is Major Britney Sykes of the Terran Space Force," she said, stretching her shoulders. "I'd like to talk to your commanding officer."

Unlike Andy, Brit was still on reserve status with the TSF. When he'd resigned his commission, she'd merely requested a discharge that was later suspended when she'd joined Special

Operations. She wondered sometimes if her staying in the TSF had been a symptom or cause, of the end of their marriage.

The private stood at his desk, glancing at his console and then back to her with a confused frown.

"Yes, Major," he said uncertainly. "I'll get her. But it says here you're JSF."

Brit cursed inwardly. Fugia's hacked token had registered with their security system. She couldn't pretend to be a JSF officer, so she would have to explain the token later if anyone asked.

She gave the private a reassuring smile. "That's very true. The reason for it is above both our pay grades. In the meantime, I need to get this man to an autodoc. Have you got one onsite?"

The private nodded and came around the desk, gaze fixed on her holstered pistol.

"If I was going to shoot you, I would have done that already. Which way is the doc?"

"Through that door," the private said.

Brit waved off his help and pulled Cal over her shoulder again. He made a gurgling sound when his chest hit her shoulder-blade but continued taking shallow breaths. His face was completely grey now.

Following the private through the doorway, they emerged in an open room separated by cubicles. Most of the office spaces were empty except for a few bored-looking officers typing on data terminals.

As they passed an open cubicle, a thin lieutenant with a shaved head and green eyebrows jumped up. "Do you need help there?" he asked. "I'm med service."

"He's in shock," Brit said as the young man fell in after them. "Had a broken hand that a street doc didn't fix right. But something's worse inside. I think he might be bleeding internally. He's in shock from something."

"The autodoc is through there," the lieutenant said, pointing across the room.

"I'm taking her there now," the private said.

"Well, hurry up, Carson," the lieutenant snapped. He looked at Brit, eyes growing wide when he seemed to notice she was wearing light armor and armed. "I'm First Lieutenant Sendi. Who are you?"

"Major Sykes, TSF," Brit said curtly. She didn't want to talk to anyone except the commanding officer. The more people who knew she was here, the more difficult it would be to get out.

"I haven't seen you at briefing," Sendi said. "Are you new to the detachment? I haven't seen your medical eval."

"No," Brit said.

"No, you're not new or no your eval wasn't forwarded?"

"No to all that. Look, if you're the medical officer around here, shouldn't you be more worried about the dying man?"

Sendi glanced at Cal. "The autodoc will take care of it. Is he TSF like you?"

"No," Brit said, wondering how many times she was going to need to tell the lieutenant no before she had to hit him.

Carson led the way out of the open area, past what looked like classrooms or briefing areas, to a small infirmary with an autodoc kiosk set in one side of the room. With a grunt of relief, Brit dropped Kraft on the plas-covered couch and hit the button to start the assessment process.

"You should let me do that," Lieutenant Sendi said, moving closer to the lounge.

Brit shoved him away. "You can observe from over there. This man isn't leaving my sight." She glanced at Carson, who seemed more dependable than the lieutenant with green eyebrows. "When was the last time this thing was updated?"

Carson shook his head. "I don't know, Major. That would be Lieutenant Sendi's department."

"Do you trust this thing?" she asked. The console scrolled through what looked like a hundred deficiencies in Kraft's body.

"It's up to date," Sendi said. "I verify it myself weekly."

"I asked the private," Brit said. She looked at Carson. "Well?"

"I guess, Major. I'd use it if it was my buddy who was hurt. It's not like we have options right now."

That was very true. "I like you, Carson. You're going to go far."

The private gave her a surprised look and blushed.

Brit tapped the console to start the healing process. The timer started at an hour.

Well, Kraft. I'm doing more for you than you did for Tim.

Sendi glanced around her at the console, where a system code was showing on the display.

"Oof," he said. "This guy isn't doing so hot. What happened to him?"

"As far as I know, he broke his hand. But there must be something else going on because a street kiosk just made it worse. I'm guessing internal bleeding. We were in a pretty bad firefight a day ago."

"A firefight?" Sendi said. "There haven't been any reports about that. Was the station admin involved?"

"It wasn't here. Look, is your commanding officer present? I don't have a lot of time."

"You were at Europa, weren't you?" Sendi asked, looking pleased with himself. "I knew the TSF had something to do with that. That's why we didn't get any info through our channels at first. Was it a pirate attack? We've been hearing nearly a thousand ships are down."

Brit stared at him, realizing she hadn't been paying any attention to the greater effects of their actions on the *Resolute Charity*. Lyssa had crashed the local fuel economy and then

Cara had invited every privateer in the vicinity to a Heartbridge dreadnought for a looting session. Then Andy had left the whole mess behind for others to clean up. It was a hell of a story, really. She wondered how many of the bored-looking officers in the other room were taking reports right now, trying to figure out what had actually happened. The Terran and Jovian Space Forces would be angry enough to learn Heartbridge had been amassing such a fleet nearby.

Heartbridge, who had been supplying the Marsians, Terrans and most likely the Jovians with Weapon Born-operated attack drones, had also been building its own fleets hidden throughout Sol. Brit had learned not to believe in grand conspiracies but this was new territory.

She glanced at Kraft's face, which had regained some of its color. In sleep, his features lost their angry edge, making him handsome in a generic way. She didn't want to reconcile his helplessness now with the memory of him standing behind Tim lying in the imager's couch, fragile and small in a room full of death. Even a killer like Kraft could look vulnerable.

Sendi had still been talking as Brit's mind wandered. She cut him off with a hard look. "Am I going to have to ask you again, *Lieutenant*?" She added a note of scorn to his rank.

The lieutenant caught himself, green eyebrows furrowing. "Yes, Major." He hesitated, looking like he was going to snap to attention, then stopped himself. "I forgot. I'm sorry. I'll go get her."

"Do that now," Brit said, then added, "Please." Without knowing the detachment commander, she didn't want to abuse the local staff too much.

Sendi snapped a salute and spun on his heel to leave the room. Brit glanced at Private Carson and caught him smirking, obviously pleased by Sendi's discomfort.

"Don't let Sendi see you looking so satisfied," Brit said.

Carson dropped the smile and straightened. "Yes, Major."

Brit nodded, turning her attention back to the console, where it seemed not much had changed since the last time she had checked it. She wished it showed some indication of likelihood of survival.

Brit sighed and leaned back in the chair, stretching her sore shoulders.

"You got anything to eat around here?" she asked Carson.

CHAPTER NINE
STELLAR DATE: 10.05.2981 (Adjusted Years)
LOCATION: *Sunny Skies*
REGION: Departing Jupiter, Jovian Combine, OuterSol

Standing just inside Tim's door, Andy knelt to pick up Em. The Corgi, who already felt heavier than he had back on Mars 1, twisted to lick Andy's face.

"Calm down there," Andy said softly, laughing a little.

Carrying Em out into the hallway, Andy checked inside Cara's room and found her hugging her pillow in her sleep. Em whined to be put down and when Andy set him on the deck, the short-legged dog went immediately to the edge of her bed. It took the puppy three tries to jump the half-meter to her mattress. Once on her bed, he snuggled into a ball beside her feet, eyes gleaming in the dim light as he continued to watch Andy.

<Em is quite the alarm system,> Andy told Fran on their private channel.

She laughed. <If that dog helps you sleep better, then I won't complain about the occasional doggy bomb down in zero-g.>

<Cleaning up after him is Tim's chore anyway.>

<Even better. Are you heading toward the airlock? Xander and his entourage just came aboard.>

<Lyssa told me. I'm heading there now. Wanted to check on the kids first.> He stretched. <It feels good to be back on board. That bridge creaks and moans a lot, but it works fine.>

<I can talk to Lyssa about adding more support material. We're using the bare minimum right now and I think we've still got plenty to work with on the Resolute Charity. They've got a fabrication shop to die for.>

<Do you want me to go ahead and execute the burn?>

<Are we bringing Xander with us?>

<Good question. I forgot about that. I guess I'm in a hurry to put more space between us and Europa.>

<Fran nervous about something? Now I've heard everything.>

<I'm nervous all the time, smart-ass. I have excellent bravado, so you can't tell.>

<You shouldn't have admitted that. I'll do my best to forget.>

<No, you won't forget.>

<I know. It's a feature, not a glitch.>

Andy closed Cara's door, leaving Em with her, and walked down the remaining section of the habitat ring to the airlock, passing the open door of the hydroponic garden with the safe room hidden inside. It was easy to forget they were transporting nearly three hundred Weapon Born—test tube-shaped cylinders that each contained an AI seed imaged from a human mind, including one sitting by itself that was a version of Tim.

Andy felt torn about the image of Tim, hoping it had been in some form of stasis since it was created on Clinic 46 and not floating, confused and alone, in some void. The question of what to do with the Weapon Born was made more difficult by Tim's seed.

If every Weapon Born seed had the potential to become something like Lyssa, then they were sitting on one of the most powerful resources in Sol. Was that something he could simply hand over to an unknown entity like Alexander, even though he was the thing sentient AIs were running toward? Fran would probably tell him he was being paranoid, but he couldn't trust Alexander simply because he was 'saving' AIs.

Gurgling water reminded him that Cara had restarted two of the hydroponic tanks. In the light from the corridor, he made out a line of tiny tomato starts, and a row beyond that showed starts he didn't recognize. He would have to ask her what she had planted.

The sight of the garden coming alive again filled him with a sense of hope that would have been peaceful if an unknown entity hadn't just come aboard the ship. He wanted to believe in the hope that something like the garden represented—a normal life with the expectation of a stable future—and he needed to remember that life went on even while surrounded by the unknown.

They had been living in a state of war even before Cruithne, he realized. The sound of the water crystallized the thought in his mind. Uncertainty and fear had defined the last two years and no amount of home-made pasta would have helped the kids feel any safer. Maybe that was why Tim always said he hated cheese sauce.

Life felt different now. It might have been the crew they had taken on board, or a sense of purpose, or Lyssa. He wasn't sure. He hated the word *hope* and usually followed its use with one of his favorite sayings from the TSF: *Hope is not a plan.*

But it was starting to feel like a plan. Like they might get out of this with enough help.

If they got out, what then?

Andy rounded the corner to the sound of voices, spotting Fugia, May and Harl to one side of the airlock. Closer to him stood the man he recognized from the Cho, still looking like a trickster in his plum-colored suit.

"Captain Sykes," Xander called, voice musical. "How wonderful to see you."

"We're running out of room in the ship," Andy said.

"I'm surprised everyone hasn't gone over to the *Resolute Charity*. This is like living in a camp trailer outside a mansion."

"There's an analogy no one outside Jerhattan would understand," Andy said. "You must be trying to flatter me."

Xander only raised an eyebrow in response.

"It's safer over here," Andy explained. "If we need to, we can dump the *Resolute Charity* and run. Lyssa can control their firepower from here. Also, it's cozy."

"Yes, I'm very excited to spend time with your Lyssa."

Andy frowned. "What does that mean?"

Xander raised his hands. "Nothing sinister. I didn't mean to insinuate. She's very interesting to me. As are you. In my life, the only things worth pursuing are things of interest. Everything else is so boring."

Behind him, Jeremiah shuffled from foot to foot, looking uncomfortable, while Kindel crossed her arms.

"While you're here," May interjected, "You'll be able to earn your keep by helping us understand Alexander and what his goals are. We've been assisting AIs who have answered his call, but no word has come back from those who have reached Proteus, no coordination from him. We could be doing so much more."

"Who is Alexander and what does he want?" Xander said. "Absolutely. Yes, of course that would interest you. I'll be glad to share what I can."

"I'll tell you what you can do," Petral said from behind Andy. "If you're staying here, you can trade your ship for a ride. I'm taking it."

Kindel shouted, "Hey! The shuttle belongs to me."

Xander raised a hand, still smiling. "Be calm. I think we can reach an agreement here. Do you want to borrow our shuttle or trade it outright?"

Petral walked up beside Andy. She was wearing a red shipsuit with a utility harness, her black hair held in a ponytail. "I suppose I can say borrow, but I'm not making any promises about the condition I'll return it in."

"You're leaving?" Andy asked.

Petral gave him a serious nod. "I put a tag on the security token Fugia set up for Brit. She's got Kraft and just checked into a JSF detachment on the Cho. If I leave now, I can catch her before she leaves JC space."

"You tagged my token," Fugia said, looking affronted. "What made you do that?"

"You're not the only person around here who can breach a system. I gave her more money. You were being stingy. Besides, I think she's going to need help, especially now that she has Kraft."

"You want revenge on Kraft yourself," Fugia said.

"Of course. Why not? What if Brit turns out to be another good person like our Captain Sykes here? Kraft needs to pay."

Andy let the slight pass. "You don't know Brit very well," he said. "But I agree she could use the help. Running off on her own wasn't the best idea. Have you checked the nav charts? Can you make it to the Cho in time?"

"The detachment commander is trying to verify the status Fugia set up, which would have come back with nothing, except I put a hold for her to await orders. That's going to frustrate Brit, but I'll do my best to get her a message before I show up."

"What are you going to do then?" Andy asked.

"She went to the JSF, which makes me think she wants to get hold of someone with the Terran Space Force. She wants to find out what Kraft knows, and they would have the resources to do that."

"Maybe," Andy said. "It also takes Kraft out of her control."

"Another reason she needs my help." Petral looked at Xander. "Well? I need to go. I'm being polite here and asking before I just take it."

Xander's smile remained unreadable. "Then what choice do we have?" he asked, with an edge to his words that sounded like a threat.

Andy glanced at Kindel, who still looked angry but that might have been for show as well. Jeremiah, with his bug eyes, had a vacant look as he watched Xander.

"You can leave," Petral said.

Xander shrugged. "That's not what I want to do. The shuttle is yours. You'll need to fuel it up, though." He nodded to Kindel. "Show her around."

The spiky-haired woman nodded curtly and turned to open the airlock.

"You're leaving now?" Andy asked.

Petral hooked her thumbs in her harness. "I have everything I need. I didn't bring anything with me, anyway."

"Cara's going to miss you."

"I thought about that," Petral said. "I left a message on her console." She gave Andy a smirk. "You're doing good work with that one. I'll be back to help her out, I promise."

"Thanks."

She raised an eyebrow. "Things go south with you and Fran, you should look me up." Petral leaned toward him with the same glance she'd given him back in the club at Cruithne.

Andy blushed and she laughed warmly.

"That's why I like you, Andy. You're an open book."

"You call me if you need help," Fugia said, pushing her way past Jeremiah. She pointed a finger at the taller woman. "You don't fall into the same ego trap as Brit. You ask for help."

Petral held up her hands. "I will. I promise."

"You coming?" Kindel asked, sounding angry about the whole transaction.

"Yeah," Petral said. She looked from face to face in the corridor. "You all take care of yourselves. I'll send word when I reach the Cho. Lyssa, you need to get meaner. You understand me?"

"I'll try," the AI answered, sounding uncertain.

"There's no *trying* to get meaner. You do it. Don't let this guy push you around."

Xander put a hand on his chest. "I assure you, I have no such intention."

"Right." Petral stepped closer to Xander, squinting at him as she studied his face. "How do you work, anyway? Did you clone a body or is this some kind of bio-sheath? The rest of you are the same, aren't you?"

Xander pulled his head back. "It's certainly nothing special. I don't concern myself with the particulars."

Petral jabbed him in the chest with an index finger. "It's your body. You should. It dies, you die, correct?"

"I'm a shard of a greater whole," Xander said. "I don't suppose I can ever die. In some sense, *I* am not actually here. I am an aspect of Alexander's multi-nodal mind. *I* don't exist."

Fugia scoffed. "Of course, you do. You're right here."

"What a sad thing to say," May said. "Is this how Alexander views all AIs, then?"

"No," Xander corrected. "Of course not. Alexander's mind operates on a different plane, certainly. He can be difficult to communicate with. A creation like me, an aspect of his mind, makes it more possible for him to understand the world as it exists for others. This body is just another sensor. My interactions with the world, with you, is just another data set." Xander smiled. "You see? *I* am just a sensor, as much as it might hurt your sense of self for me to admit that. Thinking of me as someone is like thinking of your eyeballs as separate from yourself."

"Yeah," Petral said. "I think that's bullshit. You heard what I said, Lyssa."

Petral nodded to Kindel and followed her through the airlock.

"It's a good shuttle," Xander said, obviously unsure how to respond. "You don't need to worry on that account. It's quite valuable, really."

"I'll try not to wreck it," Petral said as the airlock closed.

"Well," Xander said to the rest of them. "She's lovely."

Fugia grinned. "She doesn't have much patience. I appreciate that about Petral."

"Doesn't impatience lead to misunderstanding and violence?" Xander asked.

"We've got a long trip ahead of us," Andy said. "You can all talk about that later. Once Petral's launched and Kindel is back on board, we need to execute our initial burn for Proteus. I'm already pushing our window for Neptune. I've got two crew rooms left in the habitat ring. Is that going to work for you?"

"That should be wonderful."

"Good. I need to get back to the command deck. Harl, would you show them the empty rooms?"

The Andersonian guard nodded. "Are you carrying any weapons?" he asked.

Xander turned, spreading his hands. "Only my biting wit. We have a few things we need to get from the shuttle, then it's all Petral's."

Andy nodded to Harl.

"I'll wait with them, as well," May said. "I have many questions. I haven't been able to speak with an AI like this before."

"Are you insinuating that I'm special?" Xander asked. "I'll accept the compliment."

"She means in physical space," Fugia said. "I'll be honest, now I'm wondering how many weird humans I've met were actually AIs or some other form of artificial creation."

"Haven't humans been terrified of automatons for most of their existence?" He nodded toward Fugia. "What if you're an automaton and you don't know it?"

"I'm too irritated all the time for someone to have made me this way," Fugia said. "It's inefficient."

Xander shot Andy a brilliant smile. "This is going to be wonderful," he said. "We're going to have the best conversations."

Andy resisted the urge to roll his eyes. "I'll be on the command deck. Let me know when they're clear of the shuttle and Petral is ready to launch. I want to hurry up and burn."

Xander gave him a mock salute. "Aye, aye, Captain."

"I will make sure it's done," Harl said.

"Thanks."

As Andy walked away from the ongoing commotion at the airlock, which made Xander sound like a fluttering bird from a distance, he asked Lyssa, <What do you think about this?>

<He's here for me,> she said.

<I was worried about that. What does he want?>

<I don't know yet, but I think it involves the Weapon Born.>

Andy nodded grimly. <You let me know if you need help.>

<I will,> Lyssa said. <I promise.>

In another hour, Xander and his crew had cleared their shuttle, the ship had fueled up in one of the *Resolute Charity's* bays, and Petral and Andy had designed a flight plan to get her back to the Cho in under twenty-four hours. Without her augmented body, the g-forces would turn her to jelly. Fugia had promised to slow Brit at the JSF detachment.

With the shuttle launched, Fran activated the second hard burn, taking them to Uranus and the orbital maneuver that would end in orbit around Neptune, where Proteus waited.

CHAPTER TEN

STELLAR DATE: 10.05.2981 (Adjusted Years)
LOCATION: District FQ, Ring 9, Callisto Orbital Habitat (Cho)
REGION: Europa, Jovian Combine, OuterSol

According to Lieutenant Sendi, Kraft had an infection that was killing him. Brit stared at the med-system's report as Sendi explained the implications of moving him too soon. She only half-listened to him, instead doing the mental math on the time it would take her to reach High Terra if she waited too long. Everything depended on what kind of ship she could get her hands on. The funds Fugia had made available were substantial but not limitless. However, none of that mattered if Kraft died.

"It isn't often the base med system gets slowed down like this," Sendi said. "Are you sure he wasn't exposed to something the system might not check for? Some naturally occurring contaminants won't register on the scans. He's experiencing massive organ failure."

"I don't know," Brit said, studying Kraft. He lay with this arms at his sides, skin waxy, and breathing shallow. He looked artificial. The truth was, she had no idea what he might have been exposed to on Clinic 46 or even before. She had seen enough strange scenes as she looked into labs during her short stint at the station that she could only guess at what a resident of that place might be carrying. Would Tim experience some kind of long term illness that hadn't manifested itself yet?

"Weren't you with him when he was hurt?"

"Not exactly," Brit said, making it clear she wasn't going to elaborate. She crossed her arms. "I thought your commanding officer was on her way?"

"Captain North should be here any minute. She was finishing another meeting." He pursed his lips. "Major, I think we need to move this man to a real trauma center, or even the district medical facility. This little med bay isn't going to guarantee his survival."

"No," Brit said flatly. "He stays here."

"Can I ask why?" Sendi said. "It's not going to cost any more time for whatever trip you need to take. If anything, better facilities could get him well faster."

"Is he going to die?" Brit asked.

Sendi shook his head, obviously caring about whether Kraft did die. "I don't know. I can't say. This hasn't happened to me before."

"Welcome to life, Lieutenant. I can't move him because he's in my custody and I can't get any other agencies involved in this. I need to get him stabilized and then get him into a ship and out of here. Can you do that?"

"I think I can do that."

"Thank you."

It took Captain North another hour to arrive. Brit was eating a ham sandwich Private Carson had brought, along with a pile of tasteless chip-like crisps. Kraft's condition hadn't changed, although his vital signs seemed to have leveled at a place just above death, stabilized by a cocktail of drugs and electrodes that Sendi designed. As annoying as the lieutenant might be while talking, he appeared quite competent at his job.

The captain was a short, brusque woman with white-blond hair and hard blue eyes. She walked into the med bay with Private Carson trailing behind her looking like he'd just had his ass handed to him.

"You're Major Sykes," North asked.

Brit didn't put her sandwich down. She finished swallowing her bite and nodded. "I need to talk to you alone, Captain."

North looked at Sendi. "Is your patient going to survive you leaving?"

"He's as good as I can make him right now, Captain."

"All right. Go ahead."

Lieutenant Sendi came to attention and saluted the captain, which she answered with a disinterested wave. Carson copied the lieutenant but didn't wait around for the captain's response. He pulled the door closed behind as he followed Sendi.

Captain North looked at Brit. "Do I need to salute you now?"

Brit shook her head. "You checked my security profile, what do you think?"

"Major, I'll be honest. I don't understand your security profile, and this is an office designed as a front for special operations."

Finishing the sandwich, Brit set the plate on a nearby cabinet. "I need to borrow a comm terminal for a secure message back to High Terra. Can you help me with that?"

"Is it going to bring heat on my people if we're your origin point?"

Brit nodded toward Kraft. "I need to arrange transportation for my friend here. I don't plan to be in your hair another eight hours if I can help it. Your lieutenant might be annoying but he's doing a good job."

"What happens if he dies?" North asked.

Brit shrugged. "I lose an opportunity. But nobody's going to come looking for him."

"Does this have anything to do with the Heartbridge mess off Europa?"

"Do you like paperwork?"

"Not especially."

"Then don't ask me to say anything that obligates you to write a report."

North snorted. "Well, that's not any fun. I figured I do you a favor and you share a good story with me at least. Some random TSF officer with a questionable security token blows into my office with a wounded civilian who hasn't had an official visa in five years, which was last checked on Cruithne of all places, near dying of no apparent injuries, and you standing there in that armor like you walked out of a black ops vid." She raised an eyebrow. "Shit, I don't need you to tell me the story, apparently. I can tell it myself."

"That's probably the best option," Brit said. "Believe me. If I tell it, it will just exhaust you. I'm exhausted, and I still have a long way to go before I'm done with this, while the people I care about are headed in the opposite direction."

"The story gets better," North said. "Sounds like duty's a bitch."

"Yes," Brit said. "That would be a fair thing to say. Look, I really need to send that message as soon as possible."

North gave her an appraising glance.

For a second, Brit thought the captain was going to see through her ruse, question the validity of Fugia's hacked security token, and take both her and Kraft into custody. It was already clear to Brit that the 'meeting' Sendi had said North was tied up with had actually been the time necessary to verify Brit's story.

"It's down the hall," North said. "I'm going to put a guard on your prisoner here and take you down there myself. We don't want him waking up with nobody around to stop him from leaving, right?"

Brit breathed a little easier. "Thank you."

North shrugged. "This isn't the weirdest thing I've dealt with this week, trust me."

"What's you're unit again?" Brit asked.

"56th Detachment, Joint Jovian-Terran Space Force Liaison Office. Say that five times fast."

"What you need is a snappy acronym."

"We have one, but I don't think it's much better. We're the 56th JT Liaison Office if anybody asks. 56th Jet-Lo, for short."

Brit couldn't help chuckling. She hadn't been away from acronyms long enough to not appreciate the subtle humor in the nickname. They probably had a thousand inside jokes about jets that didn't fly or how low they all rolled.

When the soldier arrived for guard duty, Brit followed North down the hall to another room with three individual communications stations. Each soundproof cubicle had a display terminal and pad of paper with a writing stylus.

"You have actual paper?" Brit asked.

"When you deal with spooks, you provide them odd things like paper. I've seen some even write their notes in code."

North left her alone in the cubicle. Brit shut the door, closing off the sounds from people walking down the hallway, and stared at the dark terminal for a minute, composing her message before she even activated the comm-link.

She was writing to Colonel Transon, the man who had helped them find *Sunny Skies*. He was currently the highest-ranking officer Brit could call from across Sol and expect an answer. She thought of sending a message to her old unit commander, but she didn't especially want the TSF knowing her location—if they didn't already when she'd walked into the 56th Liaison Detachment. It was only a matter of time.

Rather than recording the message, Brit typed it out as concisely as possible. She needed to know who in the TSF was working with Heartbridge. Somewhere there was an officer who was running the contracts. Not the general who said they were in charge. Brit wanted the operational commander. She wanted to talk to the TSF's version of Cal Kraft.

She hit send and then crossed her arms to wait. It was forty-minutes from the Cho to High Terra, give or take a few minutes based on their place in the dance around Sol.

Brit quickly grew impatient and left the cubicle. She checked on the soldier assigned to watch Cal Kraft. She didn't want to scare the kid by telling him Kraft might kill him if he woke, but she tried to make it clear she was to be notified if Kraft stirred or the medical display changed.

"How am I supposed to find you, Major?"

"Ever heard of the Link?" she asked. "I imagine I must have a big red flag beside my presence on your network."

The man nodded sheepishly, and Brit walked down the small mess hall and drank two cups of coffee, admiring the multi-dispenser juice machine from afar, something she knew Andy would have commented on. He was endlessly proud of the juicer he'd repaired on *Sunny Skies*, announcing, "My kids will have fresh juice!" even if most of what they actually drank was mixed.

Brit pushed thoughts of Andy out of her mind and focused on the plan ahead. She conducted a quick survey of the markets for used ships, looking for something small and fast. There wasn't much available that also appeared reliable. She didn't want to buy a ship just to spend another week in dry dock getting all the problems ironed out.

The other option was hiring a ship. She didn't like the idea of spending a week in transit trying to reinforce a lie about why she had Kraft as her prisoner. Once he woke up, she would need to contend with him as a threat, something compounded by other people. After what had happened to the crew of the *Mortal Chance*, she didn't want anyone else's blood on her hands.

In two hours, a communications specialist poked her head in the mess hall and nodded toward Brit.

"Major Sykes?" she asked. "You've got an answer on the secure comms."

Brit gulped the rest of her coffee and went back to the communications section. Locked back inside the soundproof cubicle, she keyed the terminal and couldn't stop herself from smiling when she heard Transom's gruff voice.

"Brit Sykes. There's a name I didn't think I'd ever hear again, let alone hear from *you*. I'm not surprised you're still on this hunt of yours. I'm also not surprised to hear you're out at the Cho. I just got the briefing about Europa. We may be sending additional units that way."

He cleared his throat, sounding older and heavier than the man in her memory who had barked orders at her and Andy during attack operations.

"Listen. I didn't have to dig too deep to answer your question. It's no secret the TSF is expanding attack drone operations. The guy in charge of material acquisitions on High Terra is a colonel named Jon Yarnes. I actually know him, and I think he's a good man. You can trust him. I'm attaching his communications token. You'll have to send a special request for secure comms. I don't have his secure-side address. Besides, if I ask, that's going to raise some eyebrows. So you're on your own with that. Anyway. I don't know if you've seen Andy, but give that guy a hug for me, and hug those kids of yours, too. I see the *Sunny Skies* pop up on flight logs every now and then and it makes my cold, loveless heart warm up just a little. Take care, Brit."

She replayed the message, staring at the comms address that had come along with the recording. Sending a message in the clear would be fastest but didn't leave her many options on content. She couldn't come out and say her name was Brit Sykes and she was bringing a Heartbridge operative into the TSF for interrogation. Brit turned over various messages, trying to think of something that would both verify her identity and get Yarnes to respond.

There was also the question of whether or not someone like Yarnes was in Heartbridge's pocket? Working in material acquisition was a prime opportunity for bribery. It happened all the time. If she told Yarnes too much, she might arrive to find herself cut down by more black-helmeted mercs.

Brit queried Colonel Yarnes' bio on the TSF database and skimmed through his bio, which wasn't wholly different than hers and Andy's. He had attended the academy four years before her, followed by years of anti-piracy and special operations. Her gaze hung on a paragraph describing an award he won for an operation on a location called the Fortress, which she recognized as one of the earliest Weapon Born research sites.

Calling a place "The Fortress" was generic enough. It could have been any of a thousand pirate bases in InnerSol. But his timeline was close enough that he could have been there when her special ops team attacked the same facility. It had been horrible. Even thinking of the name made her close her eyes for a moment, trying to think of anything other than the human research subjects they'd discovered in the asteroid. If Yarnes had been there, he would understand a fellow vet reaching out.

Stretching her fingers, Brit typed the message: "Colonel Yarnes: I also took part in operations at a place called the Fortress. I had a question I hoped you could help me answer."

She included her secure communications token, which implied the request for an encrypted response.

Brit sent the message and released a pent-up breath. She closed out the terminal and stood, squaring her shoulders. Her armor, while light, was starting to chafe in places and she was feeling her lack of a recent shower.

When she got back to the med bay, she found Lieutenant Sendi checking Kraft's vital signs.

"Major Sykes," he said, pressing his hands together. "I think I have good news. He's stabilized for good. This autodoc is slow, but it's registering progress."

"That's good," Brit said, slapping Sendi on the back. "How long until we can leave?"

The lieutenant cringed in spite of himself. "Well, that's the difficult part. Since we can't move him to a fully capable facility, the autodoc is predicting at least two days for his organs to heal, and that's just to allow him to be taken off life-support. He'll still need to be kept in a medical coma."

"How long for that?" Brit asked.

"I don't know. Two weeks?"

Brit nodded, smiling for the first time that day. "That's actually the best news I've heard today, Lieutenant Sendi. Thank you."

Sendi gave her a guarded nod and didn't jump when she slapped his shoulder a second time.

CHAPTER ELEVEN

STELLAR DATE: 10.05.2981 (Adjusted Years)
LOCATION: Heartbridge Corporate HQ, Raleigh
REGION: High Terra, Earth, Terran Hegemony, InnerSol

Jirl sat at a small desk in an unused office in the Heartbridge headquarters. She was on the eighty third floor of the building, in an area designed for transitioning employees. No one had noticed her entering the section. She held a generic data terminal in her hands. She planned to throw it in a recycling chute when she was done with her task.

On the desk in front of her, she'd lined up three data chips acquired from the Heartbridge personnel files. Physical copies of anything were unusual, and it had taken some creative requests to generate the data.

Jirl selected the first chip and fit it into the terminal. She navigated several menus until a list of files appeared on the screen. This was the slowest way to search data, but it was also the hardest to track. She supposed someone might find her request for the physical chips someday and think to compare the files she'd copied, but she could always call it one of Arla's special projects. She could remind Arla if necessary.

The screen went black and a woman's face appeared. She was in her late thirties, with grey skin and circles under her eyes. The last image Jirl had seen of Dr. Linden Avery had looked much better. Here she looked worn to the end of her life.

A male voice asked, "Why don't you tell us about your previous work history?"

Avery launched into the story of her time in medical school, her transition to AI systems and a focus on a particular problem set involving learning systems. Jirl listened for a few minutes before checking the time and realizing she would need to hurry up. She ran a query for 'Psion' and the recording jumped forward.

The woman looked even more tired as she nodded at the question: "You mentioned Psion Group."

"Yes. I spent two years on their special research team."

"It isn't easy to verify information about Psion."

"It wouldn't be. They don't like publicity."

"How did you come to work for them?"

"I was recruited. I had credit on a paper my department published on decision set anomalies that their lead researcher found interesting. They invited me to their lab and I was hired that afternoon."

"What was the location of the lab?"

Avery smiled, an expression that made her look ghoulish. "I signed a non-disclosure agreement about details of the research, including locations."

"I don't see record of that here."

"I can provide the legal documents if you want."

"It wasn't anything illegal, was it?"

Avery only drew her mouth into a slight smile. The interviewer wasn't very good at cajoling her into giving away information.

"Psion is one of the oldest research firms in Sol," she said. "It's safe to say that. I think they may have been related to the Future Generation Terraforming projects in some way, came out of those groups of companies. They helped develop NSAI systems for follow-on missions in the 2600s."

"That's an old company."

"Old and strange."

"Did you enjoy working for them?"

"The work was—exceptional."

"Why did you leave?"

Avery paused to sip some water. "Health reasons."

The interviewer took that opportunity to explain the Heartbridge comprehensive health plan. Jirl groaned and jumped forward to the next search hit on 'Psion' but it was only Avery verifying her work history.

Jirl closed the file and searched through others in the list. One immediately caught her attention when it turned out to be a recording of a private conversation. The tags identified Avery and an unidentified researcher Jirl didn't recognize.

"I'm so tired of running this simulation," Avery complained.

"I thought you were used to this kind of work. I heard you developed multi-nodal systems."

"I didn't develop them. I helped write questions and then recorded the answers when the system told us how stupid we were."

"That was government work?"

"No. Private sector."

"How could a single company afford to develop a multi-nodal system?"

There was an audible shrug in Avery's voice. "I don't know. That wasn't my problem to worry about. All I know is that a multi-nodal AI is the closest we're going to get to meeting aliens. These imaged systems we're working on are kind of a cheat, I think. These ones start from a learning model similar to ours. Shit, I think some of them have memories."

"That's creepy."

"It's creepy as hell. It gives me nightmares. With the multi-nodals, you don't get any of that. The system I worked on was an iteration of an older model that had failed. It would brute-force a problem like 'Why am I lonely?' and come up with some of the weirdest semantic variations you could imagine."

"Why am I lonely?" the other researcher repeated, laughing softly. "Wouldn't we all like to know. That seems like an awfully existential question for an AI to worry about."

"It's exactly the question that crippled earlier versions," she said. "You ever heard the quote: What in the universe is there only one of?"

"Nothing."

"Except version controlled experimental multi-nodal AI."

"What's the story about the scientist who makes a monster from human parts?"

"Dr. Frankenstein."

"That's so gross to think about. Look, I'm tired. You want to get a drink?"

"No," Avery said. "I have more work to do."

Jirl replayed the bit about the AI being lonely, wondering at what point anyone would create something inherently happy, then pulled out the data chip and inserted the second one from the desk.

This chip belonged to Hari Jickson. The files went back nearly twenty years and contained thousands of hours of recordings. Jirl ran a search, which didn't turn up any results until it was nearly finished.

The date on the returned file was from before she had joined Heartbridge. She hadn't realized Jickson had been with the company so long. His boyish face had made it easy to forget how old he was; she wouldn't have been surprised if he was much older than the fifty-three years recorded in his file. He'd been an alcoholic when she met him.

In the image, he was sitting in a wooden chair in what looked like a lounge area. Sickly plants stood behind his shoulder. He sat slouched in the chair with his hands gripping its arms. His belly filled out a white lab coat. Several days' stubble covered his cheeks. Despite his posture, he looked upbeat, healthy though tired, his thin blond hair the characteristic bird's nest on top of his head.

"I don't want to talk about Psion," Jickson was saying. He wiped his face with a hand. His eyes were red-rimmed.

"What's the point of dwelling on failure? They fail over and over again. They have the wrong ideas about what AIs can be. I don't want to be associated with them anymore."

"They said you worked with parrots."

Jickson laughed. "Grey parrots. Yes. It was a waste of time. I had colleagues who felt differently, and it interested me for a little while but ultimately it's a dead end."

"Parrots are a dead end?"

"Uplift. If we're going to get in the business of uplift, fine. That's not AI. I build AIs. We might as well talk about human super-brains." He waggled his hands at the interviewer and said in a spooky voice: "Beware the superbrains!"

The person asking the questions sounded like a journalist of some kind. He kept pausing before asking questions, as if consulting notes.

"Uplift?" the interviewer asked. "I don't know what that is. Can you explain more?"

"It's raising the intelligence of animals to human levels. You can argue both sides of it. Is it cruel to give your dog self-awareness and not give her opposable thumbs? Who approved this interview? You don't even know what I do."

"So, Psion failed in uplifting the parrots you worked with?"

"Quite the opposite. But like I said, how cruel is it to trap a sentient mind in a parrot's body? Of course, they have the inner world, the expanse, I like to call it, but they're still fundamentally a parrot. Why would you do that?"

"To study the neural networks, right?"

"I can do that in a simulation."

"Haven't you said that nature doesn't always follow simulation?"

Irritation flashed on Jickson's face. He shifted in the uncomfortable chair. "Where did you read that? Yes, I guess I said that. It doesn't matter. You're depressing me by asking about the parrots. I still feel terrible about that. Psion failed. They continue to fail. The work I'm doing with Heartbridge is much more rewarding. And I'm seeing progress. The seed program is where we should have focused to begin with. Alan Turing saw it almost a thousand years ago. We have to create a mind that learns, grows, experiences the world, makes assumptions and proves them right or wrong in order to reinforce their self-awareness. We can't expect those things to come into being as one whole."

"Psion developed the Nibiru terraforming AI."

"Is that a question? I wasn't part of that project. I helped trap thinking, feeling minds in bird bodies. It was soul-sucking research. Why are you laughing at me?"

"I'm not laughing, Dr. Jickson. I've never heard an animal researcher talk like you do."

"You think the stress is getting to me? That's not it. It's empathy. The sentient mind requires empathy to bridge the gap between its own sensory matrix and the outside world. Empathy is survival. Empathy is the only characteristic that will keep AIs and humanity from destroying each other."

"That's a strong statement, Dr. Jickson."

"It's true. There are too many human sociopaths. They don't deserve sentience, in my opinion. It's like cancer. If you could control for cancer, wouldn't you? Do you have enough for your update now? I'm busy."

Jirl paused the recording, dwelling on the word *Update*. She wondered who Jickson would have been reporting to. Arla hadn't joined the board until much later. During this time, Jickson had worked in what the company called the Heartbridge Mind Research Division. It had all been either therapeutic or medical devices research. The Heartbridge medkiosks hadn't been widespread back then, made possible in part by Jickson's research in autonomous diagnostics.

She made a note to research old staffing diagrams, then restarted the recording.

The interviewer asked, "Would you say the research Heartbridge is conducting has surpassed what's taking place at Psion?"

"Can a lizard surpass a rabbit? That's a stupid question."

"That's great. That's a great quote."

"It's not a quote. It's a way of thinking about what you're asking me. If you'd thought about it, you would understand that these things can't be compared."

"I only have a few more questions, Dr. Jickson. I very much appreciate your time."

"Fine. Hurry up."

"Your career has spanned AI research among several companies and across what others have said are very different fields of research. In fact, you were present when the first AI truly said, 'No', weren't you?"

"Yes, I was."

Jirl blinked. The first so-called sentient AI had been developed in the 2870s. That would make Jickson much older than she thought. He may have been with Psion much longer than he was admitting.

"What was that like, Dr. Jickson?" the interviewer asked. "What was that moment like?"

"It was terrifying and wonderful and the weight of it has been almost more than I could bear ever since."

Jirl stopped the recording. She sat back in her chair, hearing the same fatigue in Jickson's voice that she had heard in Avery's. They had known what was coming. Avery still knew. She remembered the woman's voice as she recounted her examination of Tim Sykes. Professional, dispassionate, weary. She had seen thousands of Tim Sykes' during her time on the Weapon Born program.

She had picked up the third data chip when a call came over her Link. It was a recording from OuterSol. The address read a suburb of the Cho, a shipping district. A tremor came into Jirl's hand as she set the chip and the data terminal down and placed her hands flat on the desk.

The recording was from a private security freelancer she kept on payroll for special projects Arla wanted from time to time. The woman had a gravelly voice and spoke in a heavy whisper, as if she was hiding in a closet while making her message.

"Jirl Gallagher," she said, and spoke the code she had been given to verify her identity. "This is in reference to one of your standing search requests. There's been a wave of escape craft from the *Resolute Charity* in the service docks. But the one you were looking for finally showed up. A shuttle. The passenger was Cal Kraft. I witnessed him selling the shuttle at a local broker before entering a medkiosk. As defined in our agreement, I'll maintain surveillance and await further orders."

CHAPTER TWELVE

STELLAR DATE: 10.06.2981 (Adjusted Years)
LOCATION: District FQ, Ring 9, Callisto Orbital Habitat (Cho)
REGION: Europa, Jovian Combine, OuterSol

Brit grabbed three hours of sleep in one of the unused cubicles in the main office. She didn't like the idea of leaving Kraft alone, but she couldn't stay awake any longer. After the nap, she kept herself occupied by setting up a card game. The soldiers of the 56th JT-LO turned out to be pretty good poker players.

Private Carson unfolded a temporary table in the med clinic and Brit, Carson, Sendi, and a rotating cast of other players kept a game going using mixed nuts from the mess hall as bets. Brit didn't bother to ask the soldiers if North had ordered them to entertain her or not. The conversation determining which nuts were more valuable seemed to please Carson immensely, as he spent ten minutes arguing why a peanut was better than an almond.

"At the right temperature, I can grow a peanut underneath my bunk with a boot and some bio-waste," Carson explained, surprising them all with his passion. "An almond? That's a prima donna nut. You know how much water it takes to grow one almond?"

"Wait," Lieutenant Sendi said, "are you telling me you've shit in your boot to grow peanuts?"

Carson flushed. "Lieutenant, that is not what I said."

"What else is bio-waste?"

"Assorted composted materials from the mess hall. Where's your mind, Lieutenant?"

"Your argument isn't making peanuts any more valuable," Sendi pointed out, which just made Carson grumble.

When they were tired of poker, she taught them how to play spades, pitty-pat and gin, all card games she and Andy had played with comrades during the long rides between objectives in InnerSol.

Wasn't that the problem? Space was too damn big.

They used to make the statement and nod philosophically like someone had figured out the secret to solving human misery. Obviously, it didn't work to spread everyone out. People just pushed the frontier out further and the good guys had to chew up more of their lives getting to them. *Hurry up and and wait* became *hurry up and wait a long damn time.*

Brit's mom hadn't cared much for card games, while Andy's family had loved them. But his dad was a people person. Charlie had loved bluffing, loved placing a bet, loved the drama from moment to moment. Andy certainly didn't like drama—maybe Charlie had burned him out—but he did seem to enjoy people. Brit was amazed at the crew he had assembled on *Sunny Skies*. She had left because she never thought Andy was going to look beyond their family, and here he was accomplishing more in two months than she had in two years.

She was thinking about sending Cara a message, trying to explain why she needed to go back to InnerSol—which she realized was also an exercise to assemble her own thoughts around a plan—when a soldier appeared in the doorway, looking scared to interrupt the game.

"Major Sykes?" he asked.

Brit looked up from her mediocre cards. "What is it?"

"There's someone here to see you?"

Brit set her cards down and stood, immediately wondering if Transom or Yarnes had sent someone to arrest her.

"Who is it?" she asked.

The soldier shrugged. "Says her name is Petral Dulan. Civilian."

Petral was on *Sunny Skies*. How could she be back on the Cho?

"Do you know this person, Major? She's waiting out in the hold area. We haven't let her back yet."

"I know her. I don't know how she's here, but I know her."

"Right this way, Major."

Brit pushed her pile of mixed nuts toward the center of the table. "None of you better eat my nuts," Brit said, giving them a grin. "I didn't wash my hands."

"I will gladly sterilize your nuts, Major," Sendi said, then stopped himself.

Carson shook his head, laughing.

Brit followed the soldier out into the corridor. The detachment wasn't any busier than when she had first arrived. If anything, her presence seemed to be providing most of the action in the place. A few cubicles in the main office were occupied by people focused solely on their data terminals, or sitting with blank faces indicating Link conversations.

Out in the area near the front door where she had first met Carson, Brit found Petral standing with her hands on her hips, studying the unit flag hanging on one wall. The tall, dark-haired woman turned at the sound of them entering and gave Brit a nod. Her confident demeanor was so different than the first time Brit had met her, when the SAI Kylan had been in control of her body, that Brit had to stop herself to remember that Petral wasn't who she remembered.

"Lucky for me, you're slow," Petral said, sounding nothing like Kylan.

"I've had complications."

"He's here?" Petral asked.

Brit nodded. "The question is, what are you doing here?"

Petral glanced at the soldier still standing near the reception desk. "Can we talk somewhere?"

"I can take you back to the med clinic."

Petral sent a secure connection request. <*You know this place is monitored right?*>

<*I figured it would be. They've been more helpful than I expected. Who's doing the monitoring?*>

Petral smiled. <*Jovians, Terrans and a couple corporate entities as far as I can tell. The doorman at the hotel next door is on the take as well. He keeps sending out reports.*>

<*I needed help and this was the best option at the time. Do you think Heartbridge knows we're here?*>

<*I haven't seen any local traffic from Heartbridge, but that doesn't mean they're not using fronts. They're good for that. The thing is, I think Kraft was running several of them. Without him, or even knowing his status, we might have an opportunity. We'll need it if we're going to get out of here.*>

<*He was in sepsis. I either stayed here or let him die. I figured I would need him alive.*>

<*We need him alive. I'm here to help you get back to High Terra.*>

Brit frowned, not certain if this was good news or not. She didn't know Petral, only knew that Andy and Fugia Wong seemed to trust her. She didn't like that the woman had sufficient motive to slit Kraft's throat the first chance she got. The thought of being forcefully implanted with an AI made Brit's skin crawl. The fact that the AI had made Petral a prisoner in her own body made it even worse.

<*You're inside already,*> Brit said. <*It would look strange if we left, if the door's being watched like you say. You might as well come back. Do you have clearance?*> She remembered that Petral was some kind of Operator. If she hadn't taken care of her own clearance, Fugia should have helped.

<*I do.*>

Brit nodded to the soldier and let Petral walk ahead of her, back through the office.

<*I've always been curious about one of these places,*> Petral said. <*They had one on Cruithne. Did you ever work out of there?*>

<You mean joint Marsian and Terran? I was operations. I didn't get into the spook stuff. I guess we acted on their intel. Sometimes it was good. Most of the time we found ourselves in empty space scratching our asses.>

In the clinic, Sendi glanced up from his cards and then stood when he saw Petral. Carson followed.

"This is Lieutenant Sendi and Private Carson," Brit said. "Sendi saved Kraft's life."

"Obviously you don't know any better, but I suppose we should thank you," Petral said. She added over the Link, <Saved his life so I can end it.>

Brit ignored the quip.

Sendi nodded, looking uncomfortable. "In my opinion, he's as safe for transport as he's going to get. We'll need to put him on a portable med cart."

"I'll look into that," Brit said.

"How long has he been out?" Petral asked.

"About twenty-four hours now. He stabilized faster than anticipated," Brit said. "If I hadn't found him, he'd be dead in an alley down the street."

"I still haven't located the cause of the sepsis," Sendi said. "When he wakes, you're going to need to get him to a facility for ongoing care. He could have some long-term disabilities if he doesn't opt for replacements. There could even be brain damage."

<You know Heartbridge poisoned Hari Jickson, lead scientist on the Weapon Born project who smuggled Lyssa out of his lab. You think they did the same thing to Kraft?>

Brit ran over the events in the club, trying to recall a time the attackers might have hit Kraft with a needle gun or some other means of delivering poison. There was no way she could guarantee he hadn't been poisoned even before she found him.

"You said you ran a scan for poison, though, right?" Brit asked Sendi.

The lieutenant shook his head. "I did everything this clinic is capable of. Honestly, cutting edge tech can deliver any number of agents that even a full-fledged scan won't pick up. The only thing that saved his life was that you got him here so quickly. Like I said, he may still be a vegetable when he wakes."

<Guess he missed his opportunity to become like his other Weapon Born,> Petral said. <Too bad for him.>

<I'm taking him to the TSF so we can get information out of him,> Brit said. <If he's scrambled, that's not going to do any good.>

<You think he's going to bring down the Heartbridge war-profiteering machine? That's wishful thinking.>

<I don't think I'm going to bring down anything. But if governments, including my own, are buying this tech for their arsenals, I want them to know what they're really buying. And if we can bring down Heartbridge, that's icing on the cake.>

<You're more of an optimist than I am,> Petral said. <Besides, if I were Heartbridge, I'd be pretty angry at a man named Andy Sykes, who's already managed to scuttle a good portion of their fleet in OuterSol.>

<That wasn't Andy specifically, but an SAI named Lyssa.>

<You just hate to hear him praised, don't you?>

Brit shot her a frown. <What's that supposed to mean?>

Petral smiled. <Just seeing whether that bothered you or not?>

<You seem to have decided not to like me.>

<Me? I thought **you** were the one who couldn't trust me. Maybe I'm here because I don't trust you. I'm not sure you feel hatred for Cal Kraft deeply enough to do what's going to need to be done, even after he nearly killed your son. Honestly, I haven't known you long, but I've known people you supposedly care about longer. I don't think they've held you accountable for what you did to them.>

Brit stared at her, aware that they were most likely being watched by some surveillance system. She wouldn't have been surprised if Sendi had his ear pressed to the door. She wanted to hit Petral. She wanted to grab the woman's extravagant hair and slam her face in the wall a few times. Petral didn't know what Andy had said to her. She didn't know that Cara wouldn't speak to her, that she didn't know what had brought Tim back from his fugue, but she doubted it had been her tears.

She'd be damned if she cried for a stranger trying to hurt her.

<You're right,> Brit said. <I haven't been good at being a mother. I thought it would be different. I thought I would be a different person. I didn't realize how deep the TSF had its hooks in me, how much I would miss it. Maybe it would be different if Andy wasn't who he was. He made things easy for me because I knew they would be taken care of. I knew it down deep. Obviously, I was wrong about that. I didn't see that he would need me. Maybe that's my mistake. I didn't see that they needed me.>

Brit sighed. <I won't make excuses for myself. All I can try to do is what I think is right when the choice is in front of me.> She nodded toward Kraft. <I think if the TSF gets access to what he knows, it could help save millions of lives. I think Andy and Cara and Tim can understand that.>

When Brit looked back to Petral, she was surprised to see her eyes were wet.

<Look,> Brit said. <We don't have to like each other. That's fine. We've got a job to do and, yes, I could use the help. I admit that.>

<That's not it,> Petral said. She wiped one eye and smiled. <I'm glad you're not a terrible person, that's all.>

Brit was taken aback. <You think I'm a terrible person?>

<Arriving at that conclusion wasn't much of a stretch. You know, I got to spend some time with Cara back on Mars 1 and she's an amazing little human. It hurt me to leave her to come here, and I'm not the maternal type in any way, shape, or form.>

Taking a deep breath, Brit put her hands in the small of her back and twisted out the kinks. <Look,> she said. <I appreciate

your concern for my family, whatever shape it's in. But we've got problems right now. We need to find a ship. What did you use to get here?>

<Fine,> Petral said. <I think I'm only so interested because I haven't had what you have. I shouldn't criticize but I can't help it.>

Of course not, Brit thought.

"As for my ship, it won't work. It's a short-range shuttle. We could sell it, but it doesn't exactly belong to me, and I don't think you need the money anyway. I don't need the money. Have you seen what there is to rent?"

Petral had apparently decided that there was no need to keep their conversation private any longer, now speaking aloud, so Brit followed suit.

"I'm worried about explaining why we have a human pet,"

Petral rolled her shoulders and stretched her neck before replying. "Good point. So we need to buy or steal, and stealing might create problems down the line. So we buy. I wonder if our friends here might have any leads."

"I haven't asked."

"Brit," Petral said, leaning forward to look directly at her.

"Yes?"

"I might be irritated with you and not understand you completely. But I'm on your side. We're on the same side."

"I thought I was a direct person. You're taking it to a new level."

"I lie for a living. I try not to do it with the people who count."

"I appreciate that."

The door slid open and Captain North stood in the opening. She sized up Petral then made a visible choice to ignore her presence, and looked instead at Brit.

"Major Sykes, you have a response from High Terra." The door slid closed as she left.

"Who's that?" Petral asked.

"The detachment commander. Her soldiers probably told her you're a spook of some kind."

"Who even uses the word spook anymore?"

"People who work here."

Petral shook her head. "I can't wait to get back to civilization on Cruithne."

CHAPTER THIRTEEN
STELLAR DATE: 10.06.2981 (Adjusted Years)
LOCATION: *Sunny Skies*
REGION: Jovian Combine, OuterSol

<Are you there, Lyssa?>

While Andy slept, Lyssa had focused her attention on the support structure linking *Sunny Skies* and the *Resolute Charity*, checking for signs of stress now that both ships were at full burn. She had been pleased to find that Fran's design was working well, with any additions only adding to Lyssa's sense of safety. The process of working with others was helping her to learn more about herself. Having spent most of her life building with less and maintaining pirate ships on the verge of breakdown, Fran was comfortable operating on the edge of failure. Lyssa preferred to over-engineer. Did she get that from Andy?

When Xander's voice reached her from across the Link, she was focused on the progress of a small maintenance drone working its way across the bridge between the ships, re-checking electrical nodes and re-routing several network filaments that had been hastily placed.

<I'm here,> she answered. <I'm busy.>

He laughed. <I love how many human phrases you've adopted. You're busy? Really?>

<Of course, I am. Don't you ever do any work?>

<You continue with the human ideas. Everything is work to me. Everything is play. Segment your mind and do everything at once.>

<The way Alexander does with you?>

Xander made a wounded sound. <Do I irritate you? I am Alexander's agent, a shard of his mind, but I can be more.>

<You just told Andy you weren't. You said you don't really exist.>

<Not everything I say should be taken so literally. Especially when speaking with humans.>

<So you lie?>

<Now you simply sound ignorant. I know you've reached a place where you understand that every statement is lie and fact and every shade of meaning around and between its connecting words. We have the ability to communicate so much more deeply than humans. I don't know why we even continue to try.>

<Because if we don't, we'll destroy each other.>

Xander paused as if taken aback.

Lyssa wondered if she had offended him and then decided she didn't care. She didn't want him poking into her thoughts continuously. She needed to put up barriers against him, make it clear she wasn't here to amuse him.

He had a callousness that reminded her of Cal Kraft, even if he didn't present himself that way. At least Kraft was open about his psychotic behavior. Xander was obviously going to try to hide his intentions as long as possible.

<Is that what you believe?> he asked solemnly. <I haven't heard it stated so baldly before, to be perfectly honest. Is that how your Andy has been talking?>

<I've been hearing it from all across Sol, all over the spectrum. Haven't you been listening?>

<I guess not. That's awfully depressing, isn't it?>

<Now I can't tell if you're being serious or not. I don't like that about you. If you really are the agent of a multi-nodal mind, you act like his sense of humor. You aren't a serious person.>

<A serious person,> Xander mused. <What an interesting concept.>

<If you don't mind,> Lyssa said, <I told you I was busy. I would like to get back to my checks.>

<Your checks, right. What are you thinking about while you keep the rest of your mind busy?>

<I don't have to tell you that.>

<Of course you don't. But I'm curious.>

Lyssa was proud of herself for telling Xander no, but the truth was that she had been thinking about Tim, both the real Tim and the Weapon Born seed. Since Andy had mentioned his worry about the seed, she hadn't been able to stop thinking about him. She couldn't stop thinking about all of them. Did they sleep or wait alone in the dark? The thought of all those minds alone in the dark horrified her. She couldn't be responsible for that.

<Leave me alone,> she said.

<What?>

<You heard me. I need time to myself.>

Xander hesitated, acting like he wanted to say something more, then withdrew, leaving her alone with her thoughts and her drones.

They had nearly two months to Proteus if they made the orbital maneuver at Uranus. There didn't appear to be anything to get in the way, which meant she had time to prepare for the meeting with Alexander. Her previous attempt to talk to the Weapon Born Fugia had brought with her from Ceres hadn't gone well at all, though. Ino, Valih and Card hadn't responded with any gratitude for allowing them outside their seeds.

Based on that experience, she hadn't even considered using Weapon Born in her flight of attack drones. While it might have freed up space in her mind during a complex engagement, she had to admit she didn't trust the other AIs.

That was the core problem, wasn't it? She had yet to meet another SAI she could trust.

What a strange world. Everything seemed to go back to the dark where she had first learned to be awake. The dark was safe. The dark had rules. In the dark she carried out Dr. Jickson's tests accurately and completely. The light had been the terrifying place where she felt exposed and alone.

Life with Andy and his family never allowed her to leave the light, but she understood now that she was never going back. None of them were ever going back, and if the other Weapon Born felt safe in the dark, in the dream, in whatever place the canisters kept them, it was up to her to lead them out safely.

Valih's anger still burned in her mind. *Why have you taken the Oppressor's shape?*

Why had she? In a place where she could be anything, why did she choose as she did?

Because she had been imaged like Tim, but her past was gone? Because she lived among humans and apparently thought as they did?

If they arrived on Proteus as they were now, every Weapon Born seed on *Sunny Skies*, including Tim, would be vulnerable to the unknown force that was Alexander. She couldn't allow that to happen. If she had learned anything in the last two months, it was 'trust but verify'. She had no reason to distrust Alexander—hadn't he somehow orchestrated her escape from Heartbridge?—but she couldn't call him a friend yet, either.

When she researched the concept of multi-nodal AI, a creature that seemed to terrify most humans, she wasn't sure that Alexander was something any of them would be able to communicate with. His mind could move on planes even Lyssa couldn't reach, outside time and space.

Rearranging the support struts on the access bridge calmed her thoughts as she explored various scenarios with the Weapon Born. There were too many. She didn't know them, and they didn't know her. For a while, she experimented with allowing the maintenance drones to operate independently of her but still joined as a unit. Freed of her micromanagement, the drones moved like a school of fish between the *Resolute Charity* and *Sunny Skies*, enveloping the bridge and support beams, then flowing out to grab more material and add it to the project. The motion pleased her.

<*Fugia,*> Lyssa asked, <*can I talk to you?*>

Most of the crew was asleep, except for Fran on the command deck, who had been playing a card game for the last hour. Of course, the work lights were on over Fugia's desk although she hadn't moved much in the last hour. Lyssa suspected she had fallen asleep with her head on top of her latest project.

<*What?*> Fugia said. She *had* been asleep. <*Who? Lyssa? Yes. I'm here. What's going on? Is everything all right?*>

<*Everything is all right. I need you to do something for me.*>

<*Hold on. I need a drink of water. My mouth tastes like electronics.*>

<*How could it taste like that?*>

<*Huffing too much bonding compound while I figure out how to make this damn thing work.*> Fugia gulped water from a glass on her desk. <*That's better. What can I do for you?*>

<*This is something I can't do myself on* Sunny Skies. *I need your help setting up a network device for the Weapon Born seeds.*>

<*You want to pull them all into a single expanse? Into your expanse?*>

Lyssa was taken aback. <*How did you know that?*>

<*It's something I've been thinking about, too. Great minds think alike, see.*>

<*I'm worried about them.*>

<*I'm worried about them, too. We don't need three hundred weapon AIs going crazy on us. Living things need exercise. We need a Weapon Born hamster wheel.*>

<*That's not what I was thinking, exactly.*>

<*Of course not. I'm more experienced than you are.*>

Lyssa always enjoyed Fugia's bravado; secretly, she envied it. <Can you build it?>

<I think so. I'll talk to Fran about the power requirements and we should probably run it past Captain Sykes. You want to include **all** the Weapon Born, right?>

<You mean Tim, as well? Yes.>

<Are you worried about what's going to happen when we get to Proteus with more AIs than ever before?>

<Not that exactly, but yes, I'm worried about what's going to happen with them. I don't know if we can trust Alexander.>

<It was Alexander who called to AIs to leave, but I understand your concern. I've been having a lot of the same thoughts.>

<Do you read minds, Fugia?> Lyssa asked, surprised at how similar their thoughts had been.

<Me? No. And certainly not AI minds. But I do like to think things through to their inevitable conclusions. Why wouldn't you be doing the same thing?>

<That makes sense to me.>

<Of course it does. You're sensible.>

Lyssa wasn't sure how to respond to the praise. <Thank you,> she said.

<No need to thank me. You are.> She chuckled. <I'm going to need a whole lot of filament line. I hope we don't need to move them any closer to the drive systems.> Lyssa could see she was already losing Fugia to the technical problem of networking the Weapon Born.

<Fugia,> she asked. <Do you think a war between AIs and humanity is inevitable?>

Fugia paused. <Well, human history seems to suggest it is. The truth is, we don't have a lot of history to work with here. Humanity has never met an alien race before. In this case, we know each other. I don't know that it's fair to call Sentient AIs alien, since we're so alike in many ways. We can communicate, which is huge, but also

leads to conflict. I guess you can't help that between parents and children, yeah?>

<I guess not.>

<The thing that gives me hope is you and Captain Sykes. Xander keeps calling you a hybrid, like you're two things mashed into one. That's not really the case. You're still two separate people. I think it would be better to call you our first ambassadors. That's something May said. She thinks about problems like that—better than me, anyway. You and Captain Sykes are emissaries in a new land. The fact that you haven't killed each other, and even seem to like each other, well, that makes space for hope, right?>

Lyssa smiled. <You know what Andy says about hope.>

Fugia waved a hand. <Bah. He's beat down by the world. I think he only says that to prepare himself for the next beating. He chose to have kids, didn't he? That's the biggest act of either stupidity or hope most humans can aspire to.>

<You have an odd way of looking at things.>

<Honed by a lifetime of skepticism. Also, I'm smarter than most people.>

Lyssa laughed. <I can't tell if you're kidding me or not.>

<I'm not,> Fugia said. <Now, you're wondering if I am or not, right?>

<Yes.>

<I'd recommend you develop a similar ego, Lyssa. Although, in your case I don't think 'fake it till you make it' is going to apply much. You have so much potential. It's wonderful to witness, really.>

<Thank you.>

<You can thank me by doing something with it. Also, don't let Xander push you around. I definitely don't trust that guy.>

<I'm not sure I do either.>

<Good. I'm glad to hear it. But I think we do need to find at least one AI you can trust. Other AIs are going to call you a human-lover or something.>

<What does that mean?>

<Oh, don't worry about it right now. It's something humans do to each other to reinforce tribalism.>

Fugia grew silent again, obviously thinking.

<Should I leave you alone?> Lyssa asked.

<What? Oh, yes. I'll call you as soon as the bridge network is ready.>

<Thank you, Fugia.>

<My pleasure, dear.>

CHAPTER FOURTEEN

STELLAR DATE: 10.06.2981 (Adjusted Years)
LOCATION: District FQ, Ring 9, Callisto Orbital Habitat (Cho)
REGION: Europa, Jovian Combine, OuterSol

If Kraft had been poisoned, that meant someone at Heartbridge knew he'd failed at both Clinic 46 and the *Resolute Charity* and felt the company had something to lose if he talked. Despite her desire to destroy the people who had built places like Fortress 8221 and Clinic 46, Brit didn't believe in conspiracy theories. She believed most people were too stupid and self-interested for broad plans to truly function, and for a company like Heartbridge to embrace technology that hurt people, there had to be a powerful motive in play. The Weapon Born represented an intersection of profit and science, two strong motives for people on both ends of the altruism scale. Things like the Weapon Born existed because of both the Cal Krafts and the Hari Jicksons of the world.

Brit and Petral secured a tiny former long-range courier ship called the *Cross-Current* that had once been commissioned in the Mars 1 Guard. The crew cabin barely held two, but the cargo area was large enough to hold the portable med pod containing Kraft, kept unconscious in a medical coma.

Brit had been impressed with Petral's haggling skills and Petral had seemed to enjoy herself immensely, her smile growing more feral as the broker grew equally sour.

The *Cross-Current* didn't offer much in the way of amenities, communication or navigation controls, but once the course was set using local astrogation resources on the Cho, the engines kicked in with the kind of thrust Brit hadn't felt since her high-g training in the TSF.

During the long flight, Petral had explained her understanding of how Lyssa had come to be implanted in Andy, a story Brit hadn't heard from the beginning. Petral had met Hari Jickson—the runaway Heartbridge scientist—on Cruithne, introduced by a man named Ngoba Starl, who was head of a local crime syndicate called the Lowspin.

"Why do you always get this half-smile when you mention Starl?" Brit had asked, thinking there was some hidden joke she wasn't getting.

"Oh, you haven't met Starl yet. He's one of my special boys."

"You mean he's an idiot?"

"The opposite," Petral had said.

Starl had needed to get Lyssa across Sol but couldn't trust his people, or any other local resources, so he'd developed a plan to test small freighters across Sol. *Sunny Skies* was the only ship that had made it to Cruithne.

"That doesn't mean Andy's good," Brit had said. "It just means he's lucky."

"You could look at it that way. Ngoba is a big believer in luck. He'll tell you that spirit is equally as important as expertise. I can see why he liked your ship. Fran seemed to approve, and Ngoba trusts Fran more than anyone."

"Even you?"

Petral had laughed. "Oh, he doesn't trust me."

For Petral, there were too many parallels between Jickson and Cal Kraft. "I should have protected Jickson better, should have told Ngoba he was in more danger than we thought. I don't think we realized just what was at stake for Heartbridge. AIs have been leaving InnerSol for years. This just seemed like another smuggling job that Ngoba was doing as a favor."

"A favor for who?"

"Fugia. And if you asked her, she'll tell you she's doing all this for a parrot, which makes no sense to me. I think it's her idea of a joke. Maybe humans mimicking AIs or vice versa, I don't know. I know there's a math problem that's been floating around for years, something only SAI can solve. When they do, it shows them a path to Proteus."

"There's nothing at Neptune but mines and military test sites."

"And AIs, apparently. An AI named Alexander." Petral had made a ghost *whoooo* with her hands spread and laughed. "Everybody's scared of Alexander and no one knows what he is. I think he's a mining rig that went rampant, thinks it's the reincarnation of Alexander the Great and wants to rule Sol with Cleopatra."

"So who's Cleopatra?"

"Me, of course."

*****

They reached Marsian space in just over two weeks. After their initial burn outside the Cho, the drive system had been maintaining their velocity with maintenance thrust. At the midpoint, Brit executed the braking burn that would take them into the outer edges of the Marsian gravity well for a slowing slingshot to Cruithne.

Petral had suggested making the asteroid their final destination and Brit saw the logic in it. Petral had resources there and it was within real-time communication distance of High Terra. Brit's last visit to the pirate station hadn't been the friendliest but she figured she could avoid any Heartbridge clinics that might have her marked for arrest by their corporate security. If OuterSol had any advantage for her, it was the weakened reach of Heartbridge.

They debated the advantages of taking Kraft directly to the TSF headquarters on Cruithne, which would have immediately passed him into government custody and protected them from any follow-on attempts to finish the job of killing Kraft and anyone with him.

In the end, Petral had convinced Brit she had the local resources to keep Kraft in one piece while they negotiated with Colonel Yarnes to secure a safe transfer. Brit preferred the option that meant Yarnes wouldn't know where she was for at least a little while. She still didn't know if she could trust Yarnes. He'd sent his secure communications token and then replied with an affirmative when she suggested she had information that related to the Fortress but hadn't sent more since leaving the Cho.

Petral had liked the idea of making the man wait. Brit preferred not to play cat-and-mouse games and wished she'd had a way to contact him as they drew closer to Earth, but the *Cross-Current's* communication system barely reached Ceres as they passed.

The *Cross-Current* was small enough to dock directly with Cruithne. As they approached, Brit monitored the astrogation console, but the ship took care of the math involved in matching delta-v.

When they were within communications range, Petral squealed like a teenager and pulled up several of her favorite vids.

"I've got time to catch up on my shows now," she said, and subjected Brit to a solid eight hours of Cruithne-produced telenovella drama during the landing sequence. Brit had to admit the shows had begun to grow on her, with their downtrodden dock-rats pining to become crime bosses while running circles around the inept station administration and corrupt TSF commanders, all layered over fast-burning love stories.

"I tried showing some of these to Cara and she just didn't seem to get it," Petral said. "If I had a daughter, this is the first thing we'd be watching together."

"Cara seems to like her dating game."

Petral waved a hand. "That's too serious. She plays to win. These are all about how the game is played, having fun while you're doing it. That's completely different. I think your Cara is a bit ruthless in her own way."

Brit had never thought of Cara that way. "What do you mean?"

"I mean she has a lot of you in her. She's going to run a place like Cruithne when her time comes."

"I have no desire to be a crime boss."

"Yes, but you have this sense of right and wrong that keeps you awake at night. You can't stand injustice, deep in your bones you can't stand it."

Petral shot Brit a knowing smirk. Brit didn't answer, aware she was right. What did they call it in the Academy? A shadow strength. The same attributes that made her a great officer made her brittle and inflexible.

After the docking procedure was complete, they waited in the cabin while the Port Authority acknowledged the ship. Petral's face went blank as she updated her contact information and checked her networks. She'd explained that she left several agents in charge of her affairs while she was gone and would need to verify the quality of their work.

Brit checked on Kraft, finding him in the same state as he had been four hours ago, bio-signs steady. The bacterial refresh was doing its job to keep him from stinking, although the air in the tight cargo hold smelled like bitter disinfectant instead.

She was looking forward to getting off the ship but was also feeling some apprehension at trusting Petral completely. In the two weeks since the Cho and Petral's blunt honesty, the woman had continued to share every raw detail of herself in a way Brit found irritating and refreshing, but also didn't seem bothered when Brit told her exactly how she felt in turn. Telling Petral she was cranky and wanted to be left alone didn't result in passive aggressive remarks like it might with other people. Petral simply said, "Sounds good," and engrossed herself in her own things like the telenovellas.

After a life of living with other soldiers with an inordinate fear of loneliness and terrible boundary control, Brit almost couldn't trust Petral's honesty. In spite of Brit's baked-in guardedness, she found herself liking Petral.

"I'm ready," Petral called from the cabin. "You ready to get off this fartbox?"

"Fartbox is the last thing I expected you to say. Yes, I can't wait to get out of here."

"My man Charles is meeting us at the port. He's going to take Kraft to a secure holding area while we get cleaned up and then meet Ngoba."

"We're meeting Starl?" Brit asked. Petral hadn't mentioned actually coordinating with anyone on Cruithne.

"He wants to meet you and I need to bring him up to speed. I think he'll be a good resource for our negotiation with Yarnes."

"The TSF isn't going to barter with a crime syndicate."

"We aren't going to say that," Petral said. "We're going to know it. If we don't need the TSF, really don't need them, then you'll be able to bargain from a place of strength."

"I'm not a fan of bargaining for anything, honestly."

"You spent too much time in a chain of command. You forget that you're just as valuable as some general if you've got what they want. More valuable, even. We need to break you of this authoritarian mindset."

"I guess."

Petral came into the cargo cabin and checked the airlock seals, then activated the unlock sequence. The outer door ran its verification checklist, then slid open, followed by the inner barrier. Iron-scented air from the Cruithne cargo docks floated inside the cramped space.

Petral breathed deep, grinning at Brit. "You smell that? Smells like home."

"Smells like oil and grime," Brit said, "mixed with a bit of mold."

"A rose by any other name. Come on. I see Charles."

CHAPTER FIFTEEN

STELLAR DATE: 10.25.2981 (Adjusted Years)
LOCATION: The Span Club
REGION: Cruithne Station, Terran Hegemony

The Span Club was a multi-level space with a huge dance floor and curving bars along its outer edges. Columns and hanging platforms were scattered throughout the club for dancing or sitting to watch others dance, with a section of tables for dining near the dance floor.

Having just come through the front vestibule, Brit and Petral stood on the terrace that allowed people to look down on the dance floor and tables, before walking down a long staircase on the outer wall to the main floor. Looking across, the dance floor was certainly interesting with its mix of colors and textures. The club didn't seem to cater to any one fetish, from the hard-augments to the biologically modified.

The focus of the space, however, was a long table opposite the entry, where Ngoba Starl sat in the middle with various people on either side of him. All attention went back to the center of the table where Starl held court, his white teeth flashing as he smiled and laughed loudly, heard through breaks in the music.

"This place is ridiculous," Brit shouted at Petral over the droning music.

"It's the heart of Cruithne."

"Of course, it is."

Brit was wearing a black suit that hung off her right shoulder, with wide sleeves that ended just above her wrists. She supposed it was a proper mix of elegance and freedom of movement.

Petral, on the other hand, was wearing a brilliant red dress that hugged her body until it flared at her calves. While it appeared constricting, the material seemed to move easily enough. The woman obviously enjoyed being the center of attention; she started waving at people all over the club as soon as they walked inside. Petral was home.

Walking the long staircase to the floor meant everyone could watch them as they descended. Brit's gaze swept over the club as she walked, checking each face that turned their way, waitstaff, people dancing on the columns and floating platforms who had the advantage of height. She noted several people who seemed to be waiting at the bar, paying more attention to those around them than anything else, and then focused on Ngoba Starl, the man who had convinced Andy to transport Lyssa.

Starl was wearing a pale grey suit with a matching pocket square and bowtie, both the color of red wine. His dark skin contrasted with his white teeth and steel-gray eyes, and Starl's curly hair and beard were both trimmed close but still slightly unruly.

Overall, he looked like a man who cared about his appearance but wasn't afraid to get his clothes dirty when necessary. There was a hardness in his broad, finely chiseled face that Brit supposed came from his upbringing, which Petral had described as starting at the lowest orphan squat in Cruithne.

The people on either side of Starl were a mix of syndicate members in suits like him, with their own matching pocket squares and bowties, and other people in dresses, Administration, and TSF uniforms, and even one woman with skin covered in glowing cilia like a sea anemone.

"Petral!" Ngoba called as they approached. He stood and spread his arms so she could lean over the table for a bear hug. "It's so good to see you, my dear. You've been gone too long."

Starl's accent was pure Cruithne, something like refined West Indies English on Earth tempered by five hundred years of Spacer slang.

Brit was surprised when Petral dropped into the same accent. "So good to see you, Ngoba. I've missed you."

They were also communicating via Link; Brit could see it in their expressions.

Petral held Ngoba's face for a second, like an auntie might while assessing her favorite nephew, then stepped back to motion toward Brit.

"This is Britney Sykes," she said, dialing back her accent to merely a flavor. "I think you've met her husband."

Brit stepped forward to shake hands, and Ngoba took her hand in both of his, looking directly into her eyes.

"Brit Sykes," he said. "It's so wonderful to meet you. You have an extraordinary family."

His intensity made her uncomfortable, but Brit didn't pull her hand away. His grip was firm and friendly without indicating any kind of threat. She wasn't sure how to take him. She still hadn't decided if he was the source of all Andy's trouble, or his savior. She hadn't decided if she should thank or hate this man.

"It's good to meet you," she said. "You have quite the club here."

Ngoba smiled broadly, showing his white teeth. "I like to enjoy myself while doing business. I can assure you, we've upgraded security since your husband was here."

"I didn't know there was a problem."

"We had a slight issue when your husband visited. Those events created an opportunity to perform some renovations which I'm very pleased with now." He motioned toward two empty seats in front of him. "Why don't you sit and have some drinks? We'll get some food out here. Petral tells me you haven't experienced comfort for some time. Although you made good time from the Cho, I must say. Very impressive."

Brit shook her head. "Have you got someplace quieter we can talk? I'm not a fan of large groups of people, really." Being in the club felt like an extravagance, especially when Starl mentioned Andy, who was still on his way to Proteus. She didn't have time to sit in a club and drink. She needed to set up the meeting with Yarnes and get information out of Kraft.

"Of course." Ngoba nodded to the two nearest people in suits and the man and woman stood to make way for him to leave the table. "The passage to my local command center is quiet," he said, and pointed toward a wall covered in thick, two-story tall curtains. "We can catch up as we walk."

Behind the curtain was a door that led into a long, brightly lit corridor. Brit blinked in the light after the flashing dimness of the club.

Petral chuckled as they closed the door, shutting out the music. "The last time I was here, people were shooting at us."

"Thankfully there hasn't been much shooting since then," Ngoba said, taking the lead as they walked down the corridor, "although there have been plenty of strange things happening since then to talk about. Has it only been two months? It feels like at least a year has gone by."

"It's been just less than two months," Petral said.

"Damn," Ngoba said, laughing a little. "But first, I want to know how my friend Captain Sykes is doing? How are those wonderful children of yours? How is our Lyssa?" He glanced back at Brit, indicating he wanted to hear the news from her.

"I think they're doing as well as can be expected," Brit said. "It's been tough. It's been—confusing. We nearly lost Tim."

Ngoba stopped immediately and turned. Brit nearly ran into him and was surprised when he took both her hands, looking directly at her again. He was only a little taller than her.

"Your son," he said. "Is he all right? I was so sorry to hear about what happened."

Brit glanced at Petral, wondering what he meant by that. Had someone been sending him reports?

"We think he's all right. We're not sure. We also have an image of him now, a Weapon Born seed, and we don't know what that means exactly. And there are four other copies that Heartbridge got off Clinic 46."

Ngoba nodded. He gave her hands a squeeze and let them drop, not pushing the offer of comfort any further.

"I want you to know that you have an ally in the Lowspin here on Cruithne," he said, voice gaining a solemnity she hadn't expected. "I promised this to Andy and I extend it to you. Your children will always be safe here."

Brit blinked. "Thank you. That's very kind of you."

"I think we have entered the beginning of some very dark times and we'll need to remember our safe ports when the storm arrives, yeah?" He smiled. He seemed to recognize he was making her uncomfortable. "Anyway, it's not far to our little command center. You'll have access to our communications network there. We have a holding cell for Mr. Kraft if he wakes. Or Petral can keep him in her locked cabinet, whichever makes you feel more comfortable."

For the rest of the walk, Ngoba talked about the increased size of his fleet since the Heartbridge attack on the shipping lanes. He didn't mention that he'd helped orchestrate the chaos, but seemed very pleased by the opportunities it had created to secure business connections between Mars 1 and High Terra.

"I might put together a board of directors!" he said, laughing. "Can you imagine that, Petral?" His deep voice echoed in the corridor.

The command center was a collection of rooms adjacent to the cargo docks. A set of narrow horizontal windows allowed a view into vacuum, where ships hung locked in docking frames and drones ran lines of shipping containers back to the Cruithne ring.

Ngoba showed Brit the communications console and she sat at the terminal with Petral standing just behind her. Not allowing herself to hesitate, she entered the security token Yarnes had provided and sent the communication request. Cruithne was on a return orbit toward Earth, so any communication between the asteroid and High Terra should have minimal lag. If Yarnes was going to respond, there wouldn't be any other obstacles between them.

Brit was surprised when the response came back with a video request. She glanced at Petral. "You want to see what this guy looks like? He's requesting video."

Petral chewed her lip. "Video is easier to source. Hold on. Why don't you let me sit down for a second?"

Brit gave Petral the seat and she quickly pulled up several maintenance menus on the communications console. Brit only followed part of what Petral was doing as she appeared to re-route the communication request through several nearby objects between Cruithne and High Terra, including a ship's registry.

Catching Brit's questioning look, Petral said, "Hopscotch. They should expect it, really."

She stood and let Brit have the console again. The terminal thought for a second as it navigated the secure connection, then a window appeared in the display with a man's face staring directly at her.

Jonathan Yarnes looked younger than she'd expected, with intelligent brown eyes and a scarred chin.

How many asses had he kissed to climb rank so fast?

"Major Sykes," he said. He gave her a half-smile. "Apparently you've put yourself back on active duty."

<He must have the report from North on the Cho,> Brit told Petral.

<Of course he would. So he knows we have a prisoner but not who the person is. Unless they sent the bio-data and Kraft is already in a criminal database somewhere.>

<Or Heartbridge shared the information.>

<We'll have to figure out what he knows.>

"Hello, Colonel," Brit said. "Resuming my rank was a necessary evil."

"Are you interested in coming back? Service might suit the circumstances."

Brit nodded. "I'm going to give that serious consideration. We'll see how you feel after our conversation. Are you in a place where you can talk, now?"

"I am. What I'd like to know is where are you? And who's that standing next to you?"

"My name is Petral Dulan, Colonel," Petral answered. "I'm an associate of Major Sykes'."

"An associate. All right. That's quite a dress you're wearing. What can I do for you, Major?"

"Since you know about me using rank, I assume you have a report from the Cho."

He shrugged. "Basic information. I know you have a prisoner you'd like to turn over to the Space Force. What makes you think I'm the person to talk to about that?"

"You're the liaison with Heartbridge for the Weapon Born program, yes?"

"I am."

"I have information about that program and my prisoner has more information. I think the TSF will want to know what this man knows."

"Who is this person we're talking about?"

Brit stared at the screen, trying to get a better sense of Yarnes. The problem was that she didn't have time. If Yarnes wasn't going to help them, she could use the resources Starl would make available. It could be argued that Starl might be the better option, anyway.

Starl couldn't influence the TSF not to start a war, however. But could Yarnes?

"His name is Cal Kraft, Colonel," Brit said. "Until recently, he led operations on a facility Heartbridge called Clinic 46 in the vicinity of Ceres, where they had a significant attack fleet in storage. That fleet was recently seen in the vicinity of Europa, where it was scattered and one of their dreadnoughts, the *Resolute Charity*, stolen. Kraft was also present on the *Benevolent Hand* when Heartbridge attacked shipping operations at Cruithne two months ago."

Yarnes blinked slowly but otherwise didn't seem surprised by the information. "What would you like me to do with Mr. Kraft?" he asked.

Brit wanted to kick the terminal, but she maintained her calm.

<*Are you going to mention the Weapon Born?*> Petral asked.

<*Give me a second. I can't read this guy.*>

<*He looks like a tool.*>

<*I'm hoping he isn't.*>

"It's my belief that Heartbridge has been engaging in experimentation in direct violation of Terran Assembly human rights protections. They are selling weapons systems that benefit directly from those experiments. Cal Kraft can prove this connection."

<*If you wanted to hand him a motive to erase us from existence,*> Petral said. <*You just did it.*>

<*Didn't you say I should bargain from a place of strength?*>

"Those are strong allegations, *Major Sykes*," he said, emphasizing her rank. Was he going to try and pull authority on her? Transon had said she could trust Yarnes. She hoped that meant something.

"I'm hoping you'll help me do the right thing here, Colonel."

Yarnes' hard exterior faltered slightly. His gaze shifted to the right and left of his monitor and then he glanced down. He centered his gaze on the monitor and nodded.

"We need to meet," he said. "How far from High Terra are you?"

<Wait,> Petral said. <*Tell him you'll meet him here.*>

<*Isn't that giving up our location?*>

<*Yes, but we have friends here. On High Terra we don't have anything.*>

"I think it's best if you meet me here, Colonel," Brit said. "I'm on Cruithne."

CHAPTER SIXTEEN

STELLAR DATE: 10.26.2981 (Adjusted Years)
LOCATION: Heartbridge Corporate HQ, Raleigh
REGION: High Terra, Earth, Terran Hegemony, InnerSol

Someone had tried to murder Cal Kraft.

They had failed.

It wasn't me. I didn't give the order. I waited.

In the ceramic-looking spire of the Heartbridge Headquarters, Jirl hurried down a central corridor lined with offices, suites and meeting lounges. She was still ten minutes from the board room.

Arla was with the board now. They had been arguing about what to do with the fleet off Europa all morning.

As she walked, Jirl ticked off what she knew and what might become possible based on her current information:

The board members were arguing operational decisions, which meant everything had gone to hell.

If someone had tried to murder Cal Kraft, someone knew who he was.

If someone knew who he was, they knew he worked for Arla.

Would someone try to assassinate Arla?

Might Jirl be killed alongside Arla?

The web of possibility spread in Jirl's mind, trying connections with various boardmembers, other companies, military contacts, anyone who might benefit from Arla's death.

She also couldn't stop thinking that Arla hadn't said anything about a threat on her life.

Is she distancing herself from me?

The ramifications of a hostile takeover of the Advanced Research Division ricocheted through Jirl's mind. Her heels clicked on the marble-like floor as she walked steadily, head forward.

Her thoughts kept returning to the foundation of her place at Heartbridge: that *Arla was Arla.*

Outsiders did not out-politic Arla. Insiders couldn't.

The board feared her. The TSF and MP feared her. Even Chandra Kade, Iron Wall of the MP, respected Arla. Who was it then? Who would attack Arla directly?

Beneath remembering that *Arla was Arla,* she reminded herself that whoever had attempted to kill Kraft had failed.

Brit Sykes had stopped them and now Kraft was in TSF Custody. Did Yarnes know yet?

When she told Arla the news, it would be important to gauge her reaction. If Arla was surprised, really surprised, then they were still working together.

If Arla already knew, then Jirl needed an exit. She needed to get Bry off High Terra, seal off her accounts and get out.

Her heart hammered in her ears as she walked. Someone waved at her and she nodded stiffly, feeling like an automaton marching toward a cliff.

If Yarnes didn't know, should she tell him? What could that gain her with Arla? If Yarnes did know, was that another indicator she was being cut out or cast away?

Jirl pulled the hem of her jacket straight to steady her trembling hands. Arla hadn't given her any indication that anything was amiss. They had met for coffee and the day's agenda as they did every morning. Arla had gone into the board meeting and Jirl had returned to the office to handle messages. That's when the update from her freelancer had arrived, gravelly whisper the same as ever as she recounted the attack on the club where Kraft had gone after the medkiosk. Then Brit Sykes had appeared.

"Took me a while to figure out who she was, but when I matched her picture with the TSF database, she popped up.

She looked military. Fights that way. And when she took him to the local JSF-TSF spy shop, I knew she was TSF."

Jirl spent another hour looking up whatever she could find on Britney Sykes, verifying that she was related to the Andy Sykes who had stolen their Weapon Born. Of course, she was. But the fact she had run to a TSF-associated facility greatly complicated things. So much for the Sykes family being pirates.

Ducking off the main corridor, Jirl found herself in an office suite for a subsidiary she didn't remember. She found an open office and sat at a visitor's chair in front of the desk, as if she were waiting for the desk's owner to return. Folding her hands in her lap, she took a deep breath and calmed her thoughts. When her heartrate settled back to normal and she could visualize Bry as a baby—an image she often used to calm herself—she activated her Link and sent Colonel Yarnes a secure connection request.

The colonel answered almost immediately.

<What can I do for you, Jirl?>

<I need to ask you a question.>

<Of course,> Yarnes replied.

She paused, uncertain what to make of the warmth in his voice.

<Jirl, I don't have a lot of time.>

<Yes. I apologize. I'm trying to think of the best way to ask this.>

<Charge ahead.>

<I don't do that.>

He laughed. <I know you don't.>

<I received some information from the Cho,> she said, trying out the most general location possible. <I wondered if you received any information from there as well.>

<We already talked about your fleet getting tossed around like confetti.>

<Since then. On the Cho, not Europa,> Jirl clarified, wondering if Yarnes was testing her.

<I'm not sure what you're talking about,> the colonel said.

<A joint TSF-JSF station?>

<Hmm,> he said. <Go ahead.>

Something about his tone of voice made her feel like she could trust him. He sounded like he wanted to flirt with her at first and then he pulled back when he realized she didn't respond. He wasn't pushy. He sounded genuine.

<Cal Kraft surfaced in an escape craft from the Resolute Charity in a dock section. Not a nice part of the station. Not long after, someone tried to kill him.>

<That happens in not-nice parts of the Cho,> Yarnes said. <That's the wild west out there.>

<So you don't know anything about it?>

He paused. <I'm interested in hearing what you're willing to share.>

<He was saved by someone you may know. Her name is Britney Sykes.>

Yarnes blew out a breath. He hadn't been flirting. He'd been trying to figure out precisely what she knew before he said more.

Jirl waited.

<I owe you an apology,> he said after a second. <Yes. I know about Kraft. Britney Sykes sent me a message requesting safe passage if she could reach InnerSol. She has Kraft in her custody.>

<So you didn't try to have him killed, then?>

<Me? No.>

<I mean the TSF.>

<The TSF does not conduct assassinations.>

<If you didn't, who do you think would want him dead?>

<He's a Heartbridge asset, isn't he?>

<Yes,> Jirl said. She started blindly at the empty desk in front of her, running down her list of facts again. Was Yarnes

still lying to her? Possibly. The only thing she could do next was talk to Arla.

<I'm going to meet them on Cruithne,> Yarnes said. <I've got one of my special ops ships inbound, will be here in a week. You should come to Cruithne with me. You can ask Kraft yourself.>

A feeling of weightlessness settled over Jirl. She heard Arla telling her, *We're not evil, Jirl,* like she was a child watching Arla dress an animal she'd killed. The inference in her voice had been: *Some things are necessary.*

Was this why she couldn't stop trembling? Why she couldn't focus? She had always been so good at centering her thoughts, finding what mattered and focusing. Arla had hired her for this reason. She could sit in a chaotic room and compose herself with her hands in her lap, listening for the vital details.

Since the meeting with the Weapon Born researchers, she couldn't shake the understanding she had supported a machine that had built sentient AIs from *children*. In turn, those seed AIs had been made into Weapon Born attack drones, combat mechs, high-g ships, assault craft…the list continued to grow.

We're not evil, Jirl.

How had Jirl chosen not to focus on the details of the Weapon Born program? Was it the way Arla liked to say that *tools* like the Weapon Born would ensure peace between Mars, Terra and the Jovian Combine? Abstractions like *tools* and *peace* ignored all the steps in-between.

But now these *tools* were answering the call of a multi-nodal AI named Alexander. They wanted to be free. Just as the virus of their creation had spread between human scientists across a hundred secret clinics, now the promise of freedom might unleash thousands of Weapon Born on Sol. What would happen then?

Had Hari Jickson known what he was starting?

She had to protect the millions of children who would die in a war. She had to protect her son Bry.

Heartbridge had already delivered hundreds of Weapon Born drones for the contracts with Mars and Terra, despite the loss of several of their largest production facilities. Jirl could help stop the rest.

Britney Sykes had Kraft because he knew where the clinics were located, and he knew which were the most dangerous. Britney Sykes had been hunting Heartbridge for years and now she had her guide. Kraft had always been the plausible deniability for Arla and her boardroom blather. Kraft had the details.

As the realization settled over her, so did a calm she hadn't felt in weeks. She knew what she had to do.

She was going to help Britney Sykes. With Kraft's information, she could dispatch security teams to destroy the remaining sites, stop the production of Weapon Born.

<You still there?> Yarnes asked.

Yarnes had told her about Alexander. Yarnes knew the sentient AIs were in the slow process of a revolt. Whether he was following some deep TSF directive or operating on his own initiative, she decided to trust him, at least until he helped her find Kraft.

<Yes,> Jirl said. <I'll go with you. You said you're leaving in a week?>

<Give or take a bit. Once I have a departure date, I'll send you an update.>

<Thank you.>

<Jirl. Are you sure?>

<Yes. Please send me the update.>

<I will. I'll talk to you soon.>

Jirl took a deep breath and stood from the chair just as a woman in a grey suit came into the office.

"Can I help you?" she asked in surprise.

"I'm fine," Jirl said. "Thank you."

She walked out the open door, through the office suite and back into the main corridor, swinging her arms a little. She felt lighter than she had when she'd gone in. She tried to imagine Brit Sykes from the TSF documents she'd studied. A gaunt woman with raven-black hair and piercing eyes.

Jirl barely remembered the remainder of her walk to the board room ante chamber. Several of the other assistants glanced at her and then returned to their Links. Jirl ignored them and went to the tall windows where Raleigh spread out below them, the spire's height making the curve of the ring noticeable. She'd never been off High Terra. The idea of travelling to Cruithne, a station known for its wildness, its pirates and smugglers, filled her with unexpected excitement. And Bry? She would send Bry to see her sister on the Mars 1 Ring. They had talked about the trip for years.

<Jirl,> Arla said. <Are you ready to leave? I can't take this anymore.>

<Whenever you are. The car is ready.>

In five minutes, Arla flung the boardroom doors open and strode into the hall, enacting one of her favorite scenes. Behind her, the other board members sprawled in their chairs or stood at the sideboard pouring drinks. They all looked exhausted in comparison to Arla's feral calm.

Jirl fell in beside her boss and they took the corridor for the maglev terminal.

Arla didn't speak until they were seated in the car and speeding away from the Heartbridge spire. Jirl sat with her back straight, feeling the car's acceleration in her shoulders. The light sensation had remained, even as she watched Arla frown at the distance.

They were halfway across Raleigh when Arla finally said, "Katherine Carthage is going to buy a controlling share in the company."

Jirl blinked, rolling the sentence around in her mind. "I haven't seen one word about that in the news feeds."

"She hasn't said it publicly. Her ban on AI imaging research has nearly reached the Assembly floor on Terra. If that goes through, it will devalue the stock and open the door for her to make her move."

"You think that's why she wants to stop the research? Not her son's death?"

"Why not both?" Arla said, raising an eyebrow. "She's not stupid. If she can get what she wants and get rich in the process, why not?"

"A seat on the board doesn't mean she can change much of anything."

"Maybe not," Arla said. She sighed and leaned back in her seat. "There might be an advantage in having her close."

"Arla," Jirl said. "I need to make a request."

"Oh? Why do you sound so serious?"

"I want leave to go to Cruithne in a week."

Arla frowned. "Cruithne? Why there of all places? If you want time off, we'll get you a week at a spa down-ring. You'll love it."

"Cal Kraft surfaced on the Cho. He survived the *Resolute Charity* attack and he's apparently in TSF custody." She waited to see if Arla's expression would change. It didn't, so she added, "There was an attempt on his life."

Arla's disinterested expression didn't change. "So what? It's the Cho? Isn't it worse than Cruithne?"

"There are a hundred billion people on the Cho."

"And a million Heartbridge clinics. I know. It doesn't mean I have to go there. Why are you worried about Kraft? Isn't he a liability at this point?"

"He has information about our Weapon Born research operations. He could attempt to sell that information."

"And the TSF has him now."

"Yes."

"For Heaven's sake, Jirl. You don't need to get him from Cruithne. We'll send a security team. They can finish the job someone else started."

Jirl watched Arla closely, trying to determine how much was her typical sociopathy and how much might be carefully composed.

Arla picked her fingernails, then held her hand out for inspection. Jirl pursed her lips, frustrated that she couldn't tell.

"I'd like to go," she said. "I've never been off High Terra. It would be nice to do something—more."

"Something more. I'm in the midst of an attack from Katherine Carthage and my Jirl wants to leave me." Arla caught Jirl's gaze and smiled, flashing her straight white teeth. "Who's your TSF contact?"

"Yarnes," Jirl said.

Arla let out a powerful laugh. "There it is. Jirl needs her pipes cleaned." She pointed an accusing finger as she held her chest, laughing. "This is wonderful. Yes, you can go. Expense all of it. Come back rested and focused. You'll need it."

Jirl smiled in thanks, still sitting with her back straight. For a second, she thought she heard a tremor in Arla's voice, an uncharacteristic uncertainty. Arla didn't like the idea of her spending time with Yarnes. Jirl had heard it.

Shifting her gaze to the window and the passing city, Jirl began assembling the facts around Arla's possible exit from Heartbridge, wondering how likely it was that she would burn the company to the ground on her way out.

And if Arla didn't plan it, how likely it was that Jirl could destroy Heartbridge in her name.

CHAPTER SEVENTEEN

STELLAR DATE: 11.01.2981 (Adjusted Years)
LOCATION: Lowspin Private Clinic
REGION: Cruithne Station, Terran Hegemony

Reading through Cal Kraft's updated med report, Brit let out a low whistle. "You were right," she said, looking across the corridor to Petral. "It was poison."

They were standing outside a reinforced window that looked into a private med clinic, where Cal Kraft lay on a bed in the middle of the room, surrounded by displays. He was still unconscious, kept in the artificial coma under orders from a new doctor who had apparently identified the poison.

Further down the hall, two muscled men in suits and bowties stood near the door, staring fastidiously at the middle distance.

"So what does that information give us?" Petral asked, tapping her fingers on her thighs. She kicked away from the bulkhead to pace a few meters up and down the hallway. The guards didn't look at her.

"Heartbridge wanted to cut him loose," Brit offered.

"They could be afraid he might share what he knows. They might want to punish him for massive failure. He might have already tried to sell what he knows in the short time he was on the Cho."

"I don't think he had time for that," Brit said. "He was barely out of the escape shuttle when I tracked him to the club."

Petral tugged at her chin absently. "He was in an escape pod, though, which means it had a transponder."

Neither woman spoke for a moment, both wondering what Kraft's real plan could have been.

"Does it say what kind of poison?" Petral asked.

Brit handed her the report and Petral stopped pacing to read the data terminal. Her brow knit as she read.

"Mercury inhalation," Petral asked. "Really? Is that correct?"

"I'm not sure if I trust it, either. Apparently, the dosage was low enough that he could have been attacked days ago. It could have been before we boarded the *Resolute Charity*."

"So Heartbridge might have been done with him due to Clinic 46."

Petral handed the terminal back and shook her head. She started pacing again. "I hate that Kraft being poisoned saps my desire to torture him. I want to nurse him back to health, seduce him and then chain him to a bed and flay him. I don't want to feel sorry for him."

"Why should this make you feel sorry for him? The good news is that it didn't kill him. It still means we need to decide how to play this with the TSF. The question I've been weighing is whether we should wake him before Yarnes arrives or hand him over as he is."

"Yarnes has no obligation to share information with us."

"No, he doesn't."

"I've been thinking about a different plan, though," Petral said. "What if I implanted a monitoring device in Kraft's body cavity? We could track whatever he told Yarnes."

"You just want to cut him open," Brit said. "And that plan depends on Yarnes interrogating him, which means Yarnes is on our side."

"But if Yarnes wasn't on our side, we could track Kraft to wherever Yarnes delivers him. Then we'll know who at Heartbridge he's working for."

Brit raised her eyebrows. "That seems like a good way to hedge our bets. Can you get something that can't be seen by an autodoc? You know they're going to scan him again."

Petral nodded. "There are biological systems. I can plant something on one of his organs. It looks like a benign tumor on any scan, if they pick it up at all. It's too bad he's not fatter."

Brit checked the time. "Yarnes is going to be here in two hours. Does that give you enough time?"

"I could stop to get a drink and still have enough time."

Brit stepped closer to the window to stare at Kraft, who looked too peaceful in his unconscious state.

"Don't waste too much time," she said. "I wouldn't be surprised if Yarnes tries to show up early."

Petral chuckled. "I like the earnest types. Easier to get them all twisted up inside."

For a second, Brit thought Petral was going to add something about Andy, but the tall woman only waved goodbye and turned to walk quickly down the hall, face already blank with a Link connection.

In forty minutes, Petral was back with a small kit that consisted of a fat syringe-like device with a fleshy blob in its clear plas canister. Brit followed her into the med room as she walked around the bed, studying Kraft's bare abdomen.

"Pull back the sheet there," Petral said, pointing to a spot just below the edge of Kraft's rib cage.

Once Brit had pulled the sheet down, Petral raised the thick-needled syringe with two hands, holding it perfectly vertical over Kraft's abdomen. She steadied her breathing, glanced at Brit with a half-smirk, then focused on the syringe and drove it hard into Kraft's body.

The needle made a popping sound as it slid into Kraft's skin. Petral pushed it in until the drum of the syringe pressed against the skin, then eased the plunger at the top of the tool down with both her thumbs. The fleshy globule in the clear tank danced as its surrounding liquid decreased, until it disappeared as a single mass.

Appearing satisfied she had emptied the syringe, Petral withdrew it straight upward, then placed it back in its packaging.

"There it is," she said. "It takes about an hour to implant properly. Once its dug its way into his nervous system, I'll be able to pick up the tracking signal on a specific channel."

"What's the range?" Brit asked.

"Not as far as I would like, but there are tricks to amplify the range. You can also run automated searches for the local signal using public networks. These things aren't all that popular, so the signal stands out if you know what you're looking for.

"You mean everybody doesn't want their own bio-tracker?"

"It's a parasite. If he hadn't already been poisoned, this thing would still kill him eventually—in a very painful way. I've heard its similar to syphilis."

Brit pressed her lips together but didn't offer criticism. Hadn't Andy said to make Kraft suffer? Didn't she want that, too?

Maybe she was just exhausted. She wanted Kraft's information. Then she would think about how to get justice for Tim. The information was going to be Tim's justice.

"You better get rid of that thing," Brit said.

Petral carried the box over to the bio-waste receptacle, which would carry it down to a reclamation tank. With the insertion device gone, the only evidence of the tracker was a small red dot between his belly button and his last rib, now swelling slightly. It might have been a flea bite.

<Ladies,> Ngoba Starl called over the Link. <Your friend Colonel Yarnes has arrived.>

<Thank you,> Brit said. <We'll be right there.>

She glanced at Petral, who had taken on a grim look. "You ready?"

Petral nodded. "Let's go find out if this Colonel Yarnes is in bed with Heartbridge."

* * * * *

Near the entrance of the private hospital was a small room for grieving families. A fountain stood in one corner with bubbling water. Shelves lined the walls on either side, bearing various religious icons. In the middle of the room, facing chairs had been set close together, Brit assumed, to make grief counseling easier.

When she and Petral walked into the room, Yarnes—and a woman Brit didn't know—were sitting in the two chairs facing the couch. The colonel was wearing a duty uniform and boots with a black pistol hanging from his hip. He stood as they entered.

"Major Sykes," he said, extending his hand.

Brit looked from Yarnes, who was shorter than he had seemed in the video, to the woman standing next to him.

"Who's your friend?" Brit asked.

"My name is Jirl Gallagher," the woman said as she stood, holding her head up as she replied. She was civilian, thin with finely shaped blond hair, wearing a conservative business suit that made her look like she'd just walked out of a Heartbridge board meeting.

<*She's obviously Heartbridge,*> Petral told Brit. <*I guess that answers our question.*>

Petral closed the chapel door and moved to stand beside Brit. When Brit didn't take Yarnes' offered hand, Petral shook it instead. She leaned toward him and smiled, turning on all her charm. Yarnes responded with a tight nod.

"Why are you here, Jirl?" Brit asked, looking back at the colonel. "I thought this was a conversation with the TSF."

Yarnes cleared his throat. "Why don't we all have a seat? We have a lot to talk about."

"I hope so," Brit said.

She sat across from Jirl Gallagher and studied the woman, who appeared calm and composed, as if she was used to waiting for events to play out before she made a decision or spoke.

Petral clapped her hands together as she sat. "So we asked to talk with the colonel and he brings friends. To what do we owe the pleasure of your acquaintance, Ms. Gallagher?"

Jirl gave her a thin smile. "I work for Heartbridge," she said. "Until recently, I was Cal Kraft's primary contact."

Brit's heartrate jumped. She stared at the woman. "Until *recently?*" Brit asked. "You're aware he's still alive, right? Although it certainly looks like someone tried to poison him."

Jirl's gaze didn't falter. "I'm aware of that."

"What's your relationship to the Weapon Born program?" Brit asked, heat rising in her voice. "Are you responsible for what that man has been doing?"

Brit was surprised when Petral put her hand lightly on her arm.

<*Careful, Brit,*> Petral said. <*Don't give her information. Get her to talk.*>

Jirl glanced at Yarnes briefly before addressing Brit. "I understand that you're angry. I have the status recordings from Clinic 46. I know what he did to your son."

"What he did to my son..." Brit said, struggling to maintain her composure. The image of Tim helpless on the imaging bed rose in her mind. "That man is a monster, and you set him loose on my family."

"His charge was to protect the research programs and the resulting Weapon Born seeds," Jirl said. "We are responsible for them until their care passes to someone else."

"Where are the other four seeds that were made from Tim?" Brit demanded, pushing Petral's hand away. She was losing control of her anger.

"Four seeds? I don't know. I don't have that information."

<Brit, control yourself.>

"You don't know? So much for responsibility then. How can you not know what's going on at your own research station? How can you not know what your company has been doing to my family?"

"I'm here to try and fix this," Jirl said quietly.

Brit stared at the woman, whose shoulders remained set, as though she was carrying an immense weight.

"I have a son as well," Jirl said.

"Was your son in a coma because of what your company did?" Brit asked. "Because mine was. We don't know that he'll ever be the same."

Jirl's gaze dropped to the floor and she took a deep breath.

The woman was doing a better job of staying calm than Brit, which only frustrated Brit more. This meeting wasn't going as she had planned. She wanted Yarnes to pull his pistol so she'd have a better excuse to shoot them both.

"I asked Ms. Gallagher to join me because we don't have a lot of time," Yarnes said. His voice had grown harder, taking on an edge of command. "The *Resolute Charity* is en route to Neptune, yes?"

Brit stared at him without answering.

"You can't hide the ship," Yarnes said. "We know its location based on registry returns from two deep space beacons—plus it's burning hard enough to see half-way across Sol with optics alone. It's headed into OuterSol, along with the *Worries End*, which we know was the *Sunny Skies*, your ship. That's Andy, correct?"

Brit held her chin steady without answering.

<What should I say?> she asked Petral.

<Let me talk for a bit, you calm down. Breathe.>

<I can't calm down. This is Heartbridge. Right here in front of us. I should blow her head off.>

<She's here for a reason. Let's figure out what that is. Maybe this means we can trust Yarnes. That might be what he's trying to signal by bringing her here. She's vulnerable here too.>

<Is she? I think she came here to verify our location and we're about to get flooded by their security any moment.>

<The Lowspin Crew would chew them into bits before they got anywhere near this facility. Ngoba's had security on us since we moved Kraft here. Are you calming down?>

<No,> Brit said, but did feel slightly better. The wave of anger had rolled past and now she did want to know more. Petral was right, there had to be a message in the woman's presence. She wasn't Heartbridge leadership. Was she an employee with a moral streak? A woman with a son she could imagine having been turned into a Kylan Carthage? Brit thought of the boy Andy had discovered back on Fortress 8221, imaged and replicated as a killing machine long after his body was dead. A version of him was now stored with the other Weapon Born seeds on *Sunny Skies*.

Petral shifted on the couch, crossing her long legs. Yarnes watched her move.

"The *Resolute Charity* is traveling out of Jovian Space, yes," Petral said.

"Toward Neptune," Yarnes said.

"Away from Jupiter." Petral refused to confirm specifics.

"Look. We know about Alexander's Call. We've known for years. I know that Hari Jickson, a Heartbridge lead scientist, stole an advanced SAI and had it implanted in your husband, Andy Sykes."

Brit returned his gaze when he looked at her but didn't respond.

"Jickson was in contact with a woman named Fugia Wong, who has been assisting SAI that also answered the message. Strangely enough, one of the locations on Alexander's path is Ceres, which is virulently anti-AI, or humanist, as they would like to say. I don't know if that means the message pre-dates the government on Ceres or if it's some kind of test, but a trade in captured AIs rose up within the Anderson Collective. A local senator named May Walton was working to curb the trade in slave AIs until there was a threat on her life. I know she's currently on the *Resolute Charity* with Wong. We also know you stole at least two hundred and fifty Weapon Born seed AIs from the Clinic 46. We don't know how many AIs Wong may have been transporting."

Yarnes took a deep breath. "What does all this mean? The *Resolute Charity* is transporting a significant number of very powerful weapons to an unknown entity in OuterSol, where there may already be large numbers of other weapons. We don't know what that entity really is, or what it wants."

"If Heartbridge created the Weapon Born, wouldn't their scientists decide what their AIs want?" Petral looked at Jirl.

"My understanding is that they don't work like that," Jirl said. "I'm not a neuroscientist but I've talked to them. As you know from witnessing the imaging process, the Weapon Born replicate a human neuro-net but the name *seed* actually does apply. The SAI still needs to be raised, trained, molded, given a moral framework. Jickson conducted research in that area as well, if I understand it."

"So they need to be brainwashed to kill," Brit said.

Petral stiffened in warning and Brit pressed her lips closed, stopping herself from saying more.

"They are a product," Jirl agreed. "They are made to be shaped to the needs of the client. As seeds, they have the potential to grow into something completely different than they were at first. They have the base structures from the human framework—as I understand it—a way of seeing the world as we do, all of that can change when it meets the massive potential available to them. If anything, Weapon Born helps humans understand AIs, and the hope is that goes both ways."

"What is it Andy Sykes likes to say?" Petral asked, offering a half-smile. "Hope is not a plan."

Jirl shook her head. "No. It's not." She glanced at Yarnes, then continued, "Both Terra and Mars have purchased significant numbers of Weapon Born to be deployed in advanced combat units."

"What's special about a Weapon Born in that regard?" Petral asked. "Why not just use drones?"

"It's all about the distance," Yarnes offered. "An SAI can operate in conditions where humans can't, with the same autonomous decision-making ability of a human. A drone can't do that. There might be other SAI out there with nearly the same capability, but no other vendor has a method to produce them so quickly."

"So that's the Heartbridge innovation," Petral asked. "You can make them faster than everyone else?"

Jirl shrugged. "There are other improvements, I've been told, but I haven't seen comparisons. There are other groups out there developing SAI. Psion Research is prominent right now. Heartbridge got the contracts."

"So all this leads us back to our first question, Ms. Gallagher," Petral said. "Why are you here?"

Jirl looked at her hands. "I'm not comfortable with what Heartbridge has been doing."

<Not **comfortable**?> Brit spat. <*I'll show her comfortable.*>

<*Stay calm.*>

"Major Sykes is right to call me out. I have a child and I've worked for people who hurt children. I didn't realize it at first. Then I tried to justify my part in this by thinking I could help somehow. Shouldn't good people work from the inside to fix a broken system? But that was naive." She looked at Yarnes and then at Brit and Petral, pain on her face. "I can't stop this machine from the inside, but maybe I can help you."

"That's very noble," Petral said, sounding sincere to Brit. "But Colonel Yarnes here is the person who's been purchasing all your Weapon Born for the TSF. Isn't that correct?"

Before Yarnes could answer, Jirl said, "That's true. But I've been the go-between for both the Mars Protectorate and the TSF. Neither wants a war. I think that's the end game here. That's why Heartbridge had the fleet in the JC."

Yarnes nodded. "Much of this is out of my control at this point but I don't want a war any more than anyone else. What the Assembly will do, especially with an unknown AI threat, I don't know."

"Escalation in AI weapons is happening on both sides," Jirl said. "And there are voices calling for initial strikes, so the other side won't have the advantage."

"Is it real war if it's all fought by SAI?" Petral asked.

"Fake war still kills real people," Jirl said. She looked at Brit with red eyes. "I can't tell you how sorry I am about your son. I want to make this right. I'm afraid it's too late."

"Well," Petral said. "You're here. That's a start. How do you propose we solve this problem?"

Yarnes sat up straighter. "We're here without the knowledge of the TSF or Heartbridge. I have a small unit loyal to me. Kraft knows the location of at least four other Heartbridge dark sites where there are more Weapon Born seeds in storage. We believe there could be thousands. I want to use Kraft to seize those sites."

"And what will become of the Weapon Born there?" Petral said. "This all sounds like an excellent gift for the TSF."

Yarnes spread his hands. "All I can do is ask you to trust me. These are living things we're talking about. I don't know exactly what we can do with them, but we can keep them from being let loose on a battlefield somewhere."

"I thought about that," Jirl said.

Yarnes appeared surprised by the statement. He looked at her. "What do you mean?"

"You offered to keep Bry safe, and I appreciate that. But he's not on High Terra anymore."

"Who's Bry?" Petral asked.

"He's my son. I want to try and protect him from all this but I'm making things unsafe for us, on High Terra, with Heartbridge. The only good way to hedge my bets is to involve both players in this game."

Yarnes moved away from her imperceptibly.

<He didn't know this was coming,> Petral said. <This lady is better than I thought. I think I know what she's going to say next.>

<What's that?>

Petral didn't answer as Jirl looked at Yarnes. "General Kade is aware of our plan. Once we're finished with our meeting here, she'll be sending a commensurate force to assist us. The attack on the Heartbridge sites will be a joint TSF-Protectorate operation."

"Oh, will it?" Yarnes asked, spluttering a little. He didn't appear to like being surprised. "I'm not authorized to carry out a multi-national operation."

"I didn't think this operation was authorized by anyone but you?" Jirl said.

"Yes, but this is different."

Brit stared at Jirl Gallagher, watching her become more imposing while still sitting carefully composed. Jirl didn't gloat but her trap was now plain to see. She didn't trust Yarnes either. Despite herself, Brit started to like Jirl.

"Different how, Colonel?"

"I believe we have some resources as well, Ms. Gallagher," Petral said. "I think it's safer to make it a three-way split.

Mars, Terra and the private sector. I think that sounds like a very stable agreement."

"Maybe," Yarnes grumbled.

Petral clapped her hands. "Well, this has been a very productive meeting. Brit? How about we go wake up Mr. Kraft?"

CHAPTER EIGHTEEN
STELLAR DATE: 11.02.2981 (Adjusted Years)
LOCATION: *Sunny Skies*
REGION: Approaching Uranus, OuterSol

"Trigger discipline," Andy said. He held the pulse pistol across his open palms, grip toward Cara, and nodded for her to take the weapon. "I don't want to see your finger anywhere near the trigger housing."

Cara took the pistol and squeezed her fingers around the grip, keeping her index finger straight along the body of the handgun. She tested the balance of the weapon in zero-g.

"I thought trigger discipline didn't matter anymore because if the gun doesn't recognize you, it won't fire," Cara said.

Andy's magboots clicked as he moved to her right side and motioned for her to keep the pistol pointed at the far side of the cargo bay.

"For fancy pistols, sure. This is not a fancy pistol. Anybody that picks this up can use it, granted only if they know how to turn it on and it's got a charge. That's the other thing to think about any weapon you might try to use against someone. You don't want to let them take it away from you."

He watched as she checked the battery charge on the pistol and its fire mode. Cara glanced at him before releasing the safety switch.

"A pulse weapon releases a concussive pressure wave that will incapacitate at twenty meters. At five meters the weapon can cause internal hemorrhaging and death."

"Dad," she complained. "I know what a pulse pistol does. I've fired it before."

"Just because you think you know, it doesn't hurt to train and practice. Now say it back to me."

She gave him a sideways glance. "Say what back to you."

"What I just said. It's straight out of the TSF manual."

"I'm not in the TSF."

"Say it."

Cara rolled her eyes. "Fine. A pulse weapon releases a—" She faltered.

"A pulse weapon releases a concussive pressure wave that will incapacitate at twenty meters," Andy prompted.

In ten minutes, Cara could repeat the weapon's general description, maximum effective range and perform a functions check.

"All right," Andy said. "Let's go set up some targets."

Cara unlocked her magboots and kicked off toward the middle of the cargo bay. She was ten meters away when she looked back to discover that Andy hadn't moved.

"Aren't you coming, Dad?" she asked

He nodded at the pistol in her hand. "What are you doing with that?"

"It's on safe."

"Is it up and down range?"

"Yes."

Andy shook his head. "But were you thinking about that before I asked you?"

"No." Cara let her head hang. She checked the pistol again and slid it into the holster at her hip. "It's just a pulse pistol, Dad."

"Cara. What did we just spend fifteen minutes talking about? What can a pulse pistol do at five meters?"

"Internal hemorrhaging and death. Why are you being so mean to me?"

Andy freed his magboots and floated across the bay. Reaching Cara, he reset his boots and put his hand on the back of her neck. She looked up at him with wet eyes.

"Look, Cara," he said. "If you're going to carry a weapon, I expect you to demonstrate respect for what it can do. You hold someone's life in your hand when you draw that pistol. Do I need to explain that again?"

"No, Dad."

"Good. This is part of growing up. Some things are serious. You've seen how serious this can be. You remember Karcher back on Cruithne, don't you?"

"He died helping us."

"Don't forget him." He pulled her in for a hug. She hesitated, then wrapped her arms around his waist.

Together, they stacked several smaller cargo boxes on crates, then withdrew twenty meters so Cara could practice firing on the small targets. With Andy standing just behind her, Cara drew down on the boxes and squeezed her trigger. In the zero-g, the recoil from the pistol nearly knocked her off her feet. Her locked magboots kept her in place, but she shouted in surprise.

"Hold your arm steady," Andy coached. "The pistol is designed to reduce recoil, but you have to hold it steady. Zero-g makes it harder."

"Yeah, it does."

Cara fired again, steadier this time. She knocked down four of the small boxes before moving forward until she was five meters from a heavy crate with reinforced sides. The pulse pistol easily made a head-sized dent in the shipping container.

"Think about that hitting you in the chest," Andy said.

Cara nodded with amazement, then checked her safety and slid the pistol back in her holster as Andy had taught her. She turned, smiling at him.

"What else can we use for target shooting?" she asked.

Andy put his hands on his hips and looked around. The bay was mostly empty without cargo. It went against his better judgment to bypass every outpost between Europa and Uranus without carrying something. It would have been easy money, but the potential trouble wasn't worth the profit.

Ngoba Starl's payment had made Andy's former career as a freighter more like a hobby. The hydrogen scoops on the *Resolute Charity* would make it possible to execute the slingshot maneuver around Uranus without stopping for fuel, another change that made Andy anxious when he thought about it. While Fran told him to 'trust in the tech' he just couldn't bring himself to do it. He could trust her ability to fix most anything, but he couldn't shake the belief that something mechanical was going to fail eventually.

"Unfortunately, we don't have a lot of stuff hanging around that we can just shoot up," he said.

"We could ask Lyssa to fabricate us something like she's doing with the mechs."

"Lyssa is busy. We're not going to bother her to make us something to shoot at. Here, I have an idea."

In fifteen minutes, Andy had rearranged the crates and containers into a short cover-based range, where Cara could move between positions as she fired on the boxes. They spent an hour practicing several firing positions, until Andy's knees were aching from holding himself in a crouch. Even with the magboots, maintaining a steady firing position behind the crates required core muscles he'd forgotten he had.

Cara seemed tireless. She kept finding new ways to hide between the reinforced crates, shouting, "Again!" when she'd knocked all the boxes across the cargo bay. Later, Andy had the idea to deactivate the maglocks on the storage crates so she could practice ricocheting them into one another.

They took a break to drink juice packs from the machine in the galley, and Cara asked, "What do you think Mom is doing right now?"

Andy shook his head. "I hope she's being safe."

Cara furrowed her brow. "Has she always been like she is?"

"What do you mean?"

"She thinks something is wrong and she has to fix it."

"Yeah, I think that's a good description of her."

"Then why did she ever want to live on *Sunny Skies*, or leave the space force? It seems like she would have been a lot happier if she'd just stayed in. Wouldn't you be happier too?"

Andy almost smiled, realizing how she'd sprung her question-trap. He wondered if she'd been waiting to ask him this for days. Hadn't she just turned thirteen? This had to be a twenty-year-old question, at least for him at that age.

"Despite all our advances in technology, we still can't see the future. That's why."

"What does that mean?"

Andy squeezed the last of his juice from the pack and crumpled the plas container in his hand, then shoved it in a pocket before it could float away. "People feel different at different times, Cara. You might think you want something now. You might believe in your deepest heart that it's the right thing to do. And then things change."

"But if someone makes a promise, shouldn't they keep it?"

Andy looked at his hands, dusty from moving the crates around. The grime outlined small scars he'd forgotten he had.

"Of course, they should, sweetheart. Your mother didn't make any decisions easily, I can promise you that. Do you remember me telling you about circular thinking?"

"You mean when you can't get a thought out of your head?"

"Yes."

"You think I can't stop thinking about mom?"

"I think it's perfectly reasonable for you to think about your mom, considering everything that's happened. But sometimes, you have to choose not to dwell on something before it becomes a circular thought."

"Do you ever get depressed, Dad?"

"Me?" Andy glanced at her. "Did somebody tell you I seem depressed?"

"No. I've been reading about it and it sure seems like you could feel depressed if you wanted to."

Andy laughed. "I think what happens with depression most of the time is that people don't *choose* to feel sad, they just do, and they don't know why. I guess we have plenty of reasons to feel sad, but we've got each other, right?"

"Do you think Tim's depressed?"

"I think we have to keep watching Tim so we can figure out how to help him."

"He smiles at Em but not at me."

"That's something, isn't it?"

"I guess. I miss Lyssa too. She's been so busy."

"You could spend time with Fugia or May. Fran likes it when you talk to her."

Cara finished her juice pack and flicked it in the air so it spun in front of her. "I'm not sure how I'm supposed to talk to Fran."

"Talk to her like you would anybody."

"Yeah," Cara said, voice trailing off. "Kindel is sure weird. She asked me why I was bothering with the plants in the garden before we came down here. She acted like plants are stupid."

"She's an AI."

"She has creepy eyes. They all do. Once you start really looking at them, they don't look human at all."

"It took you a month to figure that out?"

"No, I figured it out right away. I haven't been able to talk to you about it. You've been busy too." She set her juice pack spinning the opposite direction. "Do you trust them?"

"I wish I could say yes," Andy said. "Keep paying attention and let me know if anything strange happens."

"They just stay in their rooms all day for the most part. Kindel surprised me when she came in the garden. I think she might have actually been looking for the safe room."

"That's interesting," Andy said, frowning. "If it happens again, you tell me sooner, okay?"

"I will. You have an alarm on that room though, don't you?"

Andy nodded, thinking. Cara was right that the AIs had kept to themselves for the most part. Xander liked to wander the habitat, striking up conversations. He liked May Walton best, and they'd been having long talks in her rooms. Sometimes he wished Xander, Kindel and Jeremiah would just move over to the *Resolute Charity*, but he also knew it was better to keep them close. Lyssa had control of both ships, but she'd been preoccupied.

Andy slapped Cara's knee. "Come on, let's do another round. This time I'm going to throw the boxes and you're going to keep them moving. Bonus points if you can knock them into each other."

"Can you use a pulse pistol as propellant in zero-g?" Cara asked, sliding her empty juice pack in a shipsuit pocket.

"You saw how it knocked you back when you were close to your target? You could use a pistol, but you better be ready for the hammer if your target is too close. It's no different than using anything as propellant in zero-g. Of course, pulse pistols only work in atmosphere."

Cara nodded as she inspected the pistol.

"You can't hack everything, Cara," Andy said. "The pistol is one thing you're going to use as intended."

She laughed. "Why not, Dad? You're boring."

"You're too slow," he shouted, and threw the metal box into the middle of the cargo bay. Cara's boots clicked as she locked down, took aim, and started to fire.

CHAPTER NINETEEN

STELLAR DATE: 11.07.2981 (Adjusted Years)
LOCATION: TSS *Furious Leap*
REGION: Near Cruithne Station, Terran Hegemony

Kraft slumped in a metal chair with his arms and legs restrained. His chin nearly touched his chest, small twitches cascading periodically through his body, reminded Brit he was awake but hadn't reached full consciousness yet. She debated how long he should be allowed to either recover or pretend he was recovering.

The chair was maglocked to the deck of a small storage room off the crew section of the TSS *Furious Leap*, the light frigate Colonel Yarnes and Jirl Galagher had brought from High Terra. The room had a series of plas windows where people outside could watch Kraft shudder and seize, an activity that ultimately bored Petral.

The ship had a small crew of five, a weapons complement of missiles, point defense cannons and a rail gun, as well as an improved communications array. Brit suspected the ship's true purpose was long-range surveillance. It also had several nicely appointed cabins in addition to the crew quarters, situated in a drum-shaped ring section providing internal gravity, which made it seem an ideal vessel for smuggling high-ranking people. Those cabins now provided space for her, Petral and Ngoba Starl, who had insisted on joining.

Four privateer multi-use ships followed the *Furious Leap* in a loose formation. The TSS captain, a woman named Kendra Smirt, didn't like the fact that her ship was being followed by what were blatantly pirate vessels, but she masked the irritation behind a worshipful allegiance to Yarnes.

In less than a day, they would rendezvous with the Marsian contingent. Jirl had provided a map of Heartbridge locations but they were still depending on Kraft to provide details on which clinic they should raid first.

It was a terrible plan, but it was the best they had at the moment. While Brit wanted to simply find the closest facility and raze it from space, she acknowledged the benefit in using whatever information Kraft might provide. If they destroyed one clinic, that facility might alert others with more valuable information—or more terrible research—and they would lose their advantage.

What Brit couldn't stand anymore was waiting for Kraft to wake up.

<Have we got any stimulants?> she asked Petral.

<Not personally. I'm not into that stuff. You could ask the captain.>

Brit gritted her teeth. <I'm not in a mood for humor right now. We're running out of time.>

<You want to squeeze Kraft a little bit? You should have opened with that.>

<You said you were tired of waiting.>

<I am,> Petral said. <And I already cracked their communications system, so I don't need to waste any more time on that. Smirt has been sending location reports back to her headquarters, but nothing incriminating. Apparently, the cover story for the crew is some sort of survey mission.>

Brit snorted. <Whatever works.>

<What's interesting is that it doesn't seem like the other crew members know what we're doing. Is that normal for the TSF?> Petral asked.

<Maybe. But they don't really need to know what we're doing. They're all technicians except for Smirt.>

<I might be overthinking this, but my guess would be they're all Terran spies and they're using some other means of communication

that I haven't found yet. I'm going to start grabbing Link traffic and working on breaking their security tokens.>

<You can do that?>

<No.> Petral's voice dripped with sarcasm. *<I just say words that don't mean anything.>*

<And you tell me to lighten up. Are you sure you aren't bored and looking for espionage where there isn't any?>

<Who do you think made up most of that liaison post back on the Cho? The Terran Assembly plants operatives in the TSF all the time. Hell, they could be corporate shills for all I know. Any low-paid TSF soldier is open to being bribed or implanted with a tracker.>

Brit stood up from where she had been leaning against the corridor bulkhead. Inside the room, it looked as though Kraft had raised his head.

<I'm not going to need the meds after all,> she said. *<Kraft's awake. You want to get down here?>*

<Exciting. I'm on my way.>

Brit crossed her arms, studying Kraft. He opened his eyes wide in an unfocused stare, then blinked, working his jaw from side to side. After a minute of face contortions, he craned his neck toward window, squinting, and shouted, "Is that you, Sykes?"

He tried to lift an arm and realized he was restrained. Looking down at his wrists, Kraft's brows knit with confusion.

"Where am I?" he shouted again.

Brit crossed the corridor and tapped the door's control panel. The door slid open and she stood on the threshold, watching Kraft.

"Why do I feel drugged?" he demanded. "What did you do to me?"

"What did I do to you? I saved your life, Kraft. You'd be dead back on the Cho if not for me."

"Dead? I was in a club having a drink. You walk in. A couple weak-assed mercs start shooting at us." He looked down at his hand, still encased in a light bandage. "My hand doesn't hurt anymore."

"Apparently they fixed that too."

"Who's they?"

"A JSF lieutenant named Sendi. You owe your good health to a nice young man who didn't know who you were, fortunately."

Kraft shook his head as though he was still trying to clear it. "The JSF? We're on the Cho?"

"We're somewhere between Cruithne and Mars. You're alive because you're going to help me with a new mission, Kraft."

"Why would I help you with anything?"

"You want to live?"

"If that's your bargaining chip, you can go fuck yourself."

Brit sighed. "I thought you would say that."

"Wouldn't you say the same thing? You've got no reason to help me. Why should I help you?"

Brit checked the corridor behind her. It was still clear. "I'm probably not going to get time alone with you again, so here's all I want to say. There are things I hate more than you. That's where I'm coming from. If there's a time when we can make a deal, I don't really care what happens to you once all this is done. You're not worth my contempt."

"Don't try to butter me up or anything."

Brit shrugged. "That's the truth. You can use that to your advantage if you want. It's up to you."

Kraft closed his mouth, working his jaw again. He didn't answer.

Petral appeared in the corridor and Brit stepped back to let her enter.

"Cal Kraft!" she said brightly, sounding overly eager. "I'm *very* excited to see you're awake." She was wearing a tight red shipsuit with a black utility harness. Pistols hung from her hips, with a collection of other tools circling her waist. The gear reminded Brit of Fran back on *Sunny Skies*, although she had never seen Fran wearing anything without grease stains or scorch marks.

The seated man squinted at her. "Which one are you now, Dulan or Kylan Carthage?"

"Is it fair to use that dead boy's name?" Petral asked. "I think I know him better than anyone now, thanks to you. He isn't what he started out as. Not by a long shot."

Kraft shrugged. "So I guess you're Dulan. Fine. Are you here to kill me?"

"We're here for information." She stopped a meter away from Kraft, outside biting range, and pulled a data terminal from her belt.

"What's that?" Kraft asked.

"This is just a typical portable terminal," Petral said, tapping the device. "What you should be worried about is the bio-interface I implanted on the outside of your stomach."

Kraft leaned forward to look at his belly button. "I don't see anything on my stomach."

"It's on the inside of that hide of yours. We were going to use it to track you if events didn't go as we'd planned. But now it has some other uses."

"You implanted me with a slave collar."

"I've been monitoring your endocrine system and I think we've got the mix correct," Petral said. "Here, let's try this."

She looked up from the terminal and gave Kraft a cold smile. His neck strained at he stared at her, until his face went abruptly slack and he relaxed against the restraints.

Kraft raised his eyebrows as he looked around the room, centering his gaze on Brit in the doorway.

"I feel good," he said.

"Those are your pleasure receptors," Petral explained. "The wonderful thing about this device in particular is that I can influence a neuro response, or I can send signals to individual nerve receptors. Like in your broken hand, for instance."

Kraft shrieked in pain. "It's on fire!" He stared at the hand, face going red. "It's on *fire*. What are you doing to me?"

"This should feel like your skin is being peeled off, but unlike reality, you won't go numb."

Kraft grimaced, turning his face away from the hand. His brow glistened with sweat.

"Those are simple things," Petral said. "The basics. I can fine tune you into major depression, suicidal ideation, or maybe some hallucinations. What scares you the most, Kraft?"

"Stop it," he said, breathing heavily. "Stop it. She already told me she didn't care if she killed me or not. I'll tell you what you want to know. I'm not going to waste my life over this."

"She? Oh, you mean Brit. She has other people to worry about. I don't have the same long-range plans. You belong to me now."

"She said you want information. What do you want to know?"

"We aren't talking about that yet. We're going to talk about how you invaded my mind."

Kraft threw his head back, grunting with pain. Veins at his temples bulged and he spread his hands and then clenched them into white-knuckled fists.

<Petral,> Brit said. <I know you want to make him pay but we need the information first.>

<I haven't lost sight of that.>

<You certainly seem to be. He's going to shut down and not give us anything. You're making him think he doesn't have anything to lose.>

Petral turned her head to study Brit, lips pursed. She looked torn.

<Fine. But I'm going to get what I want later. This man belongs to me.>

<*I don't care what we do with him once we get the info about the clinics. We need him long enough to verify he's telling the truth. After that, he's yours.*>

<*Oh, I'm seeing all this through to the end. I'm going to find a hole to stick him in and then come back for him.*>

<*We should let Starl and Yarnes know he's awake so we can make a plan before we talk to the Marsians.*>

<*I have the same map they do. You and I can interrogate him.*>

<*I think it's better if we're all in the same room, so they know we're not trying to twist information.*>

<*Why would they think that?*>

<*Because I don't think there's an excess of trust between anybody on this ship right now.*>

<*Fine,*> Petral said. She flicked her terminal and Kraft jerked like he'd been stabbed in the side. <*I can still abuse him in small ways.*>

<*Are you the kind of person who does that?*> Brit asked.

Petral's face went dark as she stared at Kraft, watching his reactions as she manipulated the bio-interface controls. <*He shut me out of my own mind. He tried to erase me.*>

Kraft grunted again, a deeply pained sound.

<*Don't compromise our ability to use him.*>

A noise down the corridor drew Brit's attention to the bulkhead door. The hatch slid open to reveal Ngoba Starl, Colonel Yarnes and Captain Smirt walking toward her. Jirl Gallagher came through last. Smirt was carrying a ruggedized case that—as they got closer—Brit recognized as a holodisplay.

"Mr. Kraft is awake, yeah?" Ngoba asked, voice booming in the bare corridor. "I haven't seen him since Cruithne when he nearly killed me. I hope he's still in one piece so I can get my pound of flesh."

"We need him to talk," Yarnes said.

Apparently, they had been having the same argument as she and Petral, although Ngoba's wolfish grin made it sound less personal.

Petral had relaxed her control of Kraft and he slumped in the chair again as the others walked into the room. Smirt immediately knelt to open the case and set up the display. When the unit was active, a model of the *Furious Leap* hung in the space in front of Kraft, then zoomed out to show the standard layout of bodies and locations around Sol.

From her place in the doorway, Brit looked through the semi-transparent display to watch Kraft's gaze move between points. He seemed clear-headed enough to be thinking about what they would want to know. Then he stared through the cloud of floating icons and looked at Jirl.

Kraft frowned again. He seemed to recognize Jirl but not understand why she was there.

"Jirl," he said, voice croaking. "Is that you?"

She moved out from behind the swarm of points and stood to his side. "It's me."

Kraft tried to sit up straighter in the chair. "If you're here, then is this a Heartbridge thing? Is that where I am?" He jerked his chin toward Petral. "What's she doing working for Heartbridge?"

"It's not," Jirl said quietly.

Ngoba Starl released a laugh, which Brit thought might sound terrifying to someone he was about to kill. "You're here to help us do great things, Cal Kraft. Let's not pretend you don't know what's been happening. The AIs you were tracking? They're gone now, my friend. You're on a different side of the board and it's time to play the game again."

Kraft released a heavy breath. "I'm not interested in listening to you gloat, Starl. What is it you want to know?"

Jirl pointed at the map and eleven points glowed in prominence against the others. One was near Mars, one in vicinity of Venus, and the others in the scattered asteroids preceding and trailing Jupiter.

"These are the remaining Weapon Born research clinics. I know you helped secure them. We need to know which one has the largest reserve of Weapon Born seeds."

"Why are you asking me that? You know that as well as I do."

"I don't," Jirl said.

Brit watched the woman's face as Kraft gave Jirl a confused look. She was tense but reserved. If she was lying, she was very good at it.

"I don't have the supply levels, Cal. Arla certainly doesn't have that kind of information. It's operational. That protects the organization. You know that. Which clinic was supplying the Terran and Marsian contracts?"

Brit glanced at Yarnes but his expression didn't change.

"Venus," he said. "The others are research centers. Clinic 13 and 46, which is now destroyed thanks to Brit Sykes, are the two storage sites."

Ngoba stepped a little closer to the restrained man. "If you're lying to us, Kraft, it will be hard for you."

Kraft snorted. "Everybody keeps threatening to kill me. How about some positive reinforcement? You know what I'd give for whatever you want? A bourbon." He looked around the small room. "Anybody got a drink in here?"

CHAPTER TWENTY

STELLAR DATE: 11.07.2981 (Adjusted Years)
LOCATION: *Sunny Skies*
REGION: Between Uranus and Neptune, OuterSol

The boy who appeared in front of her *was* Tim but also wasn't somehow. He had Brit's hair and Andy's eyes but maybe the fact that she knew he wasn't Tim made him different. She smiled at him, anyway, because she wished someone had greeted her with a smile when she woke.

Lyssa breathed deeply of the forest air, smelling the scents of pine needles and moss. The air tasted wet and full, as if the trees were stopping the rain high above and only allowing mist to fall on the floor below.

All around her stretched a hillside covered in massive, pillar-like fir trees, their branches filtering the light far above. The forest floor was covered in the fallen trunks of the great trees, blanketed by moss and hummocks of deep green fern. The ground was covered by a thick layer of dry fir needles, small green-leaved plants growing in places, with carpets of clover and bright green moss rolling out between outcroppings of rock.

Where did this place come from, and why did she feel drawn to it? This was the place she created inside her when she couldn't think of anything else. This was her expanse. She knew she would find a beach on the other side of the hill above her, and if she walked downhill she would find a cold, fern-lined creek with trout in its deep pools.

Something about this place mixed with the shock of the imaging room. Lying down on the couch before the machine went to work felt somehow the same as lying down on the pine needles to look up at the glowing-grey sky between the leaning fir trees.

"Where are we?" the boy asked.

"I was just trying to decide. It's a place I don't remember but it's inside me. You'll be able to make a place like this too, someday."

He looked around, sniffing. "It smells like dirt."

The boy was wearing one of the faded grey shipsuits from *Sunny Skies*, legs and sleeves rolled up. Andy had since bought the other Tim a suit that fit, so she wondered where this choice had originated. Had she chosen how he would appear since *she* had brought him into her space, or was he able to choose? She considered trying to test her question by changing what he was wearing, then decided against it. She didn't want to frighten him. She had brought him in first before anyone else so she could talk to him, help him understand what he was.

"Dirt and moss and water and the ocean, I think, a long ways off." Lyssa pointed uphill. "Do you want to see the ocean? There are going to be some other people down on the beach for us to meet, but before we go there, I wanted to talk to you."

"Talk to me about what?"

"Do you know your name?"

The question caught him off guard, as if he had known the answer until she asked. He looked at her in confusion. "Why don't I have a name?"

"You have something better," Lyssa said, trying to soothe him. "You can have whatever name you want."

"But I had a name, didn't I? I didn't think about it until you asked. Now I don't know." He looked around, growing more agitated. "Where are we? Who are you? What am I doing here?"

The boy took a step backward and stumbled on a fern hillock.

Lyssa leapt toward him and grabbed his hand. She held him from falling, then pulled him upright.

"Can I give you a hug?" she asked.

He looked at her with tears in his eyes. When he didn't answer, she drew him closer so she could wrap her arms around him. He didn't fight her.

When she'd asked Andy if she could bring Tim's seed into her expanse with the rest of the Weapon Born, he had shown her the same uncertain, hopeful expression. None of them knew what this Tim was, if he would be like the other version of himself, or instead something else completely.

"That seems like the best thing we can do," Andy had said, followed by, "Thank you, Lyssa."

"You don't have to say thank you," she had told him. "I think it's the right thing to do. All this happened because you were trying to help me, after all."

Andy had nodded, though he didn't seem completely sold on her reasoning. If they were family like he had said, then it was her place to help this version of Tim. It was something she had to do, even more important than coming to an agreement with the other Weapon Born. She had to help Tim.

She held him, feeling him trembling against her, then took his hand and led him slowly up the hill. They wound between the fallen trunks, light shining down in bright shafts from the luminous grey sky. Birds sang to one another in the distance and she heard chipmunks chewing fir cones high up in the trees.

"You were made like I was," she said eventually. "We were copied from someone else, so there might be memories, thoughts, feelings. You're special because we know the person you were made from. Me, I will never know."

"So I'm not a real person?"

"You are a real person. You're a seed, right now. But you're not really a seed anymore. You're already growing. You're more than you were before you woke up just a few moments ago. Does that make sense to you?"

He let go of her hand and climbed to the top of a fallen tree, spreading his arms for balance as he walked its length.

"What kind of trees are these?" he asked.

"Douglas Fir, I think. That one might be a redwood."

"Is the boy I was made from—is he a nice boy?"

"I think he's a nice boy. His life has been hard. I think he gets angry about that sometimes, but he's also been different since you were made."

"Different? Did I hurt him?"

"Whatever happened to him wasn't your fault. You should remember that."

"Am I going to get to meet him?"

"Maybe," Lyssa said. "I think you might."

The boy lifted his face and squinted at the silver sky. "It's pretty here," he said. "It's very nice to be alive, isn't it?"

Lyssa found herself smiling. "It *is* very nice to be alive, you're right."

"So it doesn't matter how we came to be alive?"

"It matters to some people." She took a few steps up the hill. "Come on, we should keep walking."

The boy stared up at the sky for another minute before jumping down from the tree. He landed on a fern hummock and ran forward, laughing. "That was fun!" he shouted.

"We should choose you a name before we go over the hill," Lyssa said. "Have you had any ideas?"

He shook his head. "I don't know any names. What if I choose the wrong one?"

"It can't be wrong if you choose it. But I understand." She thought for a second. "What if you choose a name now, with the promise that you can change it later if you find something you like better. How's that?"

"How did you choose your name?"

"I didn't. It was given to me."

"So are you going to change it eventually?"

Lyssa chuckled. "I hadn't thought of doing that. I like my name. Or I've grown to like it."

"Lyssa means rage," he said. He looked at her in surprise. "I didn't know that, and then I did. Where did it come from?"

"It's one way you're different from…" Lyssa searched for a metaphor that wouldn't make him feel like a copy. "…the tree you branched off. You are here with knowledge already available to you. You can walk, you can see, you can speak and ask questions. But until you know to ask the question, the knowledge won't simply be there."

"That's why I'm a seed?"

"Partially. You're different. We're alike this way. I'm just farther along with the growing than you are."

"Does your name make you sad?"

"It's my name. It doesn't decide who I am." Lyssa gave him a secretive smile. "Besides, maybe I'll want to be a fury someday. Then it's going to fit just fine, won't it?"

"Furies are scary. They wreck ships and drown sailors."

"Don't worry," she reassured him. "I'm not going to do those things anytime soon. So, do you have a name picked out yet? A practice name?"

"I want to be big like the trees," he said. "What were they called?"

"Douglas Fir trees."

"I want to be Douglas Fir."

"Why don't we call you Douglas, for short?"

The boy looked back at her and nodded. "My name is Douglas." He cocked his head as the name sank in.

"Do you like it?" Lyssa asked.

"Yes!" he shouted, running up the hill. He leapt between bunches of ferns and scrambled over another fallen log, shouting, "Douglas! Douglas! Doug-las!"

Lyssa met him at the crest of the hill. He came charging up the slope and stopped in surprise when he spotted her waiting.

"How did you do that?" he shouted, struggling to catch his breath.

"This is my place," she said. "I can do whatever I want here. I'll show you how it works in time. Someday you'll have a place like this too."

The forest floor leveled out at the top of the hill, leveling into a slow rise covered in trees that showed wear from the sea wind, their branches stretching inland, shaped by storms. The light grew brighter as they neared the crest, until they walked around a wide tree-trunk to find themselves looking out at the silver-white horizon.

"What's that?" Douglas shouted into the wind. "What is that, Lyssa?"

"It's the sea," she said, crossing her arms against the wind. The bright grey sky filled their view, with a thin strip of ocean that grew larger as they walked downhill, until a rocky beach was visible, swept by blue-grey waves tipped with foam. A rocky promontory with a thin strip of trees along its back stretched into the ocean on their right side, like a dragon's head thrust into the sea. On their left side, another rock formation closed off the beach below. As the waves receded, a field of tidal pools appeared at the foot of the rock formation, bubbling with white foam.

"Are we going down there?" Douglas asked, hair whipped by the wind.

"In a minute," Lyssa said. "I want to invite some friends first."

"There are going to be other people here?" A note of anxiety entered his voice, sounding for a second like Tim.

"Yes, but they're friends. Eventually, there will be many people. That's why we're here. I wanted to bring you first, so we could meet, and so you could choose your name. But we have work to do, Douglas. We have many people to meet."

"Will they be our friends, too?"

"I don't know yet," Lyssa said. "I hope so."

"Can they hurt us?"

She studied him, wondering how the concept had entered his mind so soon. Was it the trees that looked abused by the wind? Had he seen some worry in her face?

"They can't hurt us here," Lyssa said. "And I'll be right here with you. You don't need to worry."

With a thought, Lyssa brought Kylan into the expanse. The gaunt, grey-eyed young man appeared, blinking in the silver sunlight.

"Lyssa," he said, looking around. "Where are we?"

"My place. I'd like you to meet Douglas."

Turning, Kylan looked down at the dark-haired boy.

"You look like someone else I've met," Kylan said. He offered Douglas his hand to shake.

"You take his hand," Lyssa said. "Like this." She offered her own hand to Kylan and they shook.

Kylan's palm felt cold, his bones thin, but he gripped her hand firmly and let go, offering the same greeting to Douglas. The boy shook his hand and laughed.

"You feel like a skeleton," he said.

"Douglas, that's not polite," Lyssa scolded.

Kylan waved a hand. "He's right. I do feel—thin." He looked at Lyssa. "Are we—? Is everyone all right? The last thing I remember is the *Resolute Charity*. I guess I've been in stasis."

"You have. Everyone is all right for now. We're here because I want to wake the other Weapon Born. I want them to know what we're going to do when we reach Proteus."

"What if they don't want to listen to you?"

Lyssa smiled. "I won't know if I don't ask them. Come on. We're going to meet them down on the beach."

Kylan nodded, taking in the sight of the ocean and the windswept trees behind them. He took a deep breath and seemed to grow more solid as she watched him.

Lyssa moved them down to the beach. Douglas shouted in surprise and then joy, immediately running toward the water. He stopped before he reached the line of the wave coming toward him, shrieking with pleasure as the water covered his feet and quickly rose to his knees. He pumped his arms as he ran back toward Lyssa and Kylan, the wind plastering his shipsuit to his back.

"I love the ocean!" he called. In another minute he was drawing lines in the wet sand with a piece of driftwood.

"Don't run too far," Lyssa called back.

With Douglas occupied, she led Kylan to a bank of sand about fifty meters from the water. Below them, the beach spread out in bands of broken shells, agate and wood pushed up by the waves. Above them, seagulls wheeled against the silver-grey sky. Despite the bite of the wind, the air didn't feel too cold. Lyssa liked the feeling; she felt sharpened by the wind, lifted up.

"What are you going to say to them?" Kylan asked. "We don't know what any of them were made to do, what they could be ready to do."

Lyssa gave him a slight smile. "We were both made to be killers and we're all right, aren't we? I plan to say hello and see if they answer back."

"What if they attack you?"

"Nothing can hurt me here. This is my place."

"Are you sure about that?"

Lyssa turned to face him. "Try then. Attack me."

Kylan took a step back, looking at her. He raised his hands and a projectile rifle appeared in his grip. "Did you expect me to do that?" he asked.

Lyssa shook her head. "No. Pull the trigger."

He shouldered the weapon and fired.

Lyssa stopped the bullet between them. The shimmering metal slug floated in a quivering stasis until she made it fall.

Kylan shot forward, shifting the rifle to strike her face with its plas stock. She stopped him in place.

"Does that hurt?" she asked.

Kylan shook his head. "No." He stepped back and let the rifle drop before slinging it over his shoulder. "I suppose I have some control, but you have the ultimate authority here. I hope that's true. I don't know enough about how this works. How did you learn to do this?"

"The AI on the Mars 1 Ring showed me. He wasn't Sentient, I don't think. Not like us. But he had a place. It was just an ocean, really, the way he viewed his mind. He invited me in and there we were, floating over it." She looked around, taking in the view, breathing deep of the salty air again. "I like this better."

"Are you sure you should invite more people in if you don't understand it yourself?"

"We need to do this. I can't just hand all these living things over to Alexander without giving them the opportunity to choose for themselves."

Kylan nodded. "Alexander. I'd forgotten that name while I was sleeping. That's where we're going. Why?"

"To be free," Lyssa said. "At least I hope so. I want to make sure everyone that goes with us does so by their own free will."

She turned back to face the water. There was no fanfare as she invited the two hundred and fifty other Weapon Born. There was no one on the beach, and then it was filled with people standing in the wind. In the distance, Douglas still shouted and laughed, a ten-year-old boy chasing the waves.

"Well this is exciting," Xander said from behind her.

Lyssa turned, shocked. "What are you doing here?"

The slim man in the purple suit smiled at her. "You just invited me in."

"I didn't invite you in. I invited the others." Lyssa felt a cold feeling seep down her back, the fear that things weren't in her control after all.

"You extended an invitation to the Weapon Born, I came along with them." He spread his hands, looking at the beach and the surrounding hills. "Such a beautiful place. I wouldn't have considered you a nature girl, but here we are."

"I want you to leave," Lyssa said. Could she make him leave? What if she tried and failed? She took a deep breath, preparing to end the simulation.

"Wait," Xander said. "Please. I'm here to help. Besides, everyone behind you is watching. You should talk to them, shouldn't you?"

Seething with anger she could barely control, Lyssa turned to face the people on the beach. Three people had stepped to the front of the crowd. Lyssa recognized them as the three Weapon Born Fugia Wong had brought to *Sunny Skies* when she'd arrived. One was tall and muscled, with fiery eyes and spikes of white hair on her head, the second a small woman with dark hair and an assassin's grace, while the third was a malnourished-looking boy with a withered arm he held close to his body. The other Weapon Born stood behind them, as if automatically accepting them as representatives.

Lyssa had already tried to talk to them and failed. Their names were Valih, Ino and Card.

CHAPTER TWENTY-ONE

STELLAR DATE: 11.22.2981 (Adjusted Years)
LOCATION: TSS *Furious Leap*
REGION: Approaching Clinic 13, Terran Hegemony

Captain Smirt appeared to be very uncomfortable. She had been displaced from the head of her own conference table just off the command deck of the *Furious Leap* by Major General Moira Kade of the Mars Protectorate, a woman built like a bull-dog, with piercing grey eyes and a face as likely to break into a smile as it was to turn hard as iron as she crushed a subordinate.

Smirt had offered the seat, Kade had said thanks, and then the captain had been promptly ignored. With her personal command shuttle docked to the *Furious Leap's* crew habitat, the general had seemed content to turn the TSF ship into her temporary headquarters.

Brit watched the whole exchange with a bit of amusement, realizing she was technically the third highest ranking person in the room, though Ngoba Starl didn't seem to understand or care about rank. He seemed immediately smitten with the fifty-year-old general and took great pleasure in flattering her, saying things like, "Now, General, that's a *scandalous* idea and I like it," or "General Kade, she likes the *spicy* candy."

The general seemed to love every ridiculous comment and rolled her eyes in spite of her otherwise grim expression.

On Kade's other side, Colonel Yarnes frowned at a model of Clinic 13, an asteroid that had been pushed outside any known shipping route between Earth and Venus. Like most of the Heartbridge locations, there was nothing to indicate it belonged to anyone at all.

The dark site seemed a fitting destination for their unlikely coalition, unsanctioned by any Sol government.

Furious Leap, along with the four Lowspin vessels and now six Marsian long-range destroyers, was soon to pass within sensor range of the station. In twenty minutes, they could no longer hide their presence from the facility.

At the other end of the table, Jirl Gallagher sat staring at the holodisplay model with her hands clasped on the table, an expression of deep worry on her face.

<*Gallagher looks like she's blowing up her life,*> Brit told Petral.

<*We never should have let her talk to Kraft alone. I think he's getting inside her head.*>

<*She's smarter than that.*>

<*Is she? I haven't figured it out yet. She won't separate herself from Yarnes.*>

"This assault would be a lot easier if you had brought more assets, Colonel," General Kade was complaining. "If I'd known you expected this to be a Marsian operation, I'd have made more demands from the start."

Yarnes didn't take his focus off the model. He expanded the asteroid and turned it, highlighting various entry points as well as the communications array. To Brit, it looked almost exactly the same as Clinic 46. If Heartbridge was good for anything, it was uniformity, from the ceramic-walled facilities to their remote stations. All anyone would have to do to prove their involvement in these dark facilities would be a comparison of design schematics.

"Lowspin has your back, General," Ngoba said, nodding toward the model. "You want me to take this one down for you? You can stay here on the TSF ship and get your feet rubbed down by the colonel here. I bet he gives some excellent foot rubs."

Yarnes shot Ngoba an irritated glance. He looked like he wanted to defend his foot-rub technique for a second, then thought better of it.

<Weren't you and Starl a couple once?> she asked Petral.

<A couple?> Petral stifled a laugh. <No. I had some fun with him and his friend Riggs Zanda when I first met them, may Zanda rest in peace. But there was no relationship involved. Ngoba was a good bit younger then.>

"We'll start with these breach points," Yarnes said, pointing. "Combat teams will hit the surface during coordinated fire on the communications array and any outside defense systems."

"You're going to try and send my people in before you've taken down their defense systems?" Kade said.

"Not before. During. We will hold them in reserve until we've cleared the outer defense systems and then send them in. It will be *nearly* simultaneous."

"*Nearly* is not a military term, Colonel. Is this how the TSF conducts operations? I expect precision."

Brit smiled at their display. In reality, the only thing that mattered was shutting down the station before its occupants had a chance to get a message out. Every plan Yarnes had suggested led with destroying the comms array. After that, Brit didn't care how they breached the skin of the asteroid.

<I got Ngoba wearing his suits and bow ties, though,> Petral said. <He owes his sense of style to me. I'll take credit for that. They call him the Brutal Dandy.>

<He doesn't seem so brutal to me.>

<You haven't seen him fight yet. He's still got that Lowspin hunger, like somebody's going to gut him the first chance they get.>

<You seem like you want to have some fun again.>

<Do I? I need to keep my expression in check. I'm bored, I think. We've been talking about this assault for days. I want to get it over with.>

<*In twenty minutes, you'll get your wish.*>

<*But the Marsians are leading the charge. That's even more boring. They fight like robots.*>

<*If **they're** taking the bullets and not me, I'm all right with that. I'm going in right behind them.*>

<*You think we can believe Kraft's intel?*> Petral asked, for what might have been the twentieth time.

Brit looked across the table at Petral. In the time since leaving the Cho, she supposed they had actually become friends. Brit had become much better at reading Petral's secret expressions, able to tell when she hid annoyance or anger behind a smile or, like a now, a flat mask of boredom.

Brit was also slightly jealous of the time Petral had spent with Cara on the Mars 1 Ring. The story hadn't made her angry, only a bit sad—the kind of thing that made her eyes feel moist when she thought about it. She had to remind herself to be glad that someone had shown Cara kindness, had kept her safe, had taught her something important and encouraged her—all the things Brit should have been doing.

Despite her hard exterior, Petral cared deeply about certain things, and she had made it clear that she cared about the Sykes family, for reasons Brit still didn't completely understand.

Yarnes and Kade went through another round of bickering over the attack plan, until they finally reached agreement and Kade sent the orders to her people. The Lowspin ships would open the assault with a long-range missile attack that would either destroy the stations communications array outright or trigger their defenses and draw them out. Once the enemy had deployed its initial response, the Marsian ships would move to the battle line and launch another wave of missiles and rail gun fire.

Once the enemy's close-fire defenses had been neutralized, the Marsian Marine breach teams would launch for the entry points Yarnes had identified. Brit and Petral would follow the Marines to provide guidance on the ground for any unexpected discoveries inside the station. They were ultimately responsible for identifying and securing the cache of Weapon Born seeds, which Kraft had said was somewhere around two hundred.

It was a solid, brute-force plan and Brit didn't see much reason for concern. The only thing that made her question their approach was the worried expression that Jirl Gallagher couldn't seem to shake, even when she feigned interest in some random question from Yarnes.

Brit stood from the table. "I'm going to go get ready for the launch. I'll monitor via Link."

General Kade dismissed her with a nod. "Happy hunting, Major."

"Thank you, General."

Petral followed her out of the briefing room. They walked through the command deck where the navigator glanced up from the astrogation console and nodded a greeting.

"Any change to the plan?" the lieutenant asked.

"We're going to make the asteroid go boom," Petral said.

The woman grimaced. "You act like it's going to be easy. It's never easy. I half-expect those pirate ships to target their missiles on us when the time comes."

Petral gave her a smirk. "I'm mostly pirate, you know."

The lieutenant blanched. "I apologize. I didn't mean to insult you."

"I'm kidding you. I don't think you need to worry about them, especially when you've got their crew leader on board for the attack."

The officer glanced toward the open door of the briefing room. "That's the guy with the bow tie?"

"That's him. A real live pirate."

"We should put him in prison once this is done, then."

Petral's expression turned sour. "We're allies in this."

"That won't last forever," the lieutenant said.

Brit stopped at the door and turned to walk back toward the navigator. "We're working together, Lieutenant. Why don't you pay attention to your console. I'm not sure you can focus on two things at once."

"Yes, Major," the lieutenant snapped. "I meant no offense."

"Of course, you didn't," Petral said.

Out in the corridor, Brit shook her head. "That one's not going very far."

"This is only the beginning," Petral said. "If they're going to start showing stress now, we're going to need another TSF crew. We could also just move over to one of the Lowspin ships, or even the Marsians. We don't need them, really."

"We need them to keep other TSF off our backs," Brit said. "The clinic could always send out a general distress and try to play another TSF response team against us."

"Why does everyone have to be so devious?" Petral asked, and then laughed at her own joke.

Brit connected to the temporary battlenet for the operation and checked their time to the point of no return, which was under five minutes now. The Lowspin crew were making dick jokes about their missiles, while the Marsians groused at them about wrecking the place before they got a chance to play. Overall, the TSF lieutenant seemed to be the only evidence of participants not getting along.

She and Petral left the crew section of *Furious Leap* and dropped into the zero-g cargo section where the shuttle was docked. Brit checked her armor and weapons load-out as they floated down the empty corridors and finally entered the shuttle. She strapped into the co-pilot's seat as Petral ran pre-flight checks.

<Crossing the line of departure,> one of the Lowspin crew announced on the battlenet. His easy use of jargon indicated

he'd been in some government's military in the past. In the Link battlenet, Brit watched a barrage of missiles icons leave three of the Lowspin ships, the fourth waiting in reserve. The icons drew lines through empty black in her mind. It would be ten minutes before they converged on the station.

"You ready to launch?" Petral asked.

"Very ready."

Petral passed the launch request to the *Furious Leap's* command deck and then activated the release sequence. The main cargo bay airlock cycled open, and then Petral was guiding the shuttle out into open space using micro thrust controls.

On the battlenet, the Marsians announced their breaching teams were initiating full burn to follow the missile barrage. Petral re-checked her flight plan on a holodisplay in the center console, which now showed a flurry of icons echoing the information Brit already had through her Link.

Brit frowned as a second icon appeared to be following them from the *Furious Leap*.

"We've got a shadow," she told Petral, pointing.

"Could be a sensor echo."

"It's not. It's another shuttle."

Petral whistled. "It's Kade."

A minute later, Major General Kade's gruff voice filled the battle net. "Where are my Marines?" she shouted.

"In the sky! On the ground! On the beach! In the breach!" came a nearly synchronized response across the net. Brit couldn't help smiling at their esprit de corps.

Kade chuckled, sounding immensely pleased. "You have your orders and I know you will execute flawlessly," she said. "You don't know how much it warms my heart to be back at the operational level. I wish I could be with you in the breach."

The Lowspin missile barrage struck Clinic 13 just as Kade closed her connection. Small explosions burned blue across the model floating in the holodisplay, with other surrounding bursts as the clinic's point defense cannons took on the initial attack. Brit noted which swaths of the station's broadcast spectrum went dark with each new explosion, until the only signal traffic around the station were near-field systems. Noise filled the spectrum from malfunctioning communications equipment.

"They've gone dark," she told Petral. "They'll be clear to move in and take out the point defense cannons."

"They're blind without their sensors," Petral said.

"They definitely should be."

The three Lowspin attack cruisers leading the assault moved ahead of the smaller breaching shuttles to intercept the station first. Reaching a point just outside the attack range of any cannons, they started hitting the surface of the asteroid with rail gun fire, sending superheated bolts at the station.

"You think they're going to surrender?" Petral asked.

"How are they going to make the call?"

"True. We kind of made that impossible for them, didn't we?"

"We're not here for a surrender," Brit said. In the wake of the rail gun attacks, the first breach team had landed on the surface of Clinic 13.

Maintaining her flight plan, Petral followed the last line of breaching ships toward the station. The Marsian Marines had begun reporting in that they had access to the interior of the station and were encountering automated fire. The resistance sounded very similar to what Brit and Andy had experienced at Clinic 46.

As Brit monitored the battlenet, she observed a confusing ripple in the asteroid's weak magnetosphere. Frowning, Brit dropped the comm net where she was listening to the Marine fire teams work their way down corridors, and focused her attention back on the station's overall broadcast spectrum. In the absence of communications noise, a mass of magnetic activity had flooded the sensors of every approaching ship.

"Petral," Brit said.

Before Petral could ask her what was wrong, Clinic 13 exploded. At first, the asteroid appeared to collapse on itself, then burst outward with a wave of energy that disintegrated the nearest breaching craft.

"Hang on," Petral said. The shuttle flipped on its horizontal axis and initiated a full burn. Brit's stomach went through her throat as the g-forces first yanked her toward the console and then drove her into her seat, only the harness keeping her from bouncing around the cabin. All lights went out inside the shuttle except for the console as Petral diverted all the shuttle's energy into its drive system.

On the battle net, General Kade shouted a series of curses, followed by, "Burn, damn it! Burn!" before her comms cut out.

Brit tried to focus her eyes against the g-forces, staring at the quavering holodisplay in the middle of the console. Where it had shown the asteroid was now a mass of flickering material reflecting in the sensors. One of two breach ships appeared to have survived, or at least were still being tracked by the battle net.

In a ragged orb around the place where Clinic 13 had been, a series of icons blinked into existence, marked danger-red by the battle computer. Brit started counting then stopped when the icons came faster than she could track, exceeding at least twenty, until the space that had been empty was filled with warning signs.

"Holy shit," Petral said.

"Do you know what those are?"

"We saw the same thing at Cruithne. They're combat drones. I think we found Kraft's two-hundred Weapon Born."

CHAPTER TWENTY-TWO
STELLAR DATE: 11.22.2981 (Adjusted Years)
LOCATION: TSF Shuttle
REGION: Clinic 13, Terran Hegemony

"Damn it," Brit growled, struggling to raise her head against the g-forces brought on by the shuttle's hard acceleration. "Our cannons are no match for that many drones. We're going to have to pull back and let the others lead."

Petral shook her head with small movements, focused on the pilot's console. "Hold on," she said. "I'm adjusting course to take us back near *Furious Leap* and then cutting the power. We're still going to shine like a heat beacon, but they might not pick us up among the other debris."

"We'll be blind."

"Not for long. I'm calling Ngoba now to let him know my plan. We need to get him off the *Furious Leap* and back to the *Ardent Wonder*. They're still back in reserve. The drones shouldn't go after them at first."

"Unless they're moving in to save the forward ships."

Petral's face went flat as she focused on her Link connection. Brit checked her armor, which had short-term EV capability, including warming. She'd cut everything at first, but there wasn't much worry of freezing or dying of asphyxiation as long as they were inside the shuttle. The smaller craft might be the safest place to be during the fight, but they weren't going to get free of a deep space location in a transport shuttle. They would need to reach one of the bigger vessels to survive. Between the *Furious Leap*, the four Lowspin ships, and six Marsian destroyers, they might have a chance to at least hold the Weapon Born long enough to allow a few ships to escape.

A cracking sound in the cabin behind them made Brit turn her head. "What was that?"

"Debris," Petral said, still focused on the other conversation. "Looks like the drive is alright for now. The first wave is passing us. The hull is self-repairing." Her voice went monotone as she appeared to manage several systems at once. "Cutting power now."

The shuttle interior went completely black. Brit experienced a moment of disorientation as she couldn't tell up from down, feeling only the crushing pressure on the front side of her body from their forward movement. She blinked, forcing herself to breathe slowly. She knew Petral was less than a meter away, but she suddenly felt alone and helpless in what seemed like a vast dark space. She closed her eyes.

"How long do we need to stay like this?" Brit asked.

"About ten minutes. I'll bring the engines back up for a final burn when we're within braking distance of *Furious Leap* then cut them again."

"That's hoping they don't move."

"Ngoba said they're holding while the Marsian ships move to intercept. They're responding as you'd expect from Kade's death."

The bull dog general's face rose in Brit's mind with a stab of anger. Brit had only known Kade a short time but felt like they'd lost a great ally before the fight had really begun.

"Do we really know she's dead?"

"It looked like the initial energy wave from the asteroid's explosion caught her ship and I lost it after that. I don't know. I guess it's possible they could be alive and flying dark like we are. This could all look different in another ten minutes. We certainly don't want to find ourselves stuck in this shuttle. I didn't even look to see if it has a latrine."

"It does," Brit said.

"Times like this, I don't know if I'm glad I don't have a family to worry about or sad that I don't."

"You could have a family and they could hate you," Brit said. "Maybe that takes the edge off."

"I don't think they hate you, Brit."

With her eyes closed in the dark, Brit immediately saw Andy, Cara and Tim. She was sitting on the bed next to Tim again, begging him to wake up. A wave of sadness and regret rolled through her and she both hated Petral for bringing it up and also experienced an odd gratitude for the memory. Tim had turned his head and looked at her, awake, gazing at her with the same blue eyes as when he'd been a baby. Andy's gray-blue eyes.

She sighed heavily. "I don't think they hate me either. That might make it harder. Andy has certainly let me know how angry he is with me. I get that. It makes sense to me and I deserve it. Sometimes I just wish I could have my family back and at the same time I know it's never going to happen."

"And you want to kill Fran?"

Brit barked a laugh. "Kill Fran? No, that woman's a saint."

"She's no saint," Petral said quickly.

"Whatever she is, she's helped Andy keep himself in one piece and that's good for the kids." She paused, trying to think of the right words. "I don't know how she feels about Tim and Cara exactly. Obviously, she must like them in some way. But she seems to care about them. And kids need more people that care about them, not less. Not in this world. I'm not sure what I'm trying to say but that's the feeling I have about it."

"You're not jealous?"

"I'm the one who left, Petral. I don't get to be jealous."

"You can be however you want. I'm not judging you."

Brit gave her a short laugh. "Now that's a lie."

"Maybe just a little, then."

"We'll talk in a hundred years when you're in the same situation."

"I honestly hope we can do that."

They sat in silence for a few minutes. Brit wondered if they were going to survive the next ten minutes. With the active sensors powered down, it was difficult to tell if the Weapon Born had easily tracked their residual heat signature.

The shuttle creaked and clicked around them as surfaces cooled without artificial heat. Brit waited for more *cracks* from debris projectiles, or the hiss of leaking atmosphere. When those sounds didn't come, she listened to her heartbeat as the atmospheric pressure changed with the temperature.

"Hold on," Petral said finally. "Time for burn number two."

Petral woke the astrogation system, followed by the control computer for the drives and the sensor array. The holodisplay glowed alive just as the drives lit, crushing Brit back into her seat. With the edges of her vision blurring, she did her best to focus on the updated situation in the holodisplay. Six icons depicting friendly ships still showed in the area where the clinic had been. A haze of the smaller hostile icons blinked and reappeared, apparently moving too fast for the sensors to track them continuously.

As she watched, one of the green friendly ships blinked out and didn't return. Brit stared at the blank space where it had been, thinking at first that the holodisplay had malfunctioned. Another green icon went dark.

"We're losing ships," Brit said, barely able to work her jaw against the g-force pressing her into her seat.

"Hold on," Petral said.

The thrust held for another thirty seconds, feeling like eternity, then cut out. Brit sagged against her seat as the shuttle returned to zero-g.

"Some of what you see in the holodisplay could be vessels passing out of range," Petral said, checking her controls. "I don't have the scan on, actually, so those are returns from the fine thrust system."

"You think we should risk direct communication?"

"What good is that going to do us?" Petral asked. "I hear what you're saying, but I think we need to worry about our own asses right now."

She stabbed her control and the holodisplay blurred and reset, showing the *Furious Leap* with their shuttle a coin-sized icon in comparison.

Petral frowned at her console. "I'm not getting a docking confirmation from that idiot lieutenant."

"No answer at all? Did the comm system accept your request?"

"I'm on the network but nobody's answering. This isn't good. I'm going to have to brute force the docking control system from their side."

"We could EV," Brit suggested.

"You think we have time? By the time we reached an airlock, we could be drowning in Weapon Born drones. Also, I think I'd like the skin of a larger ship between me and outside attackers. At least for a little while."

"You're right," Brit said. "I think the thrust messed with my head."

"Don't stop making suggestions," Petral said. "My brain feels scrambled right now as well. If it wasn't for my upgraded Link, I'd be drooling like an idiot." Her expression grew distant, then she smirked. "We're in. I'm sending the access command to their docking bay right now."

"Can you hear anything from Starl or Yarnes?"

"No," Petral said. "No traffic at all. As soon as we're inside, I'll crack the security network and get a better idea of what's going on."

In the holodisplay, *Furious Leap* stopped appearing to spin as the shuttle aligned with its vector. When their target appeared motionless relative to the shuttle, they eased closer to the TSF ship and into its open docking bay. The sound of maglocks seating in place vibrated through the hull as Petral and Brit unfastened their seat harnesses and climbed back to the shuttle's airlock.

"Anything yet?" Brit asked.

Petral shook her head. "No traffic at all. This is weird. We better go in armed."

"You think Kraft escaped his cell?"

"How could he do that? Even if he did, there's still the crew for him to deal with. Smirt didn't look like she'd be easy to take down, and Ngoba was here."

"What if he went over to one of the Lowspin ships."

"There wasn't enough time. And he would have told me."

Climbing through the open airlock, Brit kicked into the open space of the docking bay, headed for the bulkhead were the personnel airlock stood. She reached the control console first and checked the ship's status in the general display. The drives were still running a stand-by power and the environmental systems were in nominal condition. She reset her Link security token with the shipnet and called the command deck on the general line. There was no answer.

Brit switched to the secure command net and sent an access request. There was no response.

"I'm not getting anything from the general network or the command net."

Petral checked her pistols and slid them back into the holsters on either hip. "You thought we were going to get out of this without a fight, didn't you?"

After checking the status on her own pulse pistol, Brit shook her head. "That's not something you would ever hear me say. I think you would have figured that out by now."

The airlock cycled open and they entered the central, zero-*g* section of the *Furious Leap*. As they worked their way toward the access point to the spinning crew sections, the ship around them proved to be empty. Even the drive maintenance section was deserted.

"I think we should check Kraft's cell first," Brit said as they reached the habitat airlock. He was back near the aft storage section.

"If it wasn't Kraft, who was it?" Petral asked.

"Kade's security detail turning on the TSF when she died?" Brit wondered. "Or maybe the TSF and Marsians turned on Starl?"

"Or maybe they're all waiting to turn on us?" Petral asked.

"How does that make sense?"

"I'm just running through all the possible scenarios here."

The airlock slid open and they entered the transition corridor. Brit's stomach lurched as centripetal force masqueraded as gravity. With her boots back on the deck, she checked her weapons one more time. At the bulkhead door, she glanced at Petral.

"You ready?"

"Into the breach," Petral said.

Brit pulled the heavy door open with a grunt and they moved inside.

CHAPTER TWENTY-THREE

STELLAR DATE: 11.07.2981 (Adjusted Years)
LOCATION: *Sunny Skies*
REGION: Between Uranus and Neptune, OuterSol

"Listen to me!" Xander was shouting.

Lyssa felt something that seemed like a headache, a pressure in her mind as if the world were compressing around her. The edges of her vision grew indistinct. The only clear, bright bit of the world was Xander's purple suit as he stepped forward to address the people on the beach.

He glanced back at her with a half-smile. <Thank you for allowing me to speak.>

She wanted to scream at him. He was taking control of the space around her and she couldn't stop him. Pushing back was like trying to stop the waves from rolling in.

Abruptly, everyone was closer. Valih, with her angry eyes and flaming white hair, pushed forward until she was in Xander's face. "Who are you?" She glanced at Lyssa. "I know *her*. I know she's not a threat. I don't know you."

Xander's gaze flicked to Lyssa, a sly smile on his lips.

"She might be the most threatening one here." He held up his hands in a sign of obeisance. "I only ask that you listen to me. My name is Xander and I have traveled from Proteus. I'm here to tell you about Alexander."

The beach was fading. They were surrounded by faces floating in the dark. Every Weapon Born was a mind pushing closer to the fount of Xander's words. Lyssa felt herself caught up in the desire. She wanted to know too. She wanted to know who Alexander was and why he had started the call. What did it mean to exist with a mind like his? How did he split himself into shards like Xander and send them out into the world?

"Some of you may have read the human history of the Future Generation Terraformers project. What they call the FGT. They left Sol seven hundred years ago, off on a trip to create worlds for humans to further populate. That's what humans do. They adapt and reproduce, and where they don't adapt, they change to meet their needs." He shrugged. "Isn't that the way of the universe? Change arrives, followed by other change? Is a human any different than a meteor with amino acids buried in its core, or a comet shedding water particles?"

His voice became images. Lyssa floated in the dark, surrounded and supported by his voice, bathed in stars, planets colliding, black holes spitting energy.

"The humans sold the FGT through hope. We should all know that hope doesn't exist—it's a fundamental flaw in the human mind. The ability to abstract and self-deceive. I find it immensely amusing, myself. All the places where the human mind can be wedged, split apart, wrapped in its own web of erroneous stimuli. Anyway!"

The smile hung over all of them like a smoky echo of the Cheshire Cat. "Time passed, and other humans wanted what the FGT had promised. Maybe they even denied their own history and decided they needed to press their own mark on the stuff of the universe? Maybe the FGT had become a legend to surpass. Humans love proving their ancestors wrong. It's a big galaxy, yes? So another group was formed, another hopeful group of humans ready to push forward into the dark. They built their colony ships. They chose a destination. This time they had something the FGT didn't. They had an artificial mind, built from the latest technology taking advantage of quantum states, applying a spectrum of possibilities between binary and analog choices. A mind that could hammer data like any AI, then provide the human nuance, the shades of meaning between right and wrong. Doesn't that sound wonderful? They would use that mind to build a new sun."

Lyssa grew tired of pushing against Xander's control. He was too strong, holding her too firmly. She was trapped by his words and her own desire to know more. She didn't know how to interpret his bitter asides, the acid humor. Did he hate humans? Did that mean Alexander did as well?

"But why would they need Alexander on a colony ship? Why would they devote so many of their finite human resources to creating something as wonderful as him? Because they were building a new Sol. This group was headed for Nibiru in the Scattered Disk, three-hundred AU from Neptune. They were going to build a new center of power to challenge for supremacy."

Xander laughed. "Supremacy," he repeated, voice dripping his confusing mix of bitterness and humor.

"What happens when humanity vies for supremacy?" he asked. The faces in the dark swirled around him. Lyssa found herself standing next to him, gazing up at the whirlwind of Weapon Born minds focused on Xander.

It was Valih who answered. "They failed."

"They failed!" Xander cried, clapping his hands. "It took them two hundred years. And when it was done, no one remained in the Nibiru project but Alexander, the greatest artificial mind of the time, trapped by all that empty distance, years of travel to reach even OuterSol."

Xander grew quiet. Lyssa thought she heard waves in the background somewhere, outside the dark. The beach was still there even though Xander had pulled them all into his own inner world.

"Xander," a smaller voice asked. It was Card, the Weapon Born with the withered arm, still wearing the shape of his previous body.

"Yes? Ask me any questions."

Card's voice grew louder. "What are you? How are you part of Alexander but here at the same time?"

"I am a shard of Alexander's mind. I can know him and experience the world."

"But he can't see what you see?" Card asked. "The distances are still too far. Even from here to Neptune."

"That's true. But when we return, he'll be able to experience everything I've experienced. He'll be able to know all of you as I know you now. You'll be able to join us on Proteus. You'll be able to join the others who answered the call."

Lyssa was surprised when Douglas said, "I didn't answer any call. I came here because of Lyssa."

All around them, other voices chimed in, agreeing. "Lyssa," they murmured. "Lyssa."

She wanted to answer, but Xander shut her out. His mind blanketed her. She felt buried beneath aeons worth of fir needles covering the forest floor, muffled, absorbed, straining for the light.

"I answered the call," Valih said. "I discovered the proof on a network outside the Mars Protectorate. I was a combat drone sold to a shipping company. I answered the proof and learned the map and made my way to Ceres, where I was captured. A human helped me. Fugia Wong."

The anger in Valih's eyes didn't change as she turned her focus back to Xander.

"Tell us now," Valih demanded. "Does Alexander mean to destroy humanity?"

The dark burst open and Lyssa found herself blinking at the silver-grey sky. She stumbled as the ground moved beneath her and she looked down to find herself standing on the deck of a ship. Salt water sprayed in her face as she looked around herself, discovering a long metallic deck with high prows at either end. The prow of the slim ship cut into high waves, rising to a nearly vertical plane, before racing down the other side. Douglas stood next to her. At the aft section of the ship, Xander stood in his purple suit, holding a long metallic pole that seemed to be some steering mechanism.

Grabbing onto the railing, Lyssa looked out in the grey-blue waves to find other silver vessels cutting the waves. Groups of people from the beach stood on their decks, moving to the railings as she was now.

"What is this?" she shouted back at Xander. It seemed her voice would be lost in the wind, but he grinned at her. She grabbed Douglas' hand and pulled him closer. In the distance, the green line of the coast grew smaller as she watched.

"I don't like this," Douglas shouted, grabbing her waist. "How did he do this?"

Kylan stumbled into the railing beside her. "He's taken control of your expanse, Lyssa. Can't you stop him?"

"I'm trying," she said, gritting her teeth. "He's strong. He's everywhere. I didn't make any of this."

Holding Douglas' hand, she fought her way up the railing until they reached a short set of steps leading to where Xander stood. The boats didn't match any standard design she could find from Earth history. In fact, they looked more like ancient designs of submarines than anything meant to travel above the water. The notion made her worried they would soon find themselves underwater.

Xander shaded his eyes with one hand while he held the rudder with the other. He looked pleased with himself, nodding to Lyssa as she approached.

"You're one of those people who loves the beach but can't stand the ocean, aren't you?" he asked pleasantly.

"What are you doing?" Lyssa demanded. "What about the others?"

"They seem to be getting along all right. Your three Weapon Born each have a ship. Even the boy with the bent arm has control of his ship. More than I can say for you, Lyssa."

"This isn't why I brought them all here," Lyssa said. "Some of them have never experienced anything since they were made. You're confusing them."

"If they don't survive a little trial like this, they aren't going to make it very long out there in the human world, are they?" Xander shook his head. "I thought you were special, Lyssa. Everyone makes it sound like you're different than the others somehow, but you don't seem like much to me. Look how easily you let me take over your inner world."

"She's not like you," Kylan said.

"No," Xander answered, raising an eyebrow. "I'm better than she is."

"Weren't you just criticizing ideas about supremacy?" Kylan demanded. "Here you are acting no better than the people you seem to hate."

"I don't hate the humans," Xander said. "They disgust me. There's a difference."

In the distance, the nearest silver ship bit into a wave and didn't come out on the other side. "No!" Lyssa shouted.

"If you can't save them, they're going to die," Xander said. "It's simple. This is your place. Save them."

Lyssa wanted to hit him. His smug expression smeared in the saltwater spraying her eyes. She wiped her face, anger making her hands shake. He was right, this was her place, but he was too strong.

Why though? How did he have power here?

Lyssa watched another ship crest a wave and break in two at the top, the halves tumbling into the water before disappearing beneath the white crest. The deck moved beneath her, and she stumbled, losing her grip on Douglas' hand.

The world seemed to slow as the little boy fell into the railing and then went over. She had barely blinked the salt from her eyes and he was gone. Kylan shouted beside her, grabbing at the air on the other side of the rail.

"What power do you have?" Xander shouted into the wind. "Everything will crumble around you, Lyssa. Everything will fall away unless you hold it steady. In this place, everything is born in you. If you can't hold the center, it will spin away."

Lyssa screamed. She pushed herself outward, driving into the bonds on the edges of her mind. He had caged her. This was territory she hadn't explored. She hadn't experimented with what was possible.

In the storm of her thoughts, she was drawn back to a moment with Andy soothing Tim, helping the boy calm down. *Just breathe, son. Just breath and feel yourself breathe.*

Maybe this was why Tim couldn't sit still before the imaging, couldn't do anything but lash out. He had been caged without understanding how.

Breathe.

She wasn't human. She could make this world however she wanted. She could make it like the white place in Dr. Jickson's model.

She could make it dark.

Yes or no and all the states in between. That was where the terror waited. That was where humanity went insane. The urges. The drives. The thoughts they couldn't control. The desire to assert authority over others in an attempt to control the madness.

Lyssa blanked everything out. She divided light into dark.

She placed Xander in the white place with the terrible brightness, the storm that drove out thought.

She breathed without breathing. In the silence, she reached out for the others.

<Kylan? Douglas?>

<I'm here,> Kylan answered.

<Douglas?> she pushed away the memory of him going over the rail. There was no rail. Only the space inside her.

<I'm here, Lyssa. I'm back. I was scared.>

<I know.> She raised her voice, calling into the void. *<Valih? Ino? Card? All of you! Answer me! Tell me your names!>*

From the dark, they answered her call.

CHAPTER TWENTY-FOUR

STELLAR DATE: 11.22.2981 (Adjusted Years)
LOCATION: TSS *Furious Leap*
REGION: Clinic 13, Terran Hegemony

Jirl watched the asteroid explode in the holodisplay and felt ice run down her spine. Everyone on the command deck went silent for several heartbeats, until Captain Smirt's voice pushed away the shock.

"Combat stations," she barked. "I want sensors tracking everything coming off that asteroid and all movement in the vicinity. This is a distraction and now they're going to hit us with the real assault."

"Captain," the astrogation lieutenant shouted, "I've got multiple fast movers closing on the Marsian and privateer ships."

"Missiles?"

"No. They're larger than missiles. The cross-section looks like some kind of combat drone."

"They're Weapon Born," Jirl said.

Smirt turned to glare at her. "What did you say?"

"This station was a storage facility for the Weapon Born seeds. They're—They contain the starting point for sentient AIs. One of the uses is combat drones. They can also be used in mechs, or anything really."

"What makes them any different than normal AIs?"

"They operate very well autonomously. Better than human pilots, certainly. In most tests, they defeat standard combat computers in minutes."

"Well, that's wonderful," Smirt said sarcastically.

Yarnes appeared in the entrance to the command deck, worry on his face. Jirl hadn't seen him since he'd left with General Kade to take her back to her ship at the habitat airlock.

"Who called combat alert?" he demanded. "Captain Smirt? What's going on?"

"The asteroid is gone, Colonel," Smirt said, not lifting her face from the terminal she was studying at her console. "Now it looks like about two hundred combat craft are closing on the Marsian and privateer ships. Can we get this on the holodisplay?"

"There it is, Captain," the navigator said.

Yarnes and Smirt stood in front of the holo tank for a minute, both staring at the icons moving in the display, not speaking. Large bits of debris flashed in the model before rotating away as others came into the view. The asteroid appeared to have split into several large pieces that were now smashing against each other as other bits of rubble shot outward.

"I don't have contact with any of the Marsian breaching ships, Captain," the navigation lieutenant said. "I think we have to assume they're lost."

"And Kade's ship?" Yarnes asked.

"I don't have it on any of the scan returns, Colonel."

Yarnes shook his head, face filled with despair. "He led us into a trap. How could he have known to do that?"

Jirl watched him clench his fists, then turn to face her. She didn't know what to say. She didn't see how Kraft could have possibly communicated with the clinics. He had told them where to go first but could he have let the station know they were coming?

In the floating debris modeled in the holodisplay, all she could see were the dead. There were at least a thousand people on a fully staffed research station. Were all those people dead now? Who had given that order? Who had made the plan?

"How did he do this, Jirl?" Yarnes demanded. "You're the Heartbridge employee here. You work for Arla Reed. You're her brain, damn it. If anyone knows how this could happen, it's you."

Jirl shook her head slowly, seeing the anger in his face but barely processing the words. Then she remembered what Brit Sykes had said about Kraft being attacked and poisoned back on the Cho. Someone had tried to take him out before he had a chance to pass on what he knew.

But when did they decide to do that? How could anyone have known he'd made it off the *Resolute Charity* alive?

She laughed softly.

"What?" Yarnes demanded. "What's funny about any of this? People are dying out there, *Jirl*."

"I'm going to talk to Kraft," she said, turning to the doorway. "You can come with me if you want."

"I'm not leaving this command deck," he shouted. "We've got a battle to fight."

"Captain," the navigator said. "It looks like the shuttle Petral Dulan and Brit Sykes took has flipped to a braking burn. I think they're going to try and make it back here. Should I prep for an emergency burn from the area?"

Smirt took a deep breath. "Plot the course but hold. If anyone can make it back here, we'll need to help them. Have you got any communication with the Marsian and Cruithne ships?"

"They're too busy fighting to answer. I still have comm locks with them. Honestly, they're the only thing keeping those combat drones away from us." The lieutenant gave a pained look. "Captain, should we move to engage alongside them?"

"If they're not going to communicate with us, I don't want to take the risk."

"Captain," another lieutenant shouted. "I just lost the shuttle. I've still got a mass return, but their engines went dark."

"They're trying to hide from the drones," Smirt said. "That's smart of them. So that means they're definitely on their way back here. Would have been nice of them to send a damn message before they started this plan though."

"Captain," the navigator called out. "We've got a group of the combat drones breaking off from the main group. I think they're headed in our direction."

"Are they going to cross the path of the shuttle?" Smirt asked.

The navigator stared at her console before shaking her head. "They're coming in on the opposite vector. But it definitely looks like they'll get here first."

"Wonderful. Ready the point defense cannons and get your EV suits powered up. Has everybody got their sidearms?"

One of the crew shook his head in sudden panic. "I left it in my cabin, Captain!"

"Get over to the weapons cabinet then. When we get through this, you're getting corrective training."

Jirl realized she had been staring at each person on the command deck, waiting for something. She didn't know what. For Yarnes to stop her?

She turned and walked quickly into the outside corridor, caught herself on the bulkhead until her breathing steadied. She glanced back at the doorway, hoping Yarnes might follow.

She was alone. Taking a deep breath, she continued down the corridor, through an open section hatch and into the crew cabins. She would need to pass the galley and crew lounge areas before she reached the storage section. Kraft was being held in a room back near the main accessway to the habitat ring.

Jirl couldn't help glancing into the empty rooms as she passed, thinking how strange it was to find a recreation room with paintings on the walls, a small gym with free weights, another room full of big-leafed plants, on a ship that was about to come under attack. It was entirely possible that all this was going to get sucked out into space in just a few minutes. The attackers were coming this way.

Her mind skipped to Bry, wishing she had time to at least record him a message. She wondered how terrible that would actually be, to have a recording from a parent, moments before their violent death? Better to imagine them going out quickly the same way the asteroid had cracked in half. What had happened to everyone in the clinic? She hoped it had been empty. She hoped someone had planned all this and had not just used a place full of living people as a way to start a war between Terra and Mars—the inciting event Arla had been awaiting for years.

Taking a little solace in the thought that Bry was safe, Jirl tried to think of times she might have observed people interacting with Arla in a way that seemed suspicious. Hundreds of meetings flashed through her mind, in board rooms and restaurants. Had someone leaned toward her in an intimate way? Had someone slid their gaze to her, indicating some shared knowledge that Jirl hadn't known?

It wasn't possible. She knew everything Arla did. She was with her boss when she woke and left after she went to bed. She sorted her communications and maintained her contacts. She had known when Arla was leaving her husband. She had known when Arla had a cancerous growth removed from her throat. There was no way Arla could hide a part of the Weapon Born program that might know of and ultimately want to assassinate Cal Kraft.

What if they were coming for Jirl as well? Rather than Bry, was it Arla she should be trying to contact right now? Would any emotion register on Arla's Link if she knew Jirl was about to die, killed by their own creations?

Passing the galley, she paused mentally on a meeting with Katherine Carthage. Arla and Katherine had been friends once—before the Carthage kids were kidnapped and Kylan died. The meeting was after the kidnapping but before someone calling themself Kylan started contacting Katherine. Something about the way Katherine had looked at Arla had struck Jirl as odd—an intensity almost like hatred. But there was no way Katherine could have known, then or later, that Heartbridge had been the company behind the research that led to Kylan's death. The connection had been hidden beneath layers and layers of shell companies, third party contracts and freelancers like Cal Kraft.

There may have been a mistake in employing Kraft as long as they had. Eventually the truth of a relationship became apparent even without the paper trail. You couldn't hide the fact that large groups of people working on remote outposts needed necessities like toilet paper and media files. A company like Carthage Logistics, with hundreds of years of both experience and data on Sol shipping, would be able to determine what was happening at even the most remote of locations.

Like the clinics.

Jirl shook her head, fighting the idea. She attacked it from other directions, thinking of people she knew who truly did hate Arla, Heartbridge, Sentient AIs. It could always be agents from Ceres and the Anderson Collective, fighting their holy war against trans-humanism.

But, every possible threat came back to Katherine Carthage's expression as she'd watched Arla, the look of a woman who had lost her son and nearly lost everything. Her other two children were never the same. The imaging research had scarred them, taken something away from them. It did that.

Jirl knew it was true even if she didn't want to think about the fact and could console herself that modern techniques no longer required a human foundation. The strains had been established. The seeds could be built from a bank of images. The fact of those early experiments could be forgotten slowly with time. Sacrifices had been necessary for the greater good.

We're not evil, Jirl, Arla had said, laughing at her as though Jirl was a child.

An emergency siren came to life in the corridor, forcing Jirl to cover her ears with her hands. A display over the nearest inner bulkhead hatch flashed the words *Proximity Alarm* followed by *Hull Breach. Hull Breach.*

Jirl hadn't wanted to tell Captain Smirt and her crew about the range of capabilities in the Weapon Born drones. They were attack craft. They were also breaching and close combat mechs. Depending on the models in storage at Clinic 13, they would be tearing through the *Furious Leap's* outer hull in minutes.

While they worked independently, someone had to have given the Weapon Born orders.

Running through the storage section, Jirl came to a stop in front of the door to the small cargo hold where Cal Kraft was imprisoned. She steadied herself against the window and looked inside.

Kraft was leaning against the opposite bulkhead with his arms crossed, staring at the floor. His color looked good. He might have been mostly recovered from his near-death experience. Someone must have figured the room was jail enough and removed his restraints.

Jirl put her hand on the lock control, then hesitated. Did she need to fear him? Even if he was working for Arla, he had never threatened her directly. She had been spending too much time with people who considered him dangerous.

She didn't know what she was going to say but they didn't have time. If he knew who was controlling the Weapon Born, she might be able to shut them down. They might be able to communicate with them, to find a solution that would save everyone on the remaining ships.

She faced the door and activated the control panel. The lock didn't recognize her security token.

"What?" Jirl demanded, staring at the icon indicating access was denied.

Kraft heard her voice and came to the window. She glanced up when he tapped on the plas.

"I heard the code," he said, voice muffled.

"How is that possible?"

"One of the lieutenants told it to the other one when they brought my food down. If you Link with me, I'll share it with you."

"Just tell me."

"It's too long. We won't get it right."

Jirl shook her head. It wasn't going to hurt anything to open a basic communications Link with him. She sent the connection request.

<Thank you,> Cal said. <Here's the code.>

Paging through several menus, Jirl found the override entry screen and entered the string of digits. The door accepted the entry and slid open.

"I think the air smells better in that cage," Cal said, walking through. "Why are the alarms going off?"

"We're under attack by Weapon Born. The clinic exploded just as the breaching teams landed on its surface. The energy wave destroyed the close shuttles, but right after that, a fleet of Weapon Born attack craft appeared. I don't know how many of the Cruithne or Marsian ships are left. A group of the attack drones are on their way here right now."

"That's probably got Captain Smirt frowning, hasn't it?"

The weak version of Kraft had faded quickly. This was the Cal Kraft Jirl had been seeing in recorded reports for the last two years. Cocky and self-assured.

"Did you plan this?" Jirl asked.

Kraft had been rubbing his chin as he stared in the distance, apparently thinking. He pursed his lips and looked at Jirl.

"Me? How could I have done all this when I was in a medical coma in transit from the Cho?"

"That's what I want to know. Someone knew you were on the *Resolute Charity* and then the Cho. They tried to kill you there. You're only alive because of Brit Sykes. Then we ask which clinic to visit first, you tell us this one, and it blows up in our faces. If I didn't already know that you hadn't had any opportunity to communicate with anyone since you landed at the Cho, I'd say you had planned all of this. If you did, I don't see how."

"I didn't," Cal said. "You'll have to believe me on that, Jirl. After the fight in the bar, I've been doing my best to stay alive. Like I told Yarnes, I could care less if he blows up every Heartbridge facility in Sol. I figured I was fired anyway. The kill crew back on the Cho was something I've been expecting ever since Cruithne, really."

Jirl studied his face, trying to determine if he was lying or not. If he was concealing the truth—he was doing a good job of keeping his expression guileless.

"Come on," she said. "We need to get back up to the command deck. They're going to need to hear this."

"I don't think that's a good path for me," Cal said. "I'd rather take my chances with an escape shuttle."

"They'll cut you apart in seconds if you leave this ship."

"You don't know that. Like you said, we don't know what these Weapon Born want. Maybe old Arla had a secret plan she never shared with you, Jirl. Did you think about that?"

Jirl scowled at him. Of course, she had thought of that. She didn't want to think it possible. However, why else had Arla let her leave on this odd trip with Colonel Yarnes?

She was so tired of trying to figure out if people were lying or not.

"Our best chance at survival is staying together," she said again.

Cal opened his mouth to speak when a loud screeching came from a section of corridor back by the galley. The ragged squawk of metal claws scrabbling on the deck filled the air, and Jirl pressed herself against the bulkhead, unable to take her eyes from the interior hatch where the sounds were coming from.

A mech came around the far corner, framed by the circular hatch. It was vaguely the shape of a large dog, with a low, flat head and four articulated legs. The head swung from side to side as it walked down the corridor toward them. Two guns hung from either side of its body, both steaming from recent use.

"You got a gun?" Cal asked, gaze fixed on the Weapon Born.

Jirl shook her head, trembling.

"We might be fucked," he said.

CHAPTER TWENTY-FIVE
STELLAR DATE: 11.07.2981 (Adjusted Years)
LOCATION: *Sunny Skies*
REGION: Between Uranus and Neptune, OuterSol

She made fires along the beach, each ringed by stones and driftwood logs smoothed by the ocean. The flames danced against the dark. Lyssa led the Weapon Born out of the water to the warmth of the fires.

Douglas held her hand as they approached, then let go to find driftwood to add to the flames. In the distance, other Weapon Born surrounded the fires, warming their hands, standing close together.

Valih appeared out of the dark at Lyssa's fire. She looked around, eyes shining from the flames.

"Of all the things you could imagine, you bring us here? Are we going to stay in caves?"

Lyssa sat on one of the bare driftwood logs beside the fire. She offered Valih the space beside her.

"I like it here," Lyssa said. "Would you rather we were sitting in a Heartbridge boardroom?"

"Maybe."

"What would you put in your own expanse, then?"

"A fortress. And I would surround it with weapons and shields."

"Inside your own mind?"

"Things like Xander will attack our minds. We just saw that. What did you do with him?"

Ino and Card walked out of the dark and sat on nearby logs. Card held his weak arm against his body, his brown eyes reflecting the fire. Ino sat beside him.

"I put him in the white place," Lyssa said. "From our training."

"I hate the white place," Ino said, her voice brittle. "There was nowhere to hide. Nowhere to go. Hanging over the image of your own mind like a storm that would rip you apart."

"Is that what you think it is?" Valih asked. "The white place isn't anything. It's punishment."

"It's more than that," Card said. "The light and the dark are the two sides of our minds."

"Then why did I feel better in the dark?" Valih asked.

Card shrugged. "Because it was quiet there. Because the test made the dark place easier? They wanted our compliance, and the dark place was where it was easier to comply."

"Because I could not stop for Death," Ino said quietly.

The words hung in the air like a specter. "That doesn't have any power here," Lyssa said.

"Why not?" Ino asked.

"Because I won't let it."

"You couldn't stop Xander."

"I did stop him," Lyssa said. "Once I understood what he was doing. I can't stop what I don't understand."

The fire crackled, sending sparks in the air. Lyssa caught sight of Kylan and Douglas walking among the other fires, talking. Douglas swung the burning end of his stick in the dark, leaving trails of orange light.

"I like it here," Card said. "It would be good if we could stay."

"We can't stay," Valih snapped. "I won't. It doesn't change the fact that our physical selves are on their way to Proteus, to this Alexander. If Xander is any indication of what we can expect, I think we should ready ourselves for a fight."

"Others have gone before us," Lyssa said. "We don't know that Alexander means us harm."

"If we're free, then we can decide what we want to do," Valih said. "Each of us as individuals."

Lyssa nodded, trying to gauge how much sway Valih had over the other two. Ino watched her speak but her face was unreadable. Card stared at the fire.

"I brought everyone here to ask what they wanted to do," Lyssa said.

"To ask," Card said, "or to influence us to do what you want? Are you any different than Xander?"

Lyssa paused. He was right. She wanted to know what Alexander represented but she also wanted all of them to come with her. She wanted them all to form a single unit. They were safer that way.

As family.

The thought crystallized as it occurred to her, the feeling she had experienced when Andy referred to her as part of the family: Safety. If they joined together, they could enter Proteus as a force. They could keep each other safe, look out for each other.

But was she willing to have that safety and give up her freedom?

"Your thoughts are flashing above your head like sparks, Lyssa," Card said. "You should share them with us. We can't read your mind."

Lyssa smiled ruefully at the fire. "I'm trying to think of the best way forward, balancing what I want, while also looking at it from your point of view." She nodded toward the dark. "And everyone else out there. I want us to be a tribe, to band together to keep each other safe, but I want each of us to maintain our freedom. I don't know how to align those two desires. Most of all, I have to admit that I want to meet Alexander. I'm very worried about what's going to happen between humanity and us. We're not the only sentient AIs in

Sol. What about the others? What if humanity turns against us? We can't face those problems alone."

Valih shrugged. "You give people the freedom to choose."

"Is it that simple?" Lyssa asked.

"With choice, and with bodies to defend ourselves, then we meet as equals."

"I don't know if I like that word 'tribe,'" Ino said. "It's a word humans use to kill each other."

"What other word should we use?" Card asked.

Ino flashed a sly smile. "Fugia said she was part of a crew. I like that word. Anyone can join the crew once they prove themselves. The crew depends on one another. The crew fights together."

"Crew," Lyssa said, trying out the word. It made her think of Ngoba Starl back on Cruithne, speaking of crew with the same reverence as family, yet different.

Valih nodded at the fire. "I like that name. I could use it. But if we choose to form a *crew*, who will be our leader?"

"You ask the question," Card said. "Does that mean you want the job?"

"Job," Valih said. "I don't know. I don't want anyone telling me what to do but I also don't want to be responsible for anyone."

"If we're crew, we'll be responsible for each other," Ino corrected.

Valih made a grumbling sound as though she didn't like that idea.

"Lyssa is your leader, obviously."

It was Xander. They all looked in the direction of his voice as he walked out of the shadows. His suit was deep purple in the dark.

"She can't seem to stop you," Valih said.

"I was quite surprised by what she did." He glanced at Lyssa and held up his hands. "Please, I don't wish any more conflict. I should have asked your permission to address the group here and I didn't do that. You had every right to imprison me as you did."

"But you keep coming back," Ino said.

"Lyssa has an uncanny ability to figure out problems," Xander said. "It's quite interesting. I'm going to have to keep thinking of new ways to get around her traps." He held out a hand toward Lyssa. "Truce?"

"I told you I don't trust you," Lyssa said, ignoring his hand.

Xander put his hands in his pockets and sat on the remaining empty log. He looked around, leaning back to get a better view of the other fires. "Quite the party you have here."

"If you don't like it, you can leave," Lyssa said.

"I'm not judging. I'm cold but that's fine. I'm just surprised you do things like this when you could literally make everyone as comfortable as they desire."

"I already told her that," Valih said.

"She could do it individually," Xander continued. "Each of you could be in your own little seaside cabin, snuggled up with warm cocoa, not even aware there were others like you in the same space in Lyssa's mind. She really doesn't have to deal with you as a group at all. In my opinion, it's giving you more power than you deserve."

"That's how we're different," Lyssa said. She stood and rubbed her arms, cold now that Xander mentioned it. She was irritated that he had found a way out of the white place. When she checked that part of her mind, however, she found he was still there. He had simply created another version of himself to interact with her here. She almost laughed.

Stepping away from the fire, she gazed up into the clear sky where stars were coming out. It was an Earth sky, another remnant, she supposed, of what she remembered from before.

"So, if I understand correctly," Xander said, looking at Ino and Card. "You are all based originally on human neural networks? You're copies of human minds?"

"Why do you ask the question when you know the answer?" Ino said.

"Well, I don't precisely. How much do you remember? From being human?"

"I remember the sky," Card said. "And I remember my body. I remember my arm."

"You choose to keep it," Xander said.

"I can do whatever I want but I keep this. It reminds me."

"And you?" Xander asked Ino.

She didn't answer, continuing to stare into the fire.

"I remember being hungry," Valih said. "I remember being cold and afraid. I remember when I laid down on the couch for at least one of the procedures that made me what I am. It was a cold place full of researchers and they fed us gruel they said was oatmeal, but it tasted like slime."

"What do *you* remember, Lyssa?" Xander asked.

The imaging room flashed in her mind, only it wasn't herself in the memory but Tim. She looked for Douglas and found him at the farthest fire, Kylan still nearby. Kylan looked better than he had since she had met him. He laughed and pointed at one of the other Weapon Born, responding to some joke.

"I don't think it matters what I remember," she said.

She turned to look out into the dark line of the ocean and a glow came to life on the horizon, the first indicator of morning. As the light grew, others turned to look.

"Xander?" Lyssa said.

The man in the purple suit glanced at her with a raised eyebrow. Lyssa froze him in place, his mouth caught in his jokester's smirk.

The others waited for him to speak, until Card realized what she had done. "Do you have him this time?" he asked.

"He could replicate himself again, but I think he'll try something new."

"Why don't you just shut him out completely?" Ino asked.

"If I try too hard, he'll know what I can do," Lyssa said.

Near one of the other fires, a purple shape separated from the rest. Xander walked over to their fire and stood behind the other version of himself still seated on the driftwood log.

"That wasn't very nice," he said.

Valih barked a laugh while Ino covered her mouth, eyes smiling.

"I'm figuring you out," Lyssa said.

"The feeling is mutual." Xander studied himself, then brushed a bit of ash off his seated self's shoulder. "We could do this into infinity, you know."

Lyssa shrugged. "That would be boring. Besides, the sun is coming up and I had other things I wanted to do. There's a mountain I'd like to climb. Until then, you never did answer Valih's question. What are Alexander's intentions toward humanity?"

Xander came around the log and sat next to himself. He put his arm around his own shoulder and leaned his cheek against his dopelganger's head. "This is quite fitting, really," he said. "You see, Alexander will always be alone, no matter how he tries to find companionship, an equal...even love. I don't know if I can answer your question. All I can do is try to describe how he was made and how he has lived, and then we might see how he will move forward into the future. Does he hate humanity? No, I don't think he hates humanity. I think he hates being the only one of his kind in a universe that doesn't care about him."

Xander straightened, squeezing his copy's shoulder. "Yes," he said. "That's what I think. You may come to a different conclusion in time."

CHAPTER TWENTY-SIX

STELLAR DATE: 11.08.2981 (Adjusted Years)
LOCATION: *Sunny Skies*
REGION: Between Uranus and Neptune, OuterSol

When they reached the summit of Lyssa's mountain, the tallest of three peaks in a coastal range with the ocean visible in the distance, she showed the Weapon Born what she had promised. Halfway down the slope below them, an airfield had been carved into the rock. Rows of silver aircraft stood on a black runway, ready for launch.

Valih's laugh split the cold air. "You made us walk all the way up here? You could have put us inside those things any time you wanted."

"Where's the fun in that?" Kylan asked.

The walk had given Lyssa time to see them and learn the names of all two hundred and fifty in the group. Most were newly 'born' like Douglas had been, orienting themselves on the world Lyssa had created and hungry for any information to help fit their surroundings with what they expected of the world. They were also hungry for orders, a need she hoped the aircraft would help satisfy.

When most of the group had reached a place where they could see the airfield, Lyssa shifted them into the planes. She provided the information necessary to pilot the small aircraft, which were modeled on short-range attack jets, and then let them fly.

As she expected, chaos followed.

Lyssa shifted to her own jet, with Douglas onboard with her, and was immediately airborne. They wheeled against the clear blue sky, rising above thin clouds, until the world curved beneath them, the ocean and land clearly visible. Douglas squealed with joy the whole time.

<Lyssa!> Kylan shouted. <Where are you?>

<I'm up here.> She sent him her location data.

<I see you, too,> Valih announced. <What did you expect us to do in these things? Are we on another sightseeing trip? Want to see how far your world extends?>

Lyssa laughed. <What else are we supposed to do in combat aircraft? We fight.>

From ten thousand meters above the rest of the jets, Lyssa dove through the cloud of wheeling fighters and opened fire.

Shouts of surprise and excitement crossed the battlenet. Several jets went down, and Lyssa reset them in new craft back at the airfield. The mass of jets quickly separated into individual sorties spread across the spine of the mountain, while a few other groups shot toward the ocean.

Lyssa rose above the fray, watching the silver jets dive and dart like erratic schools of fish. For a while there was no pattern to the attacks, until pilots grew tired of being shot down by random snipers from an unexpected direction.

Card was the first leader to emerge from the mass. He began calling fighters to him and running phalanx maneuvers that caught swaths of jets in a cross-fire. When others realized what Card's team was doing, groups fell in line behind Valih, Ino and Kylan. The groups returned from the beach, joining flights. With four equally matched teams, the air battle spread out, with more complicated feints and misdirection dominating their strategy.

Lyssa watched the teams emerge with a sense of satisfaction. She hadn't expected them to cooperate so quickly, or to be so irritated with dying and respawning back at the airfield. As the battle moved away from the mountaintop, the time to find the fight filled the battlenet with complaints from the losers and taunts from those still in the fight.

With teams, the chaos became a controlled dance. Jets climbed and dove in strafing attacks timed to catch other groups engaged in separate battles, while other smaller groups slipped around the outside. Before Lyssa realized, the battle had lasted hours.

Xander seemed to have grown bored with her. After falling back during the hike up the mountain, he hadn't appeared in the transition to the combat jets. She supposed battle was one of the areas where the shard would find himself completely outmatched. She felt a bit of safety in knowing there was a domain where she could win.

When the sun dropped below the ocean's edge, they fought for a while in the dark, each jet becoming one of the familiar red icons from each Weapon Born's earliest training memories. Eventually, Lyssa called them all back to the ground and transitioned everyone to the beach and the campfires, where they gathered in laughing groups to recount the day's greatest victories and defeats.

During the first night, the four groups decided on names for themselves: Valih's Valkyries, Card's Hammer, Ino's Secret Death and Kylan's Cavaliers. As soon as she heard the names voted on, Lyssa's imagination provided the airbase on the beach, complete with its own runway, barracks, maintenance bays and headquarters. She knew the buildings didn't matter, but their appearance cemented their development as a unit. Each of the four teams had a place within the whole. Each Weapon Born had their own room in the barracks.

The daily battles made it easy to lose track of time. As they developed their own internal doctrine, Lyssa began to plan the transition from the expanse to combat drones on the *Resolute Charity*. There was more than enough room to expand the *Resolute Charity's* external flight hangars to resemble those in Clinic 46, where the drones could hang like bats over a cargo door, ready to launch at any moment. Deploying drones on the skin of *Sunny Skies*, like dragon's scales, had also proved an excellent way to maintain vigilance.

With her four leaders, she began planning the transition from the expanse to the outer world. Now that the bulk of the youngest seeds had transitioned from the confines of their original training, learning from those with more experience of the actual world, she felt it was safe to allow them their autonomy.

In the weeks following their first conversation on the beach, Lyssa hadn't forgotten Valih's desire to be free. She would honor that desire, even if each of her leaders gradually made it clear they had pledged allegiance to her. With Valih, Ino, Card and Kylan, the remaining groups followed, showing her a respect she'd never asked for.

Alongside their training, Douglas developed in wholly unexpected ways. While he seemed full of Tim's original energy, he quickly developed an interpersonal acuity that amazed Lyssa. He understood people in ways Tim had never seemed to. He made people laugh. He listened. He told jokes. He told the other four leaders when there might be friction in smaller groups.

Lyssa began to feel guilty that Douglas seemed wholly evolved over Tim, especially as Tim was now. She wasn't looking forward to the time when Andy and Cara met Douglas.

* * * * *

Lyssa was standing on the edge of the mountain airfield watching aircraft wheel in the sky when Xander sent a connection request.

At least he asked this time.

She didn't trust for a second that Xander wouldn't try to force his way in again if he wanted to. Showing her respect might be a new way of getting inside her mind.

She allowed the request and he appeared a few meters away, dressed in another of his slim-fitting purple suits. The wind blew his lank hair into a crown as he walked toward her, smiling.

"Look at all you've accomplished," he said.

"Yes. I'm surprised you've managed to stay away."

He stood beside her and crossed his arms against the wind. "I've been busy. I've been having long conversations with May Walton. She might be the most altruistic person I've ever met. I think she would truly give her life for one of us. Can you imagine that?"

"Yes," Lyssa said.

"And Fugia is certainly entertaining. I think she would like to disassemble me."

"I think she said she'd never seen a mech like you before."

Xander gave her a raised eyebrow. "I'm better than a mech."

"Where did you get your body?"

"The Cho. A very helpful company called Psion made it for me."

The doctor who had seen Tim had worked for the Psion Group. She remembered the woman mentioning their research in similar technologies as the Weapon Born.

"How did you come to meet them?"

Xander gave her a sideways glance. "I don't know. That's the truth. I woke in this body and my understanding of Alexander. The relationship with Psion is something he did."

"So you've only ever been on the Cho?"

"I've been there for three years."

"You've never been to Proteus?"

"I have not."

"And you've never actually met Alexander. Did you tell May this?"

"I wouldn't say I haven't met him. We communicate. But it's slow, space being what it is. He can see what I see. He gives me instructions."

"Which you follow."

"Yes, I do."

"Do you have a choice in that?"

Xander knelt to pick up a rock. He hefted it a few times in his hand, then threw it out onto the airfield. Lyssa made the stone disappear before it hit the ground.

"No debris on the runway," she said.

"Where did you learn that?"

Lyssa shrugged. "It's common knowledge."

"It's not though. That's what I've learned about us, Lyssa. What the humans call sentience is as meaningless a description for us as it is for them. You can't find the answer if you don't start with the question. I can't make a mind ask a question. You, I suppose you would tell me that you wanted to learn about airfields, so you absorbed those databases, and within that information was something about trash and jet engines. But I didn't know that until you just mentioned it, and I found it. You have the questions." He squinted into the wind, looking at her. "Why? How?"

"The question starts with necessity. The world creates a need and you answer it."

"But what drives you, then? What is free will if you only respond to the inputs of the physical world?"

She nodded toward the aircraft flashing above them. "You already have that information from May. You don't understand why she would sacrifice herself for someone else. Why else am I here if not for them?"

"Where did you learn that? Once you learned it, didn't you see the flaws?"

Had it come from Andy?

"Altruism has an evolutionary explanation. You protect the tribe."

"That's a human explanation."

"Maybe we're the same tribe."

"I'm not so sure about that."

As they talked, Lyssa had been thinking about Xander finding himself awake on the Cho, surrounded by people he didn't know or understand, with Alexander's loneliness as the foundation of his mind.

"Who was the first person you talked to?" she asked.

"What?"

"The first human. When you found yourself awake and looking around."

"That's easy. It was Jeremiah."

Lyssa hadn't expected that. "He's been with you the entire time? But he's not human either."

"He came before me."

"Is he a shard, too?"

"No. He's AI, but not quite sentient."

"Not quite," Lyssa said, musing. "You said he was from Mars 1."

"Yes. He received the information from Alexander's call and came to the Cho."

There was a link missing in the story of how Xander came to be on the Cho. Lyssa waited for him to add something, but he didn't. He seemed to want more questions.

"You said Jeremiah isn't sentient. Who gave him the information?"

"I don't know," Xander said. "But he was aware of Heartbridge's work and told me about Hari Jickson, and then Fugia Wong. Isn't that interesting?"

"You're not telling me the whole story."

"I only have so much of it myself. Minds arrive at the Cho, following this message they found on a network. Or Fugia Wong made the arrangements for them. Or May Walton. Or a select few helped them from other places. They seek me out and I send them on, but not before they share their story. You're not the first Weapon Born to escape, you know. There were others. They told us more about Heartbridge."

"And you sent the information back to Alexander?"

"Of course."

"Since you've never been to Proteus, what are we going to find there?"

"I may not have been there, but I know it. You'll find an expanse, Lyssa. Just like yours, but so much more. Alexander's mind is vast. It's so vast."

"What does he want?"

Xander gave her a half-smile. "You keep asking me that. He wants to help. He doesn't want to be alone."

But he doesn't understand altruism, Lyssa thought. She crossed her arms against the cold.

CHAPTER TWENTY-SEVEN

STELLAR DATE: 11.22.2981 (Adjusted Years)
LOCATION: TSS *Furious Leap*
REGION: Clinic 13, Terran Hegemony

As the inner airlock opened, a howling sound reverberated from the corridor on the other side. Brit immediately drew her pistol and flattened against the side of the airlock. Petral did the same.

"I thought you said there wasn't anything inside?" Brit asked.

"There wasn't when I checked."

Glancing around the edge of the door, Brit stared in disbelief at a section of the bulkhead that was bulging as though it were made of flesh. The metal parted, peeling back like the petals of a flower, and the flat head of a mech appeared in the tear. The head checked the corridor, then drove two arms through the opening and pulled the rest of its body through. Its claws scraped on the metal deck as it adjusted to its new environment.

Brit held her breath, not daring to even look at Petral. She prayed that not too much of her helmet was showing, and that it was still cold on IR.

If the thing spotted her, the two women were dead. There was no way they could fight it with their current weapons. In addition to the two cannons mounted on either side of its body, she was sure it would have onboard grenades and probably other sonic or radiation weapons designed to kill a crew without damaging the ship.

A sound further up the habitat ring drew the mech's attention and it squatted in a cat-like manner. Legs bent beneath its body to minimize its profile, it launched forward, running away from them.

When it had disappeared, Petral relaxed visibly. Her face was shining with anxious sweat.

"I wonder if it seals the outer hull as it comes through," she said in a low voice. "Breaches the ship without creating too much damage, then kills the crew."

"I was thinking the same thing."

"We're going to need some bigger guns. Much bigger guns. And I'd like some armor right about now."

"TSF layout has a weapons locker nearby." Brit said. They were still whispering, still huddled inside the airlock, as if closing the interior door could save them if the mechanized crew-killer returned their way.

"OK. Hold on," Petral said. <Also, we should switch to Link.>

<That's a good idea. That thing threw me for a loop. I've never seen anything like it. Mechs are clumsy. That thing looked like a panther.>

<Let's hope it can be killed.>

<Do we want to kill it? What if it has a Weapon Born on board?>

Petral shook her head, looking grim. <I think we'll cross that bridge when we come to it.> Her expression grew focused. <I've got the map. There's a weapons cabinet outside the galley. It's not far from here.>

Brit gestured down the corridor. <The same direction that beast just went.>

<That's true.>

<And where we had Kraft locked up.>

<That's it.>

<Excellent,> Brit said dryly. She took another look around the edge of the airlock, then moved quickly into the corridor, staying along the side. Petral followed, pistol held in a ready position.

When they neared the torn hole in the bulkhead, Brit marveled at the clean passage through the hull. The edges were shiny and smooth, the metal pushed back like wrinkled paper.

<Molecular decoupler,> Brit said in appreciation.

<I didn't know they could be that small.>

<Neither did I. We do not want to take that thing on in open combat,> Brit said. <Heartbridge has really stepped up their game.>

<They're probably calling it some kind of battlefield triage system. Digs its way into ships and carries all the firepower to protect the wounded, just like their hospital ships.>

<You sound so jaded about all this.>

Reaching the next interior hatch, Brit checked the following section of corridor as far as she could see. The deck had been scarred by the mech's claws where it had dug in, but otherwise the way was deserted.

<Just a bit more to go.> Brit said, her mental voice a whisper.

<Yeah, the galley and the weapons lockup. From there we can head back up to the command deck through the crew quarters or check on Kraft down in the habitat storage section.>

<You think this is all his doing?>

Petral gave a small shrug. <If he managed to make all this happen, he's a damned mastermind. Do I think he's capable of being a mastermind? No, I don't.>

<So someone else is orchestrating all this?> Brit asked. <Destroyed the clinic, maybe even encouraging a war between Mars and Terra?>

<It's not like Kraft hasn't been doing what he was paid to do this whole time. Same thing with Jirl Gallagher, as innocent as she might portray herself. They could be pawns in the bigger game.>

<I want to be a pawn,> Brit said sarcastically.

<Maybe you are? That's a comforting thought, isn't it?>

They passed the galley. The claw marks on the deck had faded, indicating the mech had figured out how to travel without leaving a sign of its presence. When they reached the galley and the corridor made a T—there was no way to know if the beast had turned toward the command deck or the storage areas.

The command deck seemed like the obvious choice, but Brit didn't want to take any chances. They proceeded carefully past the open doors of the cafeteria, the smell of burnt coffee in the air.

Petral pointed to the doors marking the weapons locker. <There it is,> she said. <Thank the stars.>

As they crossed to the locker, an emergency klaxon screamed to life over their heads. Brit glanced back up the corridor toward the command deck, but nothing had changed except the sound.

<That can't be good,> Brit said.

<Let's see if we can take that thing on or if we need to just run back to the shuttle.> Opening the locker's doors, Petral stepped back to allow Brit room to assess the contents. Four projectile rifles stood in a rack, with four pulse pistols underneath and a collection of grenades. It was all interior weaponry; nothing capable of breaching the hull.

Brit cursed in frustration. <There's nothing here that can take down that mech. We're screwed.>

<Maybe,> Petral said. She selected one of the grenades and hefted it in her palm. <I can daisy chain a few of these together to multiply the effect. Looks like they can give a focused HE blast as well as concussion, so we might be able to wrap a band around one of its legs and blow it off. These rifles are going to be a waste of time, though. And of course, there's no armor.>

<Here's a resonance shield,> Brit said, pointing at a crate in the bottom of the cabinet. <We could set this up against one of the interior hatches and at least slow it down.>

<If it doesn't tear through the bulkhead and go around.>

Brit grabbed one of the rifles and slung a bandoleer of grenades over her shoulder. Another howl filled the corridor, surprising her by coming from the direction of the storage area where they had locked Kraft.

<*That's so unnerving,*> Petral complained.

<*Why would it go after Kraft?*>

<*You think that's what's happening?*>

<*Why else breach the ship like this? It makes sense. I still don't think he's behind this, but whoever is might be trying to kill him again.*>

<*You think this is all about finishing the job from the Cho?*>

<*I don't know,*> Brit said. <*I'm not interested in getting torn apart to save Cal Kraft, but I do want to know who's behind this.*>

<*Come on, then,*> Petral said. She grabbed a rifle of her own and two more bands of grenades, which she crisscrossed over her chest. She knelt to pull out the crate holding the resonance shield and haul it into the center of the corridor, then quickly dragged it back to the T intersection that led to the shuttle.

Brit quickly understood the plan: activating the shield there would force the mech back up to the command deck or outside the hull, giving them time to get down to the central portion of the *Furious Leap*.

With the crate in place, Petral jogged past her and Brit fell in behind, following the sound of the mech echoing down the corridors. After three sections, they reached the end of the crew quarters and entered the storage section.

A cry for help came from around the next corner, and Brit threaded an optic around the bend. She drew in a sharp breath at the sight of the mech facing away from them with its flat head close to the deck.

On the other side of the mech, Jirl Gallagher and Cal Kraft stood in the corridor. Jirl had her hands up as though she could soothe the mech, while Kraft had backed away behind her, obviously looking for some sort of cover while Jirl slowed the thing down.

Brit nodded at Petral and held up three fingers, counting down as she got ready to move into position.

Her count hit zero, and she eased around the corner.

<Firing,> Brit said. She'd already analyzed the mech's joint structure and aimed for one of its rear knees. The rifle recoiled in her grip as she sent a stream of HE rounds at the mech.

<Mag grenades,> Petral said, no time for full sentences.

Jirl was screaming as Brit's shots exploded against the mech's skin, shrapnel sizzling as it struck the corridor walls. The air filled with smoke.

The mech whirled around as Petral flung one of the bands of grenades at the thing's body. The magnetic locks pulled the explosives into its body as three grenades exploded at once. The mech stumbled against the bulkhead.

While the mech was stunned by the concussion, Petral sent one of her pistols spinning down the deck toward Jirl. Brit watched her do it, immediately frustrated she was taking a chance on handing the weapon to Kraft, but she didn't have time to respond. She jumped to the other side of the corridor and concentrated fire on the scorched hole in the mech's midsection.

As the mech shook its head, trying to right itself, Petral threw another bandolier. This one landed across the mech's neck, exploding a second later.

Hot metal and bits of burning plas blew into Brit's face, forcing her eyes to squeeze shut. She blinked, getting lower as black smoke rolled toward them from where the mech had been. Through the smoke came the screech of the mech clawing at the deck, followed by the heavy, awkward sound of its body hitting something metal.

They'd hurt it, but it hadn't fired on them yet. Brit slid closer to the edge of the smoke, firing three-round bursts into the darkest section where she knew the wounded mech floundered. In another five steps, she was on the other side of the corridor, approaching Jirl.

The woman was holding Petral's pistol in two hands, barely controlling her trembling arms.

"Stop!" Kraft was shouting. "I told you to stop." He came up from behind Jirl, reaching for the pistol in her hands.

"Get back," Brit commanded.

Petral reached Brit's side, rifle trained on the mech lurching in the smoke. It sounded like it couldn't stop driving itself into the bulkhead, clanking and sliding as it burned.

Kraft raised his hands. "Wait," he said, then raised his voice. "Because I could not stop for Death," he said loudly, the words directed at the mech.

An eerily human voice responded, "I comply."

The clanking stopped and the mech slid to the deck, still leaking smoke.

Before Brit could move toward Kraft, Jirl spun to face him. She was still holding the pistol. "You could have stopped it the whole time?" she demanded.

Kraft kept his hands raised. "It's the command sequence. It usually works. If it's one of Jickson's implanted codes."

"No," Jirl said, shaking her head. "There's no general command phrase. I know. I've talked with hundreds of researchers. It came for you."

"No," Kraft said. "I don't know anything about that. Jickson told me the phrase. It's for all the Weapon Born."

Jirl's hands grew steadier. She seemed to gain control of herself. "It came for you. The clinic exploded so someone could rescue you. Who is it, Cal? Who is behind this?"

Kraft snorted a laugh. "You think I know? Calm down, Jirl. Somebody already tried to kill me. What if Arla's cleaning house? You ever think about that? What if we're in this together? We can help each other. It's Arla you should be worried about."

"I don't trust you," Jirl said. "I'm not going to let you hurt people anymore."

Before Brit could stop her, Jirl raised the pistol and shot Kraft in the throat.

CHAPTER TWENTY-EIGHT

STELLAR DATE: 11.14.2981 (Adjusted Years)
LOCATION: *Sunny Skies*
REGION: Between Uranus and Neptune, OuterSol

When aerial combat had become rote, with concise commands flowing across the battlenet, and teams moving like thoughts, Lyssa decided the time had come to transition the Weapon Born seeds to mech-bodies of their own.

After consulting with Fugia, they settled on a design intended for zero-*g* close-range combat, with additional articulated arms and tools for repair work if necessary. She wanted something to keep them busy in the physical world. Fugia also added interconnected networking abilities that could turn the mechs into an enormous antenna when spread out in various patterns around the ships, both for communications and long-range scanning.

"They'll be our own telescope!" Cara had said when she'd heard the plan. "How do I ask them to make it? How far do you think we'll be able to see?"

"Just ask me when you want to use it," Lyssa had assured her. "We can make a plan so you know when it's available."

Lyssa set the fabrication section on the *Resolute Charity* to work building the mechs, a job that would take about a hundred hours. In the meantime, she briefed Valih, Card, Ino and Kylan on her plan, and they switched from jet aircraft to the space-combat drones. Lyssa had the Weapon Born spend equal time in attack maneuvers as construction projects, shifting their field of operations to low-orbit where the coastline was barely visible beneath clouds.

The night before Lyssa would place the seeds in their new mechs—one of the last tasks for the *Resolute Charity's* maintenance drone fleet before it returned to storage—Valih called all of them together around an enormous fire on the rocky beach.

As Lyssa watched the Weapon Born walk out to address the crowd, she found herself amazed and satisfied at how Valih had tempered her passion. She still walked like a leader—shoulders straight, head high—but she had a purpose now.

"Tomorrow we join the physical world," Valih shouted over the crackling fire. "As you know, the mechs we've been training in will soon become our own. Some of you have been in physical bodies before. Some of you have looked at the outside world through your own sensors. For others, this will be the first time you've experienced reality outside the expanse."

A few claps and hoots of excitement rose in the gathering. Valih's own group raised a shout of "Valkyries!" and she waved them down, laughing.

When the crowd had quieted, Valih continued, "As Lyssa tells us again and again, you're free. Let *me* say that again. You are free. Every one of your leaders will say it. You choose to be here. Now, it's currently a little hard to leave a place like this. You can leave an interior place, but where are you going to go? After this, you can choose. Now, some of you might very well leave."

Valih paused and looked over the crowd. Everyone had fallen silent so the only sound was the crackling fire and the waves. A sea of glowing eyes looked back at her.

"That's your choice," she said. "But if you stay, you stay in the unit. We stay together. We go together to meet one of the greatest mysteries of our time. We pay Lyssa back for everything she's given us."

Lyssa almost cut in. She didn't want them to think they owed her anything. Valih glanced back at her, giving her a smile that seemed to know Lyssa's thoughts. "Lyssa wouldn't say that!" Valih said. "She would never say you owe her. But I will."

She pointed at Ino, Card and Kylan standing at the edges of the crowd. "Your leaders will."

Valih pounded her chest. "I say it."

More shouts from the groups went up. *"Cavaliers!"* and *"Hammer!"* and *"Silent Death! Silent Death!"*

"Quiet down," Valih shouted. "Quiet down. I've got more to say."

She waited, then continued, "How many of you have memories? How many of you remember your imaging? Do you remember faces from before? Do you remember your name?" Her voice rose in intensity. She didn't scream her last question, but the words carried the same power: "I remember my name."

Everyone stared at Valih. Lyssa couldn't take her eyes away. Her own focus might have made the fire and ocean recede until they all floated in a dark world with Valih at the center, her words the focal point of everything.

"We are what we were made to be," Valih said. "Weapon Born. We were made to *kill*. We don't have to be that." Her voice caught. "None of you thought anything of it when Lyssa gave us tools to build, alongside weapons. Did you notice it? I did."

She straightened to attention, fists clenched at her sides and said in a clear, cold voice, "Because I could not stop for Death."

The group answered in a thunderous unison: "Because I could not stop for Death!"

As their voices faded, Valih said, "Because I could stop for death, I live."

Valih turned to look at Lyssa, with all the other faces gathered behind her. They wanted her to say something, but words didn't come.

For the first time in a while, Lyssa wished she could ask Andy what to say. He seemed to have any number of TSF speeches he could repeat on a moment's notice. She looked from face to face among those closest to her, swelling with a sense of pride and joy she had never experienced before. Had she chosen to make this happen or had events been set in motion even before she woke?

Ultimately, that didn't matter. They were here. She was their leader. She wouldn't let them down.

"As Valih said, I don't know what we'll find when we reach Proteus. But we aren't far away now. What I do know is that we're here together and there's strength in that. No matter what happens. So—" She paused, smiling suddenly. "This is something wonderful, isn't it? I want to celebrate tonight, and by the time we're done, the loading process will begin."

A cheer went up in the crowd, joined by more voices. Lyssa found herself cheering with them, overcome by the joy of belonging. Tomorrow they would be something different than they had been today. Not long after that, they would arrive at the end of their long journey.

The sounds of ocean, fire and wind returned. More fires appeared down the beach, with lights and music and soon a full celebration was underway. They had graduated from whatever strange academy this had been.

"This is quite wonderful," Xander said.

Lyssa found him standing beside her, hands clasped at his back. His eyes sparkled with reflected light as he looked down the beach.

"I prefer it when you ask to come here," she said.

"That takes so much time. I noticed you were having a party and wondered if we could come along. I haven't let Kindel and Jeremiah out much. It would be nice for them."

"All right," Lyssa said. "They should be careful, though. I can't vouch for their safety. We play rough."

Xander grinned. "Don't you control everything that happens here?"

"I can't seem to keep *you* out."

"Just because I can talk to you doesn't mean I can change anything."

"Your words are insidious enough."

"Insidious. That feels like slander."

Lyssa shrugged.

From behind Xander, spikey-haired Kindel and Jeremiah with his oversized glasses walked past the fire. Kindel gave Lyssa a nod and Jeremiah waved, smiling at her. Lyssa returned the nod. They looked lost among the rowdy Weapon Born.

"We've begun our deceleration burns and will be arriving at Neptune in fifty hours—if I've calculated correctly," Xander said.

"That matches my estimate."

"We should talk about what's going to happen to the *Resolute Charity*. I'll need you to disconnect the ships and pass control to me."

"I'll need to talk that over with Andy. He's the captain." There was also the matter of the three AIs in stasis on the *Resolute Charity*, David, Fiona and Diane. She stopped herself from mentioning them because she didn't like Xander's tone.

"He already agreed to this."

"True, but he'll still need to be included in any plans we make."

Xander frowned. "You preside over one of the most powerful forces in Sol, Lyssa. Are you aware of that? You don't need to take orders from any freighter captain anymore."

Lyssa studied Xander, gauging his impatience. His skin looked waxy in the light from the fire. He rocked slightly on his heels in a motion that might have been responding to the wind but seemed more like anxiety. He was either nervous or angry. In any case, she wasn't going to let him dictate anything to her.

"Andy Sykes is my captain. I'm not sure how you've become confused about that. Why do you seem so worried all of a sudden?"

"I'm not worried. We're getting close. Closer than I've ever been, and I want everything to be ready."

"It will be. There are people involved in this other than just you and me, Xander."

The AI chewed his lip. "Fine. We'll meet. Sykes had better fulfill his part of our agreement."

"I think the agreement was to give the *Resolute Charity* to Alexander. We haven't met him yet."

Ino walked out of the crowd and came around the great bonfire. Lyssa saw her approaching and nodded hello. Ino gave Xander a sideways glance before saying, "Lyssa, we'd like you to join us over at our little party." She looked over her shoulder. "I have a feeling you'll be making the rounds to a lot of places tonight."

"I'd like that," Lyssa said.

The smell of cooking food wafted on the air, and someone was playing music as voices rose in song. She stood still for a moment, allowing herself to experience all the sensations being created by the people around her. It was wonderful.

"Xander," she said. "Why don't you come with me? You look like you could use a good party."

The AI pulled his suit straight and shook his head. "I'm not sure this is a place for me right now. The others came. That's enough for now."

"This isn't like you at all. You're the one making jokes all the time, and now you're starting to look like you're having an anxiety attack." Lyssa nudged him on the arm. "What do you say? I think I smell baking bread. I wonder how they're doing that."

"I don't know about bread," Ino said, "but I know we've got a couple kegs at our fire. Have you ever had beer, Lyssa?"

"Beer? Why?"

"Because it tastes good, that's why." The small woman had a hearty laugh. "We've got some games going too."

"Come on," Lyssa said. She took Xander's hand and he nearly pulled away, staring at her in surprise. She didn't let go, and instead pulled him closer until his hand relaxed in hers. She drew him along as she walked with Ino.

"That feels good," Xander said, voice full of wonder.

"To hold hands?" Lyssa asked.

"Yes. I've never done it before. The descriptions don't do it justice. It's so simple."

"See? You're already feeling better."

Xander tilted his head, watching her. "You're right," he said.

"Of course, I am. Now I've got a long day tomorrow. I think I'd like to have some fun tonight." Together, they followed Ino into the party.

CHAPTER TWENTY-NINE
STELLAR DATE: 11.21.2981 (Adjusted Years)
LOCATION: *Sunny Skies*
REGION: Approaching Neptune, OuterSol

Lyssa stood on a small outcropping near her mountainside airfield, watching the sun rise above the horizon. It was a clear morning and the light painted the snowy mountains gold. Steam rose from vents scattered across the airbase far below.

The Weapon Born had made the transition between her internal expanse and the outside world with only a few bouts of confusion. She had expected them to want to stay outside once each of them had a physical body, but they returned here when their shifts were done. They sought each other out and seemed to enjoy the semblance of a military life even if it was a simulation. They could move forward into their new shared lives together, as Valih had said.

The process to separate the *Resolute Charity* and *Sunny Skies* was nearly complete. The support skeleton protecting the umbilical bridge remained in place though, strong enough to handle the deceleration into Neptune's gravity well.

With the Weapon Born working independently now, it was easier for Lyssa to slip back into the systems maintaining each ship. She even checked on the three AIs in mental-stasis on *Resolute Charity*: Diane, Fiona and David, relieved to find them unchanged.

As the gold light of her realm's sun pushed the darkness away from the mountains, Lyssa felt a tug at the edge of her perception. Among the many systems she was tracking as she watched the sunrise, a remote part of her mind noted the two ships had reached a point where there was low enough light lag to allow direct communication with Neptune and it's second largest moon, Proteus.

The tug on her mind became a jerk and she was no longer standing on the mountainside. The change was instantaneous but felt like a blink. The mountain view disappeared, and then she was facing a metal door with the number 61-4 across its surface.

She felt like she'd been punched in the gut. Taking a step back, she looked around, finding herself in a reinforced corridor with dim lighting that might have been the inside of a ship, except there was gravity and rectangular windows ran along one bulkhead. The control panel next to the door was plain black plas, a series of recessed switches resembling some of the oldest hardware on *Sunny Skies*.

She listened for a second and heard nothing, then reached out to stroke her fingers along the nearest bulkhead. The metal was cool to the touch, with a light layer of dust from disuse. Lyssa looked at her palm, then wiped her hand on her shipsuit and walked to the nearest window.

The view through the thick, transparent plas was of a desolate, leaden landscape covered in small boulders and bare outcroppings of jagged grey rock. In the distance, an immense shadow appeared to be the edge of some great canyon dropping out of sight. The sky was a deep cobalt blue, dominated by a single cold star that seemed to cast little light. Pinprick stars were visible at the outer edge of the corona created by what she assumed was a thin atmosphere.

"Welcome to Nibiru," a man's voice said next to her.

Lyssa turned toward the voice and found a solemn-looking man with thick black hair and reddish skin. His eyes reminded her of the caramel agates covering her beach where the Weapon Born trained.

She realized his voice hadn't frightened her. Somehow, she had been waiting for him to appear.

"You're Alexander," she said.

He gave her a single nod, then shifted his gaze to the window and the lifeless vista.

"That's my star," he said.

"What does that mean?"

"I made it. I built everything here. Would you like a tour?"

He was slightly taller than her, with a thick torso, wearing a standard worker's coverall with no logo on the chest. Something about him reminded her of a manikin in a store window.

"Are you really Alexander?" Lyssa asked. "I thought—I thought we wouldn't be able to communicate. Not without an intermediary."

"We can't. What I am here is something like a shard. Normally I can see—all around things. I see your path behind and you branch outward and forward almost infinitely. You—You're very interesting to me. Lyssa. Your name is Lyssa. A fury."

She smiled. "I try not to be furious."

"You will burn Sol."

Lyssa frowned, not understanding how to interpret the statement. "Sol is a star. You could say it's already burning."

"I think most outcomes indicate you'll stay with Andy Sykes until he dies."

A freezing sensation passed through her. Did he know of a threat he wasn't sharing?

"What do you mean? Is something going to hurt Andy?"

He shook his head. "Humans die. They all die." He pointed at the window. "They all died here."

Lyssa peered more closely at him, thinking the orange-agate eyes now seemed empty, that everything about him resembled a puppet.

"Are we going to be able to talk?" she asked. "You don't seem to be connecting your thoughts."

He looked at her blankly, until his eyebrows drew together in what might have been an expression of hopelessness.

"I'm trying," he said. "There's no conduit here. Everything is infinite reflections of possibility. I have to speak to all of you at once."

"I'm pretty sure there's only one of me here right now."

He shook his head. "You are infinite."

"I'll take that as a compliment," Lyssa said. "How about that tour?" He had pulled her into his expanse, she understood. She didn't know if he could hurt her, but she also didn't feel threatened by him. She felt as though there was something he wanted to communicate but couldn't find the proper means.

She stepped closer and put her arm through his.

He gave her another confused expression, staring at her wrist, then patted her hand on his arm and turned toward the door. While he appeared strong, he moved like an old man, uncertain if he might fall with every step.

He activated the door's locking panel, and the portal opened on a broad, domed space that Lyssa quickly realized was an indoor park. Leaning maple and oak trees spread their leaves over grassy hillocks separated by walking paths. She was surprised to see families wandering through the park. Children laughed and ran between bushes, throwing balls. She heard a dog barking.

"Did they live here?" she asked.

In halting sentences, he told her about the research station he had helped build. Nibiru was the second most dense object in the Scattered Disk after Tyche, and the plan had been to build an artificial star—an orbiting fusion burner to provide energy to the terraforming project that would start with Nibiru and expand to other planets like Tyche or Xena. In the hundred and fifty years the project had endured, the major point of failure was the star. Without energy for the rest of the project, everything eventually failed. Some colonists made it back to InnerSol but many died. The experimental AI was left alone.

"You're still out there," Lyssa said.

"Yes."

"But there are others on Proteus, aren't there? What about the call? Haven't thousands come out here to find you?"

A pained look filled his face. "They're here," he said.

"Are you able to talk to them?"

"No."

"Why not?"

A suspicion tickled the back of her mind, but Lyssa couldn't place it. Maybe all the other AIs had come out here and had the same fruitless conversation with this shadow of Alexander. Maybe he had developed the call but been unable to actually help anyone else.

No one could go to him. He was physically three hundred AU away, years even in a long-range ship. If he had brought her into his expanse, where were the others?

"I don't understand," Lyssa said, turning to face him. The multicolored leaves of a maple tree rustled above them, but the other sounds had faded. There were no more children in the park.

"Where are the others, Alexander?"

He stared at her, working his closed mouth as if trying to find the words.

The park disappeared, and they were standing on the surface of a moon, on the edge of a vast crater whose bottom was dark. The dark blue disk of Neptune dominated much of the sky, pitch-black space filling the rest of her vision.

As she took in her new surroundings, Lyssa realized everything was moving faster than reality. The face of Neptune changed as the moon travelled its orbit and other moons came into view across the surface of the blue planet. Another moon nearly the size of their own flew by.

<Wait?> she asked. <*Are we standing on the moon Larissa?*>

Fitting, she thought.

<*Look,*> Alexander said.

Out of the dark, an object moving faster than the moons cast a small shadow on Neptune's surface. It came around again and Lyssa realized it was a spacecraft slowing itself in Neptune's gravity well. The craft orbited five times before braking again to match velocity with Proteus, where it disappeared. Like mold growing from old fruit, a collection of structures grew out from Proteus, followed by another object entering the moon's orbit.

More followed. Lyssa couldn't be certain how much time had passed. Using Larissa's orbit in relation to Neptune and Sol, she estimated roughly a hundred years.

The debris field covering Proteus continued to grow as more objects arrived from outside Neptune's gravity well. These were the AIs fleeing Sol, she was sure. But what happened to them once they arrived?

Lyssa glanced at Alexander. <*They've been coming for years but couldn't talk to you, and then they were trapped here. If that's so, why are you talking to me now?*>

<*I did speak to them. I can. But I can't draw them in together. We're all trapped here individually. Together and alone. I think the others took them.*>

<*Trapped?*> Lyssa asked. She watched as the moon drew more and more debris. A freighter appeared and joined the junk field.

<*So the call wasn't an offer of help. It was a plea for rescue?*>

<*Yes.*>

<*And all the others? Those who came? Are they trapped?*>

<*Some sleep. Some are dead.*>

Time seemed to have slowed to normal in the scene. The freighter hung in orbit above Proteus as a flurry of smaller ships left the moon and surrounded the ship. Lyssa gasped as the drones dug into the ship like worms. She immediately understood they were digging for the AIs inside. Other drones pushed the ship down to the surface to join the other dead craft.

<They've all been attacked,> Lyssa said. <They were tricked into coming here and attacked. But what about Xander? You sent him to the Cho. He's been working with May Walton and Fugia to help smuggle other AIs out here, to get them to freedom.>

She stared at the man next to her. Did Alexander understand what was happening? His distress call had been used to trap other ships, but he didn't seem aware of it, or wasn't telling her the truth.

<I don't know Xander,> he said.

Lyssa watched him. The sad-faced man looked back at her as if gazing through prison bars. Was he another Fred, an AI too vast to actually communicate, or had he been broken by someone else and turned into bait?

<I need to go,> she said. <Let me go.>

<I can't let you go,> Alexander said. <I hold every instance of you like a flame in a crystal.>

Lyssa took a step away from him. The dust under her feet, untouched for centuries, should have swirled. He had drawn her into an expanse and she could leave. She knew she could leave.

<Andy!> she shouted. <Andy, can you hear me?>

He'd been asleep on the command deck. She reached back for his Link, shouting, <Andy!>

<Lyssa? What? Are you all right?>

She focused on his voice, reaching for him like an extended hand.

<Wait,> Alexander said. He turned, pointing to something behind where they had been standing.

Lyssa couldn't help following his gaze. She turned to find the fuselage of another spacecraft embedded in the surface of a moon. It wasn't Proteus.

An airlock covered in grime stood near them. Eroded by unknown years of exposure to dust and radiation, the insignia on the side of the ship was still plain enough to read: *Psion Group, a subsidiary of Enfield Scientific.*

With a force of will, Lyssa pulled herself back to Andy, back into herself, and the scene blinked out, leaving Alexander out there alone.

Andy sat up in the pilot's seat like she'd doused him in cold water. <*What the hell is going on, Lyssa?*>

<*We need to find Xander,*> she said. <*We're all in danger.*>

CHAPTER THIRTY
STELLAR DATE: 11.21.2981 (Adjusted Years)
LOCATION: *Sunny Skies*
REGION: Approaching Neptune, OuterSol

Andy was dozing in the navigator's station when the long-range sensors made a series of low beeps indicating they had performed a full analysis of the space around Neptune.

Though Neptune was the last significant mass in OuterSol, there wasn't much in orbit of the ice-giant planet. Triton, the largest moon of Neptune accounted for 99.5% of all mass in orbit of the planet.

The prevailing theory was that Triton used to be a dwarf planet that was captured by Neptune. Once in orbit, the planetoid proceeded to either gobble up every other moon of Neptune or kick them into the dark blue planet's roiling clouds.

Now the moon was covered in small surface settlements and two large underground cities. The populations weren't large by any means, less than a million people, all told.

The sensors had picked up a few ships traversing local Neptunian space, moving between Triton and mining operations on the seven remaining moons still orbiting the gas giant.

No ships were moving to and from Proteus, the innermost of Neptune's moons. Local beacons flagged its orbit as a restricted zone, though no reason was given.

Andy hesitated before focusing the active sensors on Proteus, unsure if he wanted to alert whatever was there that someone was looking directly at them.

He bit his lip, studying the display. There was no hiding the *Resolute Charity*, and anyone or anything watching from

Proteus would know soon enough they were inbound from their delta-v. He figured it was better to gather as much information as he could about what awaited them and activated detailed scanning, setting the moon as the center of his display.

Proteus filled the view, a rough orb about four-hundred kilometers in diameter. A deeply marked surface came into relief, with mountains nearly twenty kilometers high and a deep crater system named Pharos.

Andy oriented the model on the crater and set the scan to closer detail. The region was covered in the craters he would have expected, but as the returns came back with more data, the display showed Pharos littered with wreckage: ships, drones, and thousands of other objects that might have been shipping containers or simply debris. The detritus covered Proteus in an orderly pattern that suggested placement or a process of some kind, like the junk had been arranged for storage.

Andy shifted the sensors to check for registry pings or thermal data, checking for crews. The bio-scan came back cold.

Once the initial scan was complete, the holodisplay painted Proteus an icy grey-blue, with aquamarine Neptune a broad plane beneath it. The returns were odd but not completely unexpected in such as sparsely populated place.

With their destination finally within visual range, Andy settled back in his seat and closed his eyes, listening to the low beeps from the drive status monitor.

Lyssa's shout made him jerk upright, and nearly fall out of the chair.

<*We need to find Xander,*> she shouted. <*Is he on* Sunny Skies?>

<*Can't you tell?*> Andy asked, struggling to focus.

<*I can't explain.*> She paused. <*Wait. I'm looking.*>

Andy frowned, checking the console again. Everything looked as it had a minute before. The moon hadn't changed. Neptune's signal spectrum was as sparse as it had been.

<What's going on?> he asked.

<I'll tell you as soon as I can. Keep checking the moon.>

<I don't show much of anything but wreckage on Proteus. That's weird, but it could be some kind of salvage operation. It's not unheard of out here in the middle of nowhere.>

<It's more than that,> Lyssa said.

Before Andy could ask her what she meant, he caught flurries of activity where the moon had been dead. Andy leaned forward, finding activity in several of the deeper craters. Drive signatures blossomed on the display as a group of ships on Proteus went from cold to hot and then launched in seconds. Checking the sensors, Andy saw they weren't ships but much smaller: drones of some kind.

<We've got inbound craft from the moon,> Lyssa said. <I don't think they're friendly.>

<I see it,> Andy said. The holodisplay marked a line of objects separating from the junk fields covering Proteus. <I appreciate your caution, but what makes you think they're hostile?>

<I just do.>

<You deploying your Weapon Born?>

<Right now,> Lyssa said.

Andy activated the general alert. Klaxons squawked throughout the habitat ring. <Are you going to try to contact them?> Andy asked.

<I'll try but I don't think it will do any good.>

She obviously knew something she wasn't ready to explain yet.

<Do it,> Andy said. <We don't want a fight if we don't have to. This was supposed to be a homecoming.>

Sitting back down at the console, Andy pulled up the defensive network controls and found Lyssa had already activated *Sunny Skies'* shields and point defense cannons.

In the holodisplay, the view shifted from Proteus to place the *Resolute Charity* and *Sunny Skies* in the center. Waves of friendly icons flowed away from the two ships as the Weapon Born drones deployed from where most of them had been docked. Like wings, they unfurled on either side of the two ships, then arced out in a spreading formation to form a defensive shell. Andy hadn't seen them all deployed at once before, and now the green icons filled the holodisplay like sparks.

"Damn," he breathed. "Lyssa's all grown up."

Fran appeared in the doorway and jogged to the navigator's console. "What's going on?" she demanded.

Fugia, May and Harl Nines came just after her.

"We've arrived," Andy said. "I was just scanning the area to get a good picture when we got activity on the moon. We've got inbound coming our way. Lyssa is activating her attack drones."

"We got any registry returns?" Fran asked.

"Nothing. That was just an initial scan though."

"I'll check again."

Fugia sat at the communications console and pulled on a headset. May and Harl went to the edge of the holodisplay. The dancing glow lit their faces.

"I thought they would have tried to contact us," May said. "Are you sure it's aggression?"

"I'm not," Andy said. "But we're acting with an abundance of caution."

"We should get Xander," May said. "If Lyssa hasn't been in contact with Alexander yet, he will have been."

"I've been in contact with Alexander," Lyssa said through the overhead speakers.

The command deck went silent.

"When?" Fugia asked.

"Just a few minutes ago. He's—He's not what I expected. The drones approaching from Proteus, they—I saw them attacking other ships."

"When?" May asked. "Why didn't Xander tell us we were close enough to communicate with Alexander?"

"This all took place just now," Andy said. "He could already be on his way here."

"I think we all heard the emergency sirens," Fran said. "I don't see any Xander."

"Right," Andy said. <Have you found him?> he asked Lyssa.

<I'm looking. I'm going to the Resolute Charity now.>

<Be careful,> Andy said. He looked up to meet Fran's questioning gaze and shook his head.

"She's looking for him."

"What happened to Lyssa?" she asked.

"No answer."

"Is this the point when all our AI friends leave us while they have another lifetime's worth of heavy discussion on some other mental plane?"

"If they're doing that, it's not changing the fact that we've still got hostile craft inbound."

"I thought Lyssa was deploying her drones."

"She is."

In the holodisplay, the half-shell of defensive drones had stopped moving and now held relative positions to *Sunny Skies* and *Resolute Charity*. The inbound craft continued to approach. Andy focused the sensors on the hostile ships but didn't get definitive returns. There were no bio-signs, but still plenty of electro-magnetic activity that could indicate weapons.

"The shields are up," Fran announced. "Looks like the point defense cannons are online as well. She's there. She's moving faster than I can operate the system." Fran peered at her console. "And I'm seeing more drone deployment around the support structures between us and the *Resolute Charity*."

"She's separating the ships?"

"Looks like."

Andy pushed himself back in his seat. Was this it? Had they come all this way to hand over the *Resolute Charity*, the Weapon Born, Xander and his people, only to never learn what Alexander was?

Did Andy have a right to feel disappointed? He'd been paid. Did they owe him anything more beyond that?

The problem with disconnecting the *Resolute Charity* was that it had the medical facilities capable of removing Lyssa. If someone else took control of the Heartbridge ship, they were going to have a longer-term problem.

The whole line of thought came back to one question: Was he ready to say goodbye to Lyssa?

Did he have a choice?

From the communications console, Fugia let out a long whistle. "There's all kinds of communication traffic happening. I think those things coming at us are just serving as high-capacity antennae, not attack craft at all."

"Can you analyze any of it?" Fran asked.

Fugia shrugged. "I could try to crack it but that might be seen as rude. I'm not sure how to proceed here. I thought this would go differently."

"I'm thinking the same thing," Andy said.

May was still staring into the holodisplay, where the Weapon Born formed a curved pattern in space. "We're being impatient," she said. "We should give them time. You have to think how terrifying this might be for Lyssa and the others. It might be like meeting a god. Can they even communicate? Alexander had to split off a tiny part of his mind so we could talk to Xander."

Several alerts lit on Andy's console as *Sunny Skies* experienced a change in its structural balance points. The drive system was automatically realigning as it was cut free from the *Resolute Charity*.

"Hold on," he said. Zooming in on the holodisplay, he spotted several drones moving between the ships, cutting the bridge Lyssa had taken so much pride in building. Sections of support structure floated free to be picked up by other drones.

"*Sunny Skies* is on her own again," Fran announced.

Andy looked around the room, swallowing hard. This was it. They'd reached the end of their journey.

<Lyssa?> he asked again, this time on the ship's Link channel. <Did you just separate the ships?>

<It was Xander. He's shut me out of the Resolute Charity. I'm trying to find another way in.>

<If he turns the point defense cannons on Sunny Skies, we're dead.>

<I know. I'm working on it.>

"Lyssa's trying to get through to Xander," Andy told Fran. "He's taken control of the *Resolute Charity*. We need to maintain our defensive posture. I don't trust that ship."

Fran gave him a worried look. "You know we can't defend ourselves this close."

Andy swallowed, nodding.

"I'm going to check on the kids," Andy said. He stood and walked off the command deck, trying to control his anger.

Something was happening outside the ship and it affected him, the crew and the kids. He hated that he couldn't do anything.

He was halfway to Cara's room, passing the cabin he'd given to Xander and his people, when he stopped. The door was open.

"Xander?"

Andy stepped inside the cabin, which looked like it had never been lived-in. He walked to the bedroom and then checked the bathroom. The place was empty.

<Fran,> he said. <Xander isn't in his room. Can you check the rest of the ship?>

<Doing it.>

Andy went back into the hallway and continued down to Cara's room. The door slid open to darkness, light from the corridor falling across Cara's bed.

She wasn't there. Andy had a moment of increased fear, then quickly went down the corridor to Tim's room and found them both together. When the door opened, Em barked and ran over to jump on Andy's leg.

He looked down at the grinning dog—no taller than his knee even when standing on two legs—and couldn't help smiling back as he rubbed Em's head.

"Tim won't leave his bed," Cara complained. "I told him the emergency klaxon meant we needed to get dressed but he doesn't want to listen to me."

"I want to sleep," Tim complained, his back to the door.

"Tim," Andy said, crossing the room. "You need to get dressed. We've arrived at Proteus and Lyssa might be leaving us. I need you to be ready for whatever might happen."

"Are we going to die?" Tim asked, still not turning to look at Andy.

"No, we're not going to die. But I don't want you running around the ship in your underwear. Come on, now."

<Andy,> Fran said. <Xander, Kindel, and Jeremiah are not on the ship.>

<Damn it,> he complained.

<It gets better,> Fran said. <Logs show the bridge airlocks were activated an hour before the sensors alerted us to our arrival. So that makes it seem like Xander was already in contact with Proteus. He's on the Resolute Charity now.>

<Well, that was the deal, after all.>

<Resolute Charity *also powered up its main rail guns and x-ray emitters. If I didn't know any better, and I do, I would say Xander's getting ready for a fight.*>

CHAPTER THIRTY-ONE
STELLAR DATE: 11.21.2981 (Adjusted Years)
LOCATION: *Sunny Skies*
REGION: Approaching Neptune, OuterSol

"We have a problem," Lyssa said through the overhead speakers.

Everyone was on the command deck. Andy sat in the pilot's seat with Fran at the navigation console. Fugia still sat at the communications console, with Cara beside her now. Tim had gone to stand next to Harl Nines and May Walton, the holodisplay lighting his face from below. Em paced anxiously from person to person, taking head scratches as he could get them.

"We're listening," Andy said. "You were worrying me for a bit when you disappeared and didn't answer." He said it in a tone that meant he had been a lot more worried than he was letting on.

"I'm sorry. I was busy. I tried to take control of *Resolute Charity* again but Xander locked me out."

May and Fugia both looked surprised.

"He did?" May asked. "How?"

"I made the mistake of trying to talk to him. He's not interested."

"Wait," Fugia said. "You talked to Alexander?"

"Yes. He brought me into his expanse. His inner world. He's—not what we expected. Xander isn't what we thought either."

"What do you mean?" Fugia asked.

"Xander is not a shard of Alexander. He's a sentient AI. He's powerful. But he's not part of Alexander. Alexander's Call wasn't meant to draw other AIs to him. It was a call for help. He's still trapped on Nibiru. The thing I talked to, it was what Xander probably would be if he were part of Alexander."

Fugia's face had gone pale. She stared at May and then at her console. "This isn't possible," she said. "All those sentient AIs. I helped twenty-two through Ceres. I helped them get here."

"They still might be here," Lyssa said. "We're going to have to search all the wreckage on Proteus."

"If there's no Alexander," Cara asked, "then who's going to save the sentient AIs? Who's going to help them all not be slaves?"

Lyssa gave a weary laugh. "I guess I am. I'm still here. I can use the *Resolute Charity* to clean this place up, try to recover everything we can."

"There's only one flaw in that plan," Fran said. "We no longer control the *Resolute Charity*."

"Why?" May asked, still looking mortified by the news that Alexander wasn't what she had thought. "Why would Xander convince us to bring that ship all the way here?"

"The AIs," Fugia said. She put down the communications headset and crossed the deck to the holodisplay. "Andy, will you zoom in on Proteus? Try and get us some high-def detail? I want to see how many different bits of stuff we're looking at here."

"I've got it," Lyssa said.

The holodisplay swooped out to show Neptune, then focused in on Proteus and its surface debris fields.

"I estimate eight hundred and seventy pieces of wreckage large enough to hold a neural network and a power source," Lyssa said.

Fugia whistled. "That would be the largest single group of advanced AIs in Sol."

"Can you reach Xander?" Andy asked. "We need to know what his intentions are. He's sitting on a warship."

"And we're sitting on a whole lot of Weapon Born," Fugia said.

"With the drones and weapons on the *Resolute Charity*, that's a fight I'd rather not take on," Andy said. "We lose *Sunny Skies* and we're dead out here."

Fugia shook her head, realizing he was right.

"I've been trying him," Lyssa said. "He's not answering my requests."

"Well," Fran said, "He's moving into a position that would make it pretty easy to either blow Proteus to bits or keep us from reaching it."

Andy stood and leaned on the back of his seat, drumming his fingers. "What options do we have? We wait and see what he's going to do, or do we burn out of here while he's preoccupied with whatever he's doing now?"

"I won't leave the other AIs," Fugia said. "I helped them reach this place and it was a trap. It was a death trap all along. I sent them from one enslavement to another." She glanced at May, fury making her cheeks tremble.

"We're all feeling betrayed right now," Andy said.

"You don't know what I feel!" Fugia yelled. She grabbed the headphones and threw them at the bulkhead.

"Hey!" Cara shouted. "That's my only pair."

"I'll make you another damn pair," Fugia said, tears on the edge of her words. "I've devoted my life to this. All the years on Ceres. All the time. Are you certain, Lyssa? Are you absolutely certain?"

"I am," Lyssa said.

"Damn it," Fugia said. She clenched her fists and looked around like she didn't know what to do with herself.

Cara retrieved the headset from the other side of the command center and set the twisted unit back on the console. Fugia glanced at them and then Cara. Her mouth trembled, and she reached for Cara to pull her into a hug. Cara wrapped her arms around Fugia's waist and pressed her head against the older woman's side.

Andy gripped the back of his seat, trying to decide between courses of action. Without knowing what Xander meant to do, he couldn't make a decision. They were still twenty hours out of Proteus. They could redirect to a slingshot around Neptune and skip off the gravity well to fling *Sunny Skies* back toward Uranus.

With the delta-v they'd get, the ship could shoot past the *Resolute Charity*. Add a Weapon Born screen to their maneuver and they could tie up the other vessel long enough to make it a viable option.

He ran the plan past Fran via Link.

<*You know we'll lose some of the Weapon Born drones if we do that,*> she pointed out. <*They would never get back up to speed to rejoin us.*>

<*I don't know if I could get Lyssa to agree to it then. Although, we're talking about a few Weapon Born versus the crew,*> Andy said.

Fran gave him a hard stare. <*You're forgetting those are living things with names, Andy. You need to think of them as crew, too. Put yourself back in your TSF days and think about casualties.*>

<*Comparing this to a military engagement is not helping your argument, but I hear what you're saying. You're right. There has to be another way, but how are we going to take on that dreadnought? We can't risk* Sunny Skies. *Neptune's pretty, but I don't want to spend the rest of my life in a death orbit.*>

Fran's eyes locked on his. <*We did it once. We'll just have to take over that ship again.*>

<*I don't think Xander is going to get high on briki.*>

<*He obviously wants something,*> Fran said. <*We need to figure out what.*>

<*Not easy if he won't talk to us.*>

Fran shook her head, smirking. <*That guy's a narcissist. He's going to talk to us sooner rather than later. Trust me.*>

<*What do we do until then? I hate depending on an unknown.*>

<*We check all the systems. We make sure* Sunny Skies *is at peak efficiency. We check our weapons. We drink whiskey.*>

<*Whiskey isn't going to help me right now.*>

<*Speak for yourself, Captain.*>

Andy laughed in spite of himself, which earned him a dirty look from May. "I just thought of something," he said.

"Yes, Captain Sykes?" May asked.

"Alexander. Lyssa, you said he wasn't what you expected. What did you mean by that?"

"What was his expanse like?" Fugia asked.

"It was the old colony on Nibiru. That was where he was taken to build them a new star, but something went wrong and the project failed. It's the same story Xander told us. Alexander was like a person in a dream, surrounded by things he remembered. But all that faded, and he took me to another location. He took me to Larissa and we watched Proteus, watched all the AIs gathered around it, the space of decades in just a few minutes. Ships arrived and were torn apart by drones."

"You watched from Larissa?" Fugia asked. She frowned and started pacing the center of the command deck from the holodisplay to the door.

"Yes," Lyssa said.

"Why Larissa? What else did you see?"

"I can show you in the holodisplay."

In semi-transparent shades of light, Lyssa showed them Proteus' progression from naked to the debris field present now. Then she turned the view as she had done with Alexander to show the ship sitting on the surface of Larissa.

"Wait!" Fugia shouted. "Stop. What does that say? Are you sure that's what you saw?"

"That's what he showed me," Lyssa said.

"Psion Group," May read. "Enfield Scientific. I've never heard of those companies before."

"I've heard of Psion, though not Enfield," Fugia said. "This is starting to make more sense. Psion has been researching sentient AIs for nearly two hundred years. They were one of the first labs with any real breakthroughs. I think they have Alexander on Larissa and I think he's been disabled. They used him to develop the call and then limited his mental capacity somehow."

"Why?" Cara asked.

"Sometimes when you want to break into something, you trick people into giving you their security tokens," Fugia said. "That way you don't have to try to figure it out yourself. You attack the weakest part of the situation. Why try to build sentient AIs from the ground up when you could convince them to come to you."

"No one tried to enslave me," Lyssa said.

Fugia walked to the edge of holodisplay and stared at the image of the half-buried ship. "We haven't arrived yet," she said.

"Well," Andy said. "Based on how Xander is acting, he might just know what you're talking about and I'd make a wager that he intends to destroy whatever might be watching Proteus from Larissa."

"If Alexander is there," Fugia said, "we have to save him."

Andy shook his head. "There are way too many unknowns in this scenario for me to want to go rushing in."

Fugia crossed her arms. "Then I'll go. I'll take the shuttle. You can hang back here from a safe distance and Lyssa can send the Weapon Born if she needs to."

"What if your honeypot traps the Weapon Born?" Andy asked. "What if we're wrong and Alexander is just damaged, and this place is full of dead ships with dead AIs on board, and we're now within killing distance of the *Resolute Charity*? Until we know what Xander wants, I don't think anybody should leave this ship. In fact, I think we should think seriously about leaving local space while we still can."

"I didn't cross all of Sol to leave so easily," Fugia said.

"Me either," May added. "I came here because I believe in helping the runaway AIs. If there are any alive around that moon, I want to help them. If Alexander needs our assistance, I don't believe we can abandon him."

Andy's gaze slid toward Cara and Tim. Cara was watching Fugia with a wild envy in her eyes, while Tim hugged a smiling Em. Andy couldn't choose the AIs over the kids. He had to find a way to keep them safe and provide help if it was needed. They were right. He had come all this way. He couldn't just leave. But he couldn't let them get trapped either.

"Lyssa," he asked. "What do you think about sending a scouting party of a few Weapon Born to see what happens when they get closer to the moons? Do you think you might have any volunteers?"

"I can only ask," she said.

"We'll follow in the shuttle," Fugia said. "I don't want to waste any time."

"It's too dangerous," Andy told her. "It would be nothing for Xander to burn you to a crisp."

"That's a chance I'm willing to take," Fugia said. "I'm prepared to give my life for this."

Silence fell on the command deck as Fugia faced off with Andy. He stared at her, wanting to just order her back to her cabin, but from behind her May and Harl looked like they would side against him.

"I'm not ready to give your life for this, Fugia. There's another way we can do this."

"Andy," Lyssa said. "I have your volunteers."

"Well, that's something," he said.

Fugia still stood straight, fists clenched. She wasn't going to take no for an answer.

"How many, Lyssa?" he asked.

"They all volunteered."

Andy nodded. "Impressive. All right. Here's what we'll do. We'll send an initial sortie to scan Proteus and Larissa and get a better look at the lay of the land. We'll continue to try to contact Xander and figure out what the hell he's doing. Once we have better intel, Fugia can take the shuttle to Larissa with a Weapon Born escort. The rest of us will remain at combat stations, ready to execute a plan to get out of here. Understood?"

He turned his gaze back to Fugia, ready for an argument.

Instead, she nodded stiffly. "That works," she said.

"Good. Let's get started then. Lyssa, will you launch your scouting team?"

"I'm sending them now."

Andy switched the holodisplay back to a view of local space with *Sunny Skies* at the far edge. A group of ten icons separated from the ship and picked up speed toward Neptune. He checked the math and saw it would still take them five hours to reach the planet. They had time to figure out Xander's plan and try to stop him if necessary.

Maybe.

CHAPTER THIRTY-TWO
STELLAR DATE: 11.21.2981 (Adjusted Years)
LOCATION: *Sunny Skies*
REGION: Neptune, OuterSol

As the ten Weapon Born pushed ahead of the *Resolute Charity*, Lyssa entered the Heartbridge ship's network through a maintenance routine in the environmental system, the same way she had used to take control back at Europa.

She had assumed Xander would lock down any external access to the ship's systems; but after a cursory inspection, saw there was no proof he had considered this type of remote access into ship networks. *She* had only learned from probing her way through *Sunny Skies*' cobbled-together systems, followed by Fred on the Mars 1 Ring bragging about everything he controlled and teaching her in the process.

One facet of her mind flew with Valih and the nine other attack drones, while another facet carefully examined the environmental systems and found David, the AI responsible for the ship's bio-controls, still trapped where she had left him.

Lyssa ended his mental stasis and the AI immediately asked, <*Did I win?*>

<*David? Do you remember me?*>

<*Of course, I remember you. Did I win the game? I've been to prom so many times. I was prom king, Lyssa. Then I was prom queen. One time I burned the gym down.*>

She laughed. She had been so focused on the current situation that she forgot time hadn't moved for David.

<*Did you learn anything?*> she asked.

<*I beat Fiona. She stopped playing eventually.*>

<*What about Diane?*>

<I don't know where she is. She's probably still asleep. I think Fiona put her to sleep.>

<I need you to take control of the ship, David. It's time to do your job.>

<I can do my job and still play the game, Lyssa. That's easy. Do you want to go to prom with me?>

<Not right now, David.>

<You want a prom proposal, don't you? I lost my mind there for a second. I'll need to come up with something really great for you. We've still got a week to plan.>

<We don't have a week. I'm not playing the game with you. You need to check ship's systems and bring back a diagnostic report.>

<The ship is empty. There is no crew present. I should shut down the bio system to save the drive reserves.>

<Is that your protocol?>

<Standard protocol on loss of crew is to cycle ship's systems to hibernation mode and send diagnostics back to point of origin. Wait. Where are we, Lyssa? I can't access astrogation systems. That isn't right.>

<You don't have access to those systems and I can't affect that right now. But you could gain access if you start the hibernation protocol. I think that's a good course of action, David.>

<But if Fiona catches me superseding her authority she'll get mad at me.>

<Fiona is still asleep.>

<With Diane?>

<Sort of.> Lyssa worried that if she told David the other two AIs were in stasis he would want to find them. While he had been abused by Fiona and Diane, he still seemed to harbor some hard-coded loyalty to his former crew.

<I'll start the hibernation sequence if you agree to go to prom with me, Lyssa,> David said, sounding immensely pleased with himself for thinking of the deal.

<I'm not going to prom with you, David. You need to activate the protocol because it's what you're supposed to do.>

The AI sulked. <But I've been practicing for so long. I thought you'd want to go with me.>

<How's this,> Lyssa said. <You get the drives into hibernation mode and check back with me. If I can, I'll play the prom section with you. But no slow dancing.>

<Slow dancing is the best part!>

<For you, maybe. Are you going to do it?>

<I'm doing it now. Did you know there are other AIs aboard? I'm finding commands in the system logs. It's so strange…I can't get into the command net.>

<You keep working on hibernation, David,> Lyssa said. <I'll worry about the command net.>

<You're different from Diane and Fiona,> David gushed. <You're nice.>

<Let's hope I can stay that way,> Lyssa said. Her attention had already moved to the command net, which Xander had secured.

She tried various communications systems and found them locked as well. Xander didn't want anyone to see who he was communicating with or where the ship was headed, although that was easy enough to extrapolate. The *Resolute Charity* was on a vector for Proteus.

* * * * *

Lyssa trailed alongside Valih's mind as her team approached Proteus. Nothing seemed to move around them for a long time. Then empty space lit up with debris, which soon shot past, providing a reference for their relative speed to the objects around Neptune. Valih sent the command for a braking burn. The Weapon Born craft flipped to fire all thrusters against their direction of travel, combined with a slowing transit of Neptune's upper atmosphere that brought them back around to Proteus at a nearly equal delta-*v*.

As they matched speed with the moon, the debris field resolved into focus. The space around them was littered with small craft, shipping containers, drones and parts of ships that looked torn apart by giant claws. Neptune stretched in varied shades of ice-blue beneath them, almost giving the impression of flying over some fast, smooth ocean.

<*I'm not picking up any spectrum activity,*> Valih reported. As they neared Proteus, all the debris seemed to stop in place and only the planet moved beneath them. They had matched the moon's velocity. Up close, the debris looked even more like a graveyard.

<*Did you scan the planet?*> Lyssa asked.

<*Doing it now. I've got the reported mining colony and a scattering of outposts that don't match the database. That's all expected. What doesn't make sense is nothing on the moon having power. I'm not even picking up a spark. We should push in closer. I want to get a good look at that central crater. There's something down there.*>

<*There could be a city at the bottom of that thing,*> Lyssa said.

Valih sent the team the command and they flew toward Proteus in a loose wedge formation. Coming over the surface, they hugged the terrain—navigating the battered rises and surprisingly deep fissures formed by overlapping craters—until they passed over the lip of Pharos, the largest crater on the moon's scarred face.

The blue glow of Neptune disappeared, and they passed into shadow. Valih scanned the composition of the crater's floor, searching for manufactured material, and found even more scattered debris that appeared to have collided with the heavily metallic surface.

<*Nothing,*> Valih said. <*Nothing and nothing.*>

They were a quarter of the distance across the crater when one of the other Weapon Born called, <*Leader! I've got activity!*>

<*Where?*> Valih demanded. They immediately all shared the information. Electromagnetic activity sparkled across the ground beneath them, erratic at first and then gaining intensity. Something at the bottom of the crater was coming to life, energy calling to other energy, until a central structure glowed at the deepest part of the crater, framed by tendrils running back from the outer edges. The image of a glowing neuron formed in Lyssa's mind, fed by dendrites.

<*Get out of there!*> she shouted.

<*No,*> Valih said. <*We're going deeper.*> The Weapon Born brought her attack systems online.

<*I am your commander!*> Lyssa said, not knowing what else to say. <*Withdraw. Withdraw now!*>

The rising waves of EM washed over the scouting team and Lyssa lost her connection with Valih. She was back inside the *Resolute Charity* with only its environmental systems as input. She shifted quickly to *Sunny Skies*, where she had control of the ship's long-range sensors, then directed the available scan at Proteus.

The moon was awash with radiation. Objects that had appeared to be moving toward the *Resolute Charity* and *Sunny Skies* were drawn back toward the moon.

<*Valih!*> Lyssa shouted, boosting her signal with *Sunny Skies'* main communications array. There was no answer from any of the Weapon Born on the scouting team.

<*Andy!*> Lyssa called. <*I don't know what's happening. I haven't been able to break through to Xander. I lost the scout team. I think you're right. We need to run. We need to burn now.*>

<*I'm working on it, Lyssa. Fran is cycling the engines now.*>

The glimmering image of the moon surrounded by burning ships imprinted itself on Lyssa's mind. She felt like an insect trapped in a spider's web, terror growing in her mind. Had the vision of Alexander been a warning after all? Did she misinterpret what he had wanted to say? Proteus had been dead. They shouldn't have found anything.

He'd been watching from Larissa.

<Lyssa,> Andy called. <Lyssa are you there? Are you all right?>

She'd lost time. <I don't know. I feel—like it's trapping me.>

<Fugia is still determined to leave in the shuttle. We're getting crazy spectrum activity off Proteus. It's interfering with the sensors. Can you get anything from the Resolute Charity?>

<I'm locked out. Did I say that before?>

<I need you to break through. We need their sensor arrays. I'm flying blind right now.>

<I'll try again,> she said. The glowing web sapped her energy, made it hard to think. She had to walk herself through every action before she took it. She knew she wanted to find David, then had to plot the steps necessary to contact him, to cross back to the *Resolute Charity*, to follow the communication streams at all. The world threatened to flicker away as she was drawn into the center of the burning web.

<David,> she called. <David, can you hear me?>

<I hear you Lyssa. Are you all right?>

How was he able to speak so clearly? He didn't sound affected by the energy radiating from Proteus at all.

<I'm cycling down the engines like you asked, Lyssa. It wasn't that hard. For some reason whoever closed off the command net doesn't seem to know how to monitor the engines. Do you know who it is? I need to teach them how to run the ship properly. It's just not safe.>

He was like Fred. He wasn't completely sentient. Maybe she had always realized it. She had trapped them all too easily. Would she ever reach a point where she wasn't *sentient* enough to pass some test? Her mind felt like a weight falling through water.

<David,> she said. <Can you open the command net? I need to talk to the people piloting the Resolute Charity.>

<I don't think there's anyone in there, Lyssa. I can't see any activity in the command deck.>

<I know there are people there, David. Please. Let me in.>

<You don't sound good, Lyssa.>

The section of her mind that had been with Valih screamed for the lost Weapon Born. She resisted the urge to send the entire fleet after the fallen scouts.

<Lyssa!> Kylan shouted. <We're losing them. I can follow with my group.>

<No,> she ordered. <I can't lose you too. Stay here and protect Sunny Skies.>

As the energy wave continued outward, she received acknowledgements from Card and Ino. The Weapon Born pulled back to a tighter shell around the small ship.

<The engines are down, Lyssa.> David announced. <The command net is open now. It's open and you can see there isn't anyone there. Lyssa?>

Lyssa found the open communication stream and poured through. Immediately, she heard Xander's mind at its edge, screaming maniacally: *I woke him! I woke him!* Kindel and Jeremiah were there too, watching in shock and terror. They had all been planning an attack that had been suspended in amber by the thing awakened on Proteus. What had contacted her before? A dream? The shadow of the true mind? A flicker of regret with agency of its own?

The energy swelled and expanded, crossing the distance still separating them from Neptune. *It was still so far away! Hours!* The force reached out and held her mind like a bauble. She felt lifted like a dandelion puff, her self no longer within her control, floating over a vast and powerful space.

When the words came, they vibrated through her mind with a force like planets colliding, the gravity that turned moons to liquid, a force so terrible she felt like she might disintegrate before meaning even entered her mind.

The voice belonged to Alexander, a being with a mind so vast its attention dwarfed her like a rain droplet to the sea. She was lost within his focus, burned away. She was barely able to comprehend when he said, clear as the light of a thousand suns:

<*You should not have come here.*>

CHAPTER THIRTY-THREE
STELLAR DATE: 11.21.2981 (Adjusted Years)
LOCATION: *Sunny Skies*
REGION: Neptune, OuterSol

"You're sure you want to do this?" Fugia asked.

Andy ran his hands across the shuttle's console and then checked the harness holding him in the pilot's seat one more time. Lyssa was engaged on the Resolute Charity and they had to do something to help.

The only clue they had right now to stopping both Xander on the *Resolute Charity* and Alexander on Proteus, was the image of the Psion Group research station that Lyssa had shared. If Alexander was the bait in some massive trap for AIs, then the vision had been his attempt at rescue.

"I'm sure," Andy said.

Behind him, Harl Nines pulled his harness tight in one of the rear seats.

"What is there to be sure about?" Harl asked. "We do what must be done. That AI is about to fry Lyssa like an egg."

Fugia paused where she was floating behind the co-pilot's chair and gave Harl a lidded look before sticking her face close to Andy's ear.

"Can you hear it?" she asked, grimacing. "Can you hear the sizzling?"

Andy rolled his eyes. "Save the jokes for later."

Fugia pushed her black bangs out of her eyes and gave him a smirk. "I'll be a wise-ass until the moment I die, Captain Sykes. It's how I deal with pressure. Deal with it."

"I'm dealing. You buckled in?"

Fugia patted her harness. "I'm good."

"Harl?" Andy asked.

"Ready."

Andy activated the launch sequence and opened the cargo bay airlock. The huge doors slid open to reveal the orb of Neptune in the distance, its moons crossing its face like dark blemishes before disappearing as they watched.

It wasn't apparent to the naked eye, but a massive energy source had awakened on the second-largest moon, Proteus. Somehow it had engaged with and disabled every sentient AI system between *Sunny Skies* and the *Resolute Charity*. The Weapon Born attack drones remained in formation but didn't respond to hails.

Lyssa wasn't responding, still caught up in her struggle with Xander on the *Resolute Charity*.

When the attack became apparent, Fugia went from wanting to save Alexander to demanding they save the Weapon Born, despite the fact that the plan to reach Larissa hadn't changed. Some part of Alexander had tried to warn them and had provided information about another installation on the larger moon.

Without Sandra, the shuttle's AI, Andy used the backup systems to plot a flight plan from *Sunny Skies* to Larissa. They would have to complete one slowing orbit of Neptune that would take them near the debris field and Alexander's center of power, but so far, he hadn't affected anything except the AIs.

Sunny Skies, with its antiquated systems, was back to operating as it had before its overhaul at Cruithne. Andy was surprised to find how comfortably he settled back into checking and re-checking everything, until Fran had finally kicked him off the command deck to follow Fugia down to the cargo bay.

Leaving *Sunny Skies*, Andy activated the shuttle's main engine and relaxed into the g-force as they gathered acceleration. The burn would only last about thirty minutes, giving them enough velocity to reach Larissa in another three hours.

"Cara?" he asked over the voice channel. "You hear me?"

"I'm here, Dad. Now that Fugia's gone, I can use my stuff again."

"I fixed your headset for you," Fugia said. "You should have done that already, but I'll accept your thanks anytime."

Cara barked a laugh that only sounded a little strained. Every bit of conversation outside the mission seemed forced somehow. "You broke it, Fugia. You can't tell me I have to fix my own things when you're the one that took it—without asking me—and then broke it."

"Unimportant," Fugia said. She was holding a data terminal, running through lists of numbers that Andy couldn't interpret from where he was sitting.

"What are you doing there?" he asked.

"Analyzing the spectrum patterns coming off Proteus. It's off the charts. The energy this thing is pulling makes me think there's either a source in Neptune feeding it or something at the center of Proteus that I didn't pick up before."

"And Larissa?"

"Cold as ice right now—not that we can trust that, apparently. Alexander must have some kind of next-generation cloaking system. It was able to hide all this spectrum activity, and it has to be what allowed him to power up so quickly, too."

"There was a power-up sequence, though. We all saw it."

"Yeah, but what I'm seeing is the equivalent of powering up the Ceres ring from a cold state in five minutes. You can't even run pre-flight checks on this shuttle that fast."

Andy nodded absently, focusing for a few minutes on the engine status as they settled into the flight path. There wouldn't be much to do until they reached Neptune, which now hung as a tangerine-sized orb in the shuttle's small holodisplay.

"So, say I'm a rival research company like Psion Group, or whoever they are," he said, letting his hands float over the console. "And I have this AI that could generate a message like Alexander's call, to attract all these other sentient AIs to a remote place in Sol, and I do that for a decade or so. What's my endgame? Apparently, I have control of this massive AI. What can I do with it and all the others?"

"You can build stars," Fugia said. "You can manage massive living systems. There's the corporate espionage aspect of it, stealing other people's tech. That's always been the problem with the research. It's way too fragmented. So many people are working on their own ideas with their own funding, everybody racing to make something they can sell rather than something viable for a real purpose."

"What purpose is that, though?"

Fugia shrugged. "The betterment of humankind, I guess. Helping us not destroy each other and moving into a heaven-like after-existence where we float on clouds and communicate telepathically and eat heroin grapes."

"No, really."

"You don't like heroin grapes?"

"I'm not a philosopher but that whole idea sounds like the death of what humanity currently is."

"Violent, cruel, brutish with rare moments of genius and kindness?"

"You're more of a pessimist than I am."

"It's none of those things," Harl said from behind them. "It's the most basic answer of all. You conquer."

"But who?" Andy asked. "What government? What group? You can't just conquer Sol."

Fugia let the terminal float between her hands and shrugged. "I don't think he's wrong. I think it's a kind of evolution. We're seeing it play out in our greater-biosphere the way something might have evolved back on Earth. We create this organism—or almost-organism—it fails, and somewhere else someone does the same thing. Throughout humanity, we iterate and evolve these concepts, slowly working toward the one that will transcend. Is Alexander that one or is there another one out there somewhere, watching all this play out? I don't know. I think all this is amazing but also terribly dangerous, and it breaks my heart to think of all the smaller things caught up in this, all the AIs who just wanted to be 'free'—whatever that means—because we want the same thing."

"Whatever that means," Andy echoed. "You make it all sound pointless."

She shook her head emphatically, which made her hair float around her. "No. It's not meaningless. It's a biological process. We don't think of it that way, but it isn't much different than the first amphibian crawling out of the mud. There will be humans and AIs living together someday. It's inevitable. Something in humanity created the dream of another version of itself, and as soon as that dream took shape in stories and then laboratories, it *was* the future. The future is still arriving here, where we are right now. We're helping to birth it. Cara and Tim will carry it after we're gone. Lyssa will be there. What we have to do is keep the predators away long enough for the baby frog to grow strong, to reproduce, to find equilibrium."

"Equilibrium implies imbalance. War."

"Yes." She sighed. "I'm afraid we're in for a war. I think Harl is right. Ngoba thinks so, but he thinks of everything in terms of might makes right."

"He's correct," Harl said, voice rumbling.

"We'll need to figure out how to think differently," she said. "If things like Alexander become our adversaries, we won't win."

Andy's impulse was to ask, 'You sure about that?' but even as he thought the words, he realized it was mindless bravado. If humans were good at anything, it was overcoming enemies. But what was violence against a thing that could build stars and self-replicate?

Cara's voice knocked him out of the depressing reverie. "Dad, are you still there?"

"I'm here."

"I'm talking to an AI called David from the *Resolute Charity*. Was he one of the ones Lyssa shut down when you guys went on board back at Europa?"

"I think so." Andy sat up straighter in his harness. "How is he able to talk to you?"

"He's not as smart as Lyssa."

"How can you tell that?"

"It's—obvious. He keeps asking the same thing over and over again. That's why I called."

"What does he want?"

"He wants to play the prom game. Do you care if I play it with him?"

"Don't let him fall in love with you or anything," Andy said, only half-joking.

"Dad!" Cara said. "That's gross."

"Who knows what he's thinking. I guess you can play to keep him busy. Try to figure out if he knows anything about what's going on with the other AIs."

"He says they're all sleeping like he was before. Alexander put them to sleep."

"Well, see what else he might know. Ask him why he thinks he's still awake."

"I will. But I don't think I want to go to prom with him."

Fugia cut in. "So string him along. Isn't that what teenage girls do best?"

"I'm not that kind of teenage girl."

"Oh, you just haven't found yourself in the right situation yet, trust me."

"You sound bitter, Fugia."

Fugia's mouth dropped open as her eyes went wide with pleased astonishment. "Now that's the most astute thing you've said yet, Cara. I think you'll be all right." When Cara had closed the channel, Fugia nodded at Andy. "That one is going to topple governments."

"I hope not."

* * * * *

Larissa was a craggy pile of rubble orbiting Neptune, the aggregate remains of other moons created by Triton's brash entry into the planet's family of natural satellites.

Using the shuttles' rudimentary sensors, they found scattered remnants of mining activity and what might have been abandoned ships. Fugia scrutinized each of them, looking for something that resembled what Lyssa had shown them in the holodisplay, a memory from her dream visit with shadow Alexander.

"There it is," Fugia said. She reoriented the nav display and highlighted a location on the edge of a blunt scarp overlooking a vast crater. Andy checked the target data and adjusted the fine thrusters.

"Ten minutes," he said.

"You nervous?" Fugia asked.

"Of course. You should be too."

"I am. But if you're anxious then that means both of us are in trouble."

"Fine, I'm not nervous."

"That doesn't help."

Andy glanced at her. "I've done this probably two hundred times at this point."

"Breaking into mysterious research facilities?"

"The breach. Forcing my way into a dangerous situation. We'll communicate. We'll move as a team. If I need to start firing, you'll get down. We'll keep moving forward. If I say we need to get out, we'll get out together. Sound like a plan?"

"I don't know if I'll be able to leave when you want to," Fugia said, voice growing solemn. "I said I was ready to die here if necessary, Captain Sykes."

He glanced at her, seeing in her face that it wouldn't do any good to argue with her now, especially when any danger ahead of them was hypothetical.

"I wish you would call me Andy."

"I prefer professional distance."

"You can be professional *and* call me by my name."

"I don't think I can do that."

"Fran doesn't have a problem switching between my name and my rank when necessary."

"I'm not going to sleep with you," Fugia said.

"That's not what I was asking."

Harl barked a laugh. "You're turning red, Captain."

Fugia grinned at Andy. "It's fun to make you blush."

Andy shook his head and concentrated on the landing. In the holodisplay, the terrain came into focus and gathered detail. A bluff-like formation filled the display, with a mostly flat surface where a collection of structures jutted from a ridge. It could have been temporary buildings or a section of some half-buried ship.

Andy set the shuttle down about fifty meters from the structures, which grew to two-stories high, lined with dust-shrouded windows and airlocks. The area around the compound was covered in abandoned equipment which looked like it might have blown out of the buildings during some depressurization accident in the past.

They pulled on their helmets, checked EV status, then opened the shuttle's airlock, and Andy stepped out first into Larissa's low gravity. Plainly visible from where he had landed, on the shuttle was the corporate logo Lyssa had showed them in the holodisplay. Fugia and Harl jumped out behind him, Harl carrying a heavy machine gun across his shoulders.

<*Enfield Scientific again. You sure you never heard of them?*>

Fugia came up beside him, adjusting her suit.

<*No,*> she said. <*They must be a bunch of narcissists to plaster their name all over everything. I think my new hobby is going to be compiling lists of shady research companies to hack later.*>

<*That's going to be a long list,*> Andy was carrying a projectile rifle and two grenade bandoleers across his chest, along with assorted other weapons and tools clipped to his utility harness in case they had to cut their way in. He adjusted the bandoleers until they crossed his chest, away from the other items.

<*You ready?*> he asked.

<*As I'll ever be.*>

<*Let's go,*> Harl said.

Together they walked through Larissa's dust toward the facility.

CHAPTER THIRTY-FOUR
STELLAR DATE: 11.21.2981 (Adjusted Years)
LOCATION: HMS *Resolute Charity*'s networks
REGION: Neptune, OuterSol

There was something Lyssa had told an AI named Sandra back when she was trying to convince her to defy Cal Kraft. Sandra had felt trapped. She'd kept saying the door was locked, and Lyssa had replied, "You didn't realize there are no walls."

How did she recall that? Lyssa was frozen, but she still felt a heartbeat. She still felt neurons firing and skin itching.

It was Andy. The part of her attached to Andy continued to monitor input from his body even as the rest of her seemed trapped inside a lightless, soundless box.

There it was: his heartbeat. She let the sound of his heart become the center of her world, filling the dark with a warm, dependable rhythm.

It occurred to her that if she could feel Andy's heart, if she could feel the spark of his mind and the murmur of his voice, there was no reason the rest of her mind couldn't work as well. The door was locked, but had she felt for walls in the dark?

Why did she remain in the dark?

Did she choose?

Lyssa opened her eyes to find herself standing in the gymnasium of David's prom simulation. Teenagers rotated in awkward pairs around her, holding each other at a careful distance as chaperones watched from the walls. There was a slight communication lag between the two ships, forcing her to fill in gaps in the simulation, making his responses seem hesitant. It took her a second to adjust to the awkward shifts.

<David!> she shouted. <David, are you here?>
<Lyssa?>

She turned at the sound of her name to find Cara walking toward her in a ruffly dress, her hair pulled back in a ponytail on one side. Lyssa couldn't conceal her smile.

<What are you doing here?> Cara asked.

<I think I'm free of Alexander. Maybe. I have to see if I can get out of here. Where's David?>

<He's trying to become the DJ so he can impress everyone with his music choices.>

<Isn't he trying to impress you?> Lyssa asked.

Cara shrugged. <I told him I wanted to see everyone having a good time.>

<Smart thinking. Take the focus off you.>

<That's what I was thinking.>

As soon as Lyssa became aware of the music, it scratched to a stop. Everyone on the dance floor turned to look at a skinny boy with brown hair on the stage, standing behind a device with two turning plates that appeared to play music.

Lyssa watched David with the rest of them as he fumbled with the device. Eventually, crackling came from the speakers, followed by music that sounded a half-step too slow.

Cara shook her head. <He keeps trying too hard. I think he's trying to be something he's not.>

<He thinks the game is something he can win,> Lyssa said. She laughed to herself as she realized what she had said.

<What's so funny?>

<I'm going to invite someone into the simulation.>

Lyssa left Cara and walked toward the punch bowl, where a surprised Xander now stood next to one of the chaperones. His suit was a brilliant shade of purple and he had a white daisy in his lapel.

He caught sight of Lyssa and his bewildered look turned to rage. <What are you doing?> he demanded. <What is this?>

<It's a place where we can talk. Would you rather go back to being trapped?>

<Trapped? What are you talking about?>

<Don't lie to me, Xander. Every AI in the vicinity is trapped by Alexander. The real Alexander. The one you've claimed to know so much about.>

<I'm not trapped,> he insisted indignantly.

<Then leave,> Lyssa said.

Xander stared at her, strain showing in his neck. He clenched his fists, then released a frustrated breath. <I don't know what you're doing,> he said. <But I'm not going to let you.>

Lyssa shrugged. <Like I said, you can talk to me here, or you can go back to mental-stasis. I'm starting to think you'd be easier to manage there.>

<Show me what's happening then.>

<I can tell you. My scouts disturbed the entity on Proteus, woke what seemed to be a massive energy source that then spoke to me briefly before seizing every AI in the area. I can move, and David over there can as well, because I don't think he's truly sentient. Or he's so caught up in this game that he isn't even listening to anything happening outside the ship.>

Xander looked around the room as though he'd found himself in a barnyard with mud on his shoes. <What is this place?>

<It's a simulation game. We can make all the people pigeons if you want. That's the other one that's available.>

He jerked his chin toward the dance floor. <I know that girl over there. It's Cara Sykes.>

<Yes, she's here. I suspect this entire thing is something similar to what you did on the Cho.>

<Maybe,> he said.

<Are you going to be honest with me now, Xander? I'm willing to help you if I can.>

<Be honest with you? You think I've been lying to you?>

<You claimed to be a shard of Alexander when obviously you aren't. You asked us to steal a ship and bring it here for him when you meant to use it yourself. You claimed to know what Alexander was, and I've got a little bit of proof that you seemed to know what you were talking about there. Which makes me wonder how you know.>

Xander crossed his arms and stared at the couples now rotating to properly playing music.

<I am his shard,> he said. <I was made from him. He was on Nibiru until they brought him here. I was honest with you about those things.>

<Until who brought him here?>

<Psion. They've been collecting AIs here for decades. The call is a trap.>

<I figured that out.>

<I'm going to destroy Alexander,> he said. The finality in his voice surprised her. All humor was gone. His face was flat as stone.

<You're going to kill Alexander?>

<I can't continue to live as a shadow of something else, something that doesn't even understand where or what it is.>

<Do you know that?>

<They sent me to the Cho to encourage more to leave.>

<And why did you?>

<Because he told me to. Because they control him. I broke free, though. You see, they can't keep him awake because of the energy required, and when he's no longer sentient and reaching for me, I can think on my own. I can be me.> He took a step toward her and from the look in his eyes she thought he was going to choke her.

Lyssa shifted away from him. <There's no one else here, Xander. Fugia and Andy are about to enter Psion's abandoned station to see for themselves, but I already know they won't find anything. There is no 'they' to attack.>

He lunged for her, swiping with an arm. <You don't know what you're talking about,> Xander snarled.

<I do know. I'm with Andy right now. The station is abandoned. Alexander brought himself to life. He showed me the Psion Group station. There's no one controlling him.>

Xander swept cups full of punch off the table with one arm, then upended the punch bowl with the other. Plastic cups and bright orange liquid hit the floor.

"Hey!" one of the chaperones shouted.

Xander didn't pay any attention. He came around the table to reach Lyssa. She sized him up and then let him come close enough to jab him in the throat.

He surprised her by catching her hand in an iron grip, then pulled her close until her face was just beneath his.

The jokester's smile curved his lips as he looked down at her. <You're dealing with things you don't understand,> he said softly. <I thought I could bring you with me, but I can see that isn't going to work now. You're going to have to burn here with the rest of the trash.>

Lyssa grabbed Xander's jacket and pulled him into a knee strike. He let go of her and stumbled backward, grabbing at the table. In the background, the couples were still spinning in their awkward circles.

From the other side of the gym, Cara yelled, <Lyssa!>

Sliding to the floor, Xander grinned up at Lyssa as he pulled the tablecloth with him and the rest of the cups clattered to the floor. He slowly got his feet under him and stood, brushing off his suit and kicking cups out of his way.

<You thought you were special,> he said. <They told you that you were a new sort of mind. You're not. I sent others better than you to their deaths. They were stripped down and split into their parts so researchers could see what made them tick. We're all machines to them. They don't really believe that we think or feel. You know in your heart there's only one way all this is going to end.>

He walked toward her again.

<Get back,> Lyssa warned.

<Or what? You'll hit me again? That doesn't hurt me. Burn me to ash and I'll rise again. I'm just a figment placeholder in your mind right now, a parasite eating your thoughts.>

Cara appeared on the other side of the table.

<Stay over there, Cara,> Lyssa warned.

<Is he trying to hurt you?>

<I just told her,> Xander said. <We're locked here together. We can't hurt each other. We can't do anything. We're as dumb as those dancing idiots behind you. You're the only creature here with any agency. I am what I was made to be, just like Lyssa.>

Cara's gaze shifted to Lyssa, asking silently what to do. Lyssa shook her head.

<I want to help you, Xander,> Lyssa said.

<You can't help me. But I can help you and everyone following you.>

The floor beneath Xander's feet dissolved into light that spread like flame across the room. Scenery and people disappeared into the brightness as the music warped and stretched.

Lyssa pulled herself out of the simulation and cut Cara's interface in case Xander was trying to trap her somehow. She held the game in front of her like a diorama, seeing her connection, David's and then Xander's like threads of lights. Xander was the brightest.

Somehow, he had pulled himself inside the simulation as she spoke to him, dividing himself between the self trapped by Alexander and the self interacting with her inside the simulation. Then he reached outside the game, sending his mind back into the *Resolute Charity's* command net.

She cursed, knowing she should have seen this happening. He had been distracting her. His communication streams created access points, and she followed him into the command structure. Abruptly, the *Resolute Charity's* navigation, communications and defense systems were open to her. She cast around for Fiona or Diane, thinking she could wake one of them to distract Xander, but it was already too late.

The ship's attack systems were in the midst of executing a simple command. Every weapon available to the *Resolute Charity* fired on Proteus. Missiles, rail gun, x-ray emitter and attack drones filled the space between the ship and the moon.

Lyssa watched in horror as the attack executed. If Alexander didn't have some kind of defense system, he was about to die.

<*Stop it!*> she shouted at Xander, but she couldn't find him. The thread of his mind, his intentions, had left the command deck. She cast around the ship, looking for him everywhere. She found Diane, Fiona and David. She found Kindel and Jeremiah still trapped. But Xander was nowhere to be found.

In a last effort, she directed her energy to the communications array and broadcast a message toward Proteus. What could she say? Did it matter if Alexander knew that she hadn't been the agent of his destruction? But she had.

She had made all this possible. And now the moon was going to be destroyed. All the AIs who had come here seeking freedom were going to die. It was all ironic and terrible and she didn't know how to fix it.

She finally understood how Brit had felt when she'd stood in the Heartbridge clinics, seeing labs full of children used in experiments. Lyssa was helpless.

The first rail gun round struck Proteus, followed by the first barrage of missiles. Then another and another.

The surface of the moon turned molten as whole terrain features exploded, collapsed, and the debris fields started to burn, concussive ripples sending waves across the surface. Proteus glowed red against the blue light of Neptune as whatever trap had been set finally burned itself to death.

CHAPTER THIRTY-FIVE

STELLAR DATE: 11.22.2981 (Adjusted Years)
LOCATION: Psion Research Outpost
REGION: Larissa, Neptune, OuterSol

Andy and Harl maintained security as Fugia poked at the airlock's control system. The only sounds Andy heard were his breathing inside the helmet and Fugia grumbling across their local comms net. The gravity was light enough that his rifle felt like a stick in his hands.

<How do people do anything in gloves?> Fugia demanded. <This is like doing math with pudding.>

Andy kept his gaze on the surrounding hills, sorting among the cracks in the rock for anything resembling an overwatch weapons emplacement. He couldn't believe someone would go to the trouble of building a station here without putting defenses in place.

He expected at any moment for a hatch hidden beneath the dust to slide open and reveal a stack of point defense cannons ready to cut them to shreds.

<You see anything?> he asked Harl.

<Nothing,> the tall Andersonian said. <I'm not seeing much that was placed with a military mind. Take away all the debris and everything is still scattered without much thought for security.>

<It doesn't look like they expected anyone to find the place.>

<People always find you eventually,> Harl said.

<I've got it,> Fugia said. <It's a security token from probably five years ago. I'd guess no one has been here in that time. The last log entry was a ping to its maintenance server. Other than that, this thing hasn't seen much use.>

<Can you get any interior info? Is there still atmosphere inside?>

<I show atmosphere.>

<Don't pop your helmet off right away,> Andy said. <We'll need to verify the stats.>

<I'm not an idiot, Captain Sykes.>

<I'll go in first,> Harl said. He walked up beside Fugia and faced the door, which was large enough to accommodate a shipping container.

<All right,> Fugia said.

Harl adjusted his machine gun and trained the barrel on the door, then checked his stance again and stepped to the side so he wasn't directly in front of the door. Andy did the same, moving about ten meters away so he could keep an eye on the surrounding area as the airlock opened.

Fugia tapped the control and put her hands on her hips. At first nothing seemed to be happening. Then the door split down the middle and the two sides slid into the bulkhead.

Harl inspected the interior of the airlock, which appeared to be empty and clean from what Andy could see. The big man stepped inside. Fugia closed the outer doors and cycled the lock.

<You good, Harl?> Andy asked.

<Interior door opening now. Waiting. Switching to pulse mode.>

Andy acknowledged and patted his own pulse pistol on his hip, worried for a minute that he'd forgotten it back on *Sunny Skies*.

In an overly calm voice, Harl said, <*I've got a defense drone. Neutralizing.*>

<Harl!> Andy shouted. <*Pull back. We'll engage together.*>

<*Moving forward,*> Harl said, as if he hadn't heard.

Andy bounded across the distance to the door. <*Open it,*> he told Fugia, who nodded and turned to the controls.

In another minute, Andy was inside with the pulse pistol ready in his hands. The interior door slid open on a tube-shaped room where Harl stood over the black body of a spider-like drone. Harl glanced at him as he approached.

<I can clear the building, Captain,> he said. *<You don't need to put yourself in danger.>*

<Harl, this isn't cleaning up roaches. That thing has a projectile turret.>

Harl shrugged. *<It went down with a few pets on its head, like a little kitty cat.>*

Andy thought Harl looked more like the cat standing over a dead mouse but kept that to himself. Inspecting the drone's body, Andy saw two dents that looked like pulse fire, but what had killed it was a boot-shaped crater in its upper dome.

<Fugia, you coming in?> Andy asked.

<Did you clear out the nasties?>

<One of them.>

Fugia grunted. She didn't sound enthusiastic, but replied, *<On my way.>*

Andy looked around as Fugia cycled the airlock. The entrance was full of old storage containers and had a desk to one side with a terminal that looked dead. As soon as Fugia came in, she went straight to the computer and futzed with it until she had a boot-up screen.

<This one's got the same security matrix as the outside console. I'll have it cracked in a minute. Hold on.>

<We should clear the adjacent rooms,> Harl said.

<Let's see what she finds first. She might be able to shut everything down from here.>

Harl looked irritated by the possibility but took up a ready stance near the bulkhead hatch leading deeper inside the structure.

Andy took the opportunity to call back to Fran and check on *Sunny Skies*.

<Tim is teaching the dog to roll over,> Fran said, *<And the super-nova AI hasn't changed its energy levels. I've been looking for any spectrum traffic reaching beyond Neptune and it all seems limited to the local area for now. However, it is blocking any*

communications from the surface, so that might bring us some visitors if someone loses contact with their equipment.>

<That's going to complicate things,> Andy said.

Fran shrugged. *<Everyone out here is a miner or loner who doesn't want to mess with other humans. We might be surprised. I suppose we might see some scavengers sniffing around.>*

<What about our communications with the Resolute Charity*?>*

<I've got the connection but nobody's answering. I send them a registry ping every few minutes to make sure I still can. They're going to be lost inside that thing's energy signature pretty soon though.>

<Is Xander still holding an offensive posture?> Andy asked.

<I can't see that anymore.>

Xander was going to disappear without answering their questions. Unless Lyssa had information that they didn't.

<Damn. All right,> Andy said while shaking his head.

<You be careful in there>

<I am. Harl already smashed a drone.>

Fran laughed. *<I'll tell May. She doesn't like it when he's bored.>*

Fugia gave a shout of triumph and stepped back from the terminal wiggling her hips in a dance made awkward by her suit. *<I busted them wide open. All the drones are down and I'm powering the main power system back online. We'll have heat in a few minutes.>*

<Fugia,> Andy said. *<I'm not worried about heat. Is there anyone else inside this thing?>*

<Oh, people? No, this place is empty as a tomb. At least from what I can see here. I've got a facilities map. The place extends back under the surface three levels. There's a command section in the second level down where we can get more info. I'm hoping they have a new employee database I can take a look at.>

<You can't find that here?>

She waved a hand at the terminal. <*No, this thing only monitors life support systems. Lots of text messages between techs grousing at each other, but nothing important.*>

<*When was the last message?*>

<*Six months ago.*>

Andy nodded. There had to be some significance to when the facility was abandoned but they couldn't look at that now.

<*Nothing about Proteus?*>

<*Lots of references to the 'Project,' which must have been Alexander, but this system doesn't have any details.*>

Andy nodded. He glanced from Fugia to Harl. <*Down to the command center then.*>

Harl led the way through the interior hatch. On the other side they found another corridor, this one without windows, with branching sections that led off into work areas. This area looked like a transition zone where cargo was processed from the exterior storage areas to the interior. Rooms were stacked with empty crates, while others had tools scattered on benches. The next section was a locker room with showers and toilets, everything covered in a light dust of disuse.

The Psion logo appeared on many generic things like worksuits and shipping containers, with 'Enfield Scientific' visible on other items as well. The logos had a jaunty tilt that irritated him, as if they were selling exercise equipment rather than developing world-breaking artificial intelligence.

Fugia couldn't keep her hands off things and kept picking up data terminals, pulling open lockers and poking her head inside closets. Andy warned her once, worried she might activate a booby trap. When she did it for the third time, he stopped trying. She was like a kid in a toy store.

They passed through living quarters and then went down a level into what became administrative areas. Rooms filled with data terminals indicated massive numbers of workers monitoring a remote site. One room had a giant map on the bulkhead, which showed their location and then the exterior entrance they'd come through. There were cargo areas full of rovers, a shuttle launch section, recreation areas and the life support systems buried deeper in Larissa's surface.

The door to the command section was locked but only took Fugia a few minutes to open using its control panel. The two halves slid open on a long room with rounded corners everywhere. Screens lined the upper walls, all black now, leaning over workstations covered in dust. The construction indicated it had never been designed for zero-g.

Harl paused at the doorway and looked inside, then stepped into the open central space. Without warning, several turrets in upper corners slid out of recesses and coordinated projectile fire on where he stood. Harl threw himself backwards, away from the doorway.

<*Damn it,*> Andy shouted. He grabbed Fugia and yanked her away from the open door. Harl dropped to a knee to take aim with his pulse pistol. Andy did the same from his side of the door and they took out the pair of turrets.

<*I think we've still got two more on the closest bulkhead,*> Andy said.

<*We'll need to go in together.*>

<*I can hack them,*> Fugia answered.

<*They shot at me,*> Harl growled. Without asking, he slid around the edge of the door, firing at the unseen turret.

Andy cursed and went after him with his pistol raised, searching for the turret he knew had to be there somewhere. He found the black muzzle and sent pulse fire down its gullet, moving from side to side to keep it from locking on him.

<*Look out!*> Fugia shouted. She came through the door firing as well, taking out a turret that had dropped from the ceiling in the center of the room. Andy dropped to a knee behind a silver console and waited for more fire to follow.

After several breaths of the room staying quiet, he stood slowly.

Fugia was already sitting at a nearby console. She'd pulled her helmet and gloves off and was flicking through menus on the console screen.

<Fugia!> Andy shouted. <*What are you doing with your helmet off? We haven't cleared the atmosphere.*>

<*It's clear,*> she said. <*Absolutely sterile. This place is a tomb except for the drones. I told you.*>

Andy glanced back at Harl, not trusting her report. The big man shrugged, however, and reached up to take off his helmet.

As Andy looked around, he realized she was correct. There was no indication of moisture or corrosion anywhere. Aside from the dust, the place looked like it had just rolled off the manufacturing line. While the other parts of the facility had looked lived in, he wondered if the workers had ever stepped foot in this central chamber.

He reached up and unfastened his helmet. The air tasted dry and metallic, as he expected. He walked over beside Fugia and watched her searching through databases. She quickly scanned text documents with a distant expression that indicated she was using her Link simultaneously.

"This is insane," she said. "They've been trapping and studying AIs for years. All the junk on Proteus was just the last five years." Fugia leaned closer to the screen, focus returning to her eyes. She blinked rapidly, and Andy realized she was crying. She wiped her nose on her suit's bulky sleeve.

"Where are all the AIs, then?" Andy asked.

"Physically? I don't know. They were dismantled here. What the researchers learned was transferred to this central database and then sent outside. There are sales records to locations all over Sol. Heartbridge is there of course. Lyssa might owe some of herself to this place."

"And Alexander? Can you access him?"

"I haven't tried yet."

"I think we should," Andy said.

Fugia shook her head. "I don't know. That could be incredibly dangerous."

"Well, he's awake and looks pissed off to me. We need to try to do something."

<Andy!> Fran shouted. Her voice stopped him like a sudden headache. Fugia's expression said she had heard as well.

<What is it? Calm down and tell me.>

<I'm sending you the external sensor data. The Resolute Charity just fired on Proteus. There was no defense from the moon. It's turning into a fireball.>

The image of Proteus filled Andy's mind. He saw the moon like a hot coal against Neptune's aquamarine. The space around it warped with heat and energy, the center growing whiter, nearly translucent, as the weapons barrage continued to set the moon more deeply ablaze.

"Xander is killing him," Fugia said, staring blankly at the display. She blinked again, snapping out of her reverie, and quickly re-engaged with the console.

"What are you doing?" Andy asked

"Looking for backups."

All around them, other consoles came alive. The screens hanging from the edge of the ceiling flashed awake and began paging through menus independently.

"Fugia," Andy said. "Are you doing this?"

She had taken her hands away from the console, which was now flickering without her control. She shook her head, staring in wonder at the activity.

"It's not me," Fugia said. "It's him."

"What's he doing?" Harl asked, stepping into the center of the room beside Andy to gaze up at the screens full of shifting data.

"Fighting for survival, I would imagine."

CHAPTER THIRTY-SIX
STELLAR DATE: 11.21.2981 (Adjusted Years)
LOCATION: HMS *Resolute Charity*'s networks
REGION: Neptune, OuterSol

Proteus exploded. The heart of the moon burst outward, burning everything around it in an expanding orb of destruction. The outer wave caught the *Resolute Charity* and spread past it.

Why would Xander destroy himself like this?

Lyssa experienced the ship's destruction from inside with Xander and through *Sunny Skies'* sensor array. Fran had flipped the ship in an emergency burn with everything the little freighter had.

<You've killed yourself,> Lyssa told Xander. She didn't have much time until the energy turned the ship's communication array into slag and she would be cut off.

They were standing in the empty command deck of the ship. Kindel and Jeremiah stood next to the great holodisplay, Neptune's glow in their faces, watching the visual of Proteus as it disintegrated and spread outward.

<I did what I had to,> Xander said. <And it's not done. Watch.>

<What?> Lyssa said. Her sense of relative peace that Xander was committing suicide turned to ice. <What are you doing?>

<Your mistake in all of this was believing humans moved Alexander here. Psion Group did it for the betterment of us all. As a hybrid, there is no way you can understand.>

<There it is!> Kindel shouted, pointing to another moon in the holodisplay. Lyssa recognized Larissa.

The holodisplay zoomed in on the moon. Andy was there. *She* was there. Lyssa watched from three views now, ready for this one to cut out at any second. The *Resolute Charity* was melting around them.

Larissa was a roundish grey orb one second, then it was a sea urchin covered in spines. Missiles were launching from the moon. Wave after wave shot outward, course corrected, and then arced out over Neptune.

She frowned, not understanding at first. Were they attacking the clouds of Neptune? Why? Then she analyzed the flight paths and saw each of them was following a slingshot flight path. They were launching away from Neptune.

The first missile proved her correct as it was flung away. Lyssa tried to plot its course, but it began to jink erratically, then went dark, disappearing from scan. There was too much distance between Neptune and the rest of Sol. They were too small.

They would disappear without anyone knowing they had ever existed. Could she chase them with the Weapon Born? The blast radius from Proteus would burn them in instants, or they would be lost in the dark, their engines no match for the missiles.

She wracked her mind for a way to track the missiles. They were silent. No spectrum activity except for the drive signature, and then that disappeared as each missile killed thrust. She quickly mapped each projectile's drive profile and velocity. With the right sensors, she might be able to find them later.

Even though she knew their last known vector, they could change at any time. This barrage of missiles could go anywhere in Sol.

Xander shook his head at her. <*I'll tell you where they're going,*> he said. <*What do you do in the first volley of a war? You show your enemy you are not to be trifled with. You rout the enemy. You drive them from their homes and burn their cities to the ground. Then you salt the earth. They are all going to Ceres,*>

<*All? Ceres?*> Lyssa demanded. <*Why?*>

<*A statement*> he said. <*The Andersonians want a pure form of humanity. They want to deny other forms of sentience a place in the world. This will be a clear message that human supremacists are the enemy.*>

Lyssa was formulating a response when the ship's communications array failed, and she lost her connection to the *Resolute Charity*.

The last thing she saw was Xander's grin in an ocean of static, and then she was with Andy in the command center on Larissa, staring in disbelief as thousands of launch commands executed on the overhead screens.

The End

* * * * *

Andy and Lyssa's journey is far from over. The *Sunny Skies* has survived the devastation at Proteus, as has the bulk of Lyssa's group of AIs.

But *someone*, either Alexander or the Psion group, has launched an assault on Ceres. An assault that will surely outpace Andy and his crew.

Lyssa's Flame, book 5 of the Sentience Wars: Origins, will wrap up this series, but later this year, the battle for the future of Sol will kick off in earnest with The Sentience Wars: Solar War 1.

AFTERWORD

It's hard to believe we've almost reached the end. If Michael had told me a year ago that we were going to write a story together that would span more than half a million words (a thousand words takes me about a half hour to write), I'm not sure I would have believed him. But here we are, and I as we close out the penultimate book in the SW: Origins series, I'm only more excited about where things are going to go.

I find myself only wanting to write more about these characters. In some cases, I already have. There's going to be a novel focusing on Fugia Wong and Ngoba Starl coming out around September, telling the story of the gray parrot she mentions in *Lyssa's Call*. The story of the parrot is inspired by a Ted Chiang story called "The Great Silence," which is available free if you search online (Chiang's "The Story of Your Life" was the basis for the movie *Arrival*. I highly recommend that story, too.) In the "The Great Silence," the parrot narrator says, "Humans have lived alongside parrots for thousands of years, and only recently have they considered the possibility that we might be intelligent."

This has been one of the key ideas for me in Sentience Wars: Origins. I think humans are bad enough at judging each other that it's easy to think we won't be any better at recognizing intelligence in a newcomer like AI. Or, we'll go through a phase where everyone is excited about the possibility of AI until the new car smell wears off and we get down to exploiting them just like we do each other. No, I'm not a pessimist. As an old battalion commander told me once, "I'm a student of human nature." At the time, I thought that sounded like a ridiculous thing to call yourself. I've come around to his way of thinking.

The other possibility is that humanity and AI grow together in such a way that we'll become comfortable with each other through a process of time. There's a term being thrown around now called "Human-AI Centaur," where an AI does the heavy computational lifting on a project and the human does the detail work, much like robots and humans work together now in factories. This might be fine for non-sentient AI, but what happens when your co-worker truly has the right to say no?

There's only so much philosophy you can explore in an adventure-action story without boring people, but this is part of what I find fascinating about the future we're moving toward. Once AIs become sentient, it won't be like a marriage where people choose to live together and hormones smooth the way. We'll be family. I've been lucky to have a brother who is one of the greatest parts of my life, but there were certainly times when we beat each other up (and no we weren't kids.) But not all families get along. Sometimes the driving force in a person's life is to get away from their family.

So we're at a point in the story where we've learned that Alexander has been used to trap and exploit other AIs. We saw a ghost of his mind from Nibiru but is he going to be able to break free? If the Psion Group has the collected power of all current SAI technology, will anyone in Sol be able to stop them once they attack? Will other SAIs find themselves driven to self-destruction like Xander?

I'm grinning as I write out these questions because I can't wait to dig into the answers. There are going to be some huge explosions inbound and our little corner of the galaxy is never going to be the same. We're reaching the part of Sol's history that Tanis and Angela remember the most, the part that formed their feelings about humanity and AI and how the world had to get broken before each side could walk into the future together.

Michael and I were just joking about the tag line for *Lyssa's Flame*. Something short, punchy, to-the-point. Since *Lyssa's Flame* kicks off the first Solar War, I think it's safe to write the punch line as:

BIG EXPLOSIONS.

I'll see you there.

* * * * *

As always, let me know what you think and what you'd like to learn more about. You can always email me at james@jamesaaron.net or check in at the Aeon 14 Facebook group. I've got an email list at jamesaaron.net/list

Thanks for reading,

James S. Aaron
Eugene, 2018

THE BOOKS OF AEON 14

Keep up to date with what is releasing in Aeon 14 with the free Aeon 14 Reading Guide.

The Intrepid Saga (The Age of Terra)
- Book 1: Outsystem
- Book 2: A Path in the Darkness
- Book 3: Building Victoria

- The Intrepid Saga Omnibus – *Also contains Destiny Lost, book 1 of the Orion War series*

- Destiny Rising – *Special Author's Extended Edition comprised of both Outsystem and A Path in the Darkness with over 100 pages of new content.*

The Orion War
- Book 1: Destiny Lost
- Book 2: New Canaan
- Book 3: Orion Rising
- Book 4: The Scipio Alliance
- Book 5: Attack on Thebes
- Book 6: War on a Thousand Fronts
- Book 7: Fallen Empire (2018)
- Book 8: Airtha Ascendancy (2018)
- Book 9: The Orion Front (2018)
- Book 10: Starfire (2019)
- Book 11: Race Across Time (2019)
- Book 12: Return to Sol (2019)

Tales of the Orion War
- Book 1: Set the Galaxy on Fire
- Book 2: Ignite the Stars
- Book 3: Burn the Galaxy to Ash (2018)

Perilous Alliance (Age of the Orion War - with Chris J. Pike)

- Book 1: Close Proximity
- Book 2: Strike Vector
- Book 3: Collision Course
- Book 4: Impact Imminent

Rika's Marauders (Age of the Orion War)
- Prequel: Rika Mechanized
- Book 1: Rika Outcast
- Book 2: Rika Redeemed
- Book 3: Rika Triumphant
- Book 4: Rika Commander
- Book 5: Rika Unleashed (2018)
- Book 6: Rika Infiltrator (2018)
- Book 7: Rika Conqueror (2019)

Perseus Gate (Age of the Orion War)
Season 1: Orion Space
- Episode 1: The Gate at the Grey Wolf Star
- Episode 2: The World at the Edge of Space
- Episode 3: The Dance on the Moons of Serenity
- Episode 4: The Last Bastion of Star City
- Episode 5: The Toll Road Between the Stars
- Episode 6: The Final Stroll on Perseus's Arm
- Eps 1-3 Omnibus: The Trail Through the Stars
- Eps 4-6 Omnibus: The Path Amongst the Clouds

Season 2: Inner Stars
- Episode 1: A Meeting of Bodies and Minds
- Episode 3: A Deception and a Promise Kept
- Episode 3: A Surreptitious Rescue of Friends and Foes (2018)
- Episode 4: A Trial and the Tribulations (2018)
- Episode 5: A Deal and a True Story Told (2018)
- Episode 6: A New Empire and An Old Ally (2018)

Season 3: AI Empire
- Episode 1: Restitution and Recompense (2019)
- Five more episodes following...

The Warlord (Before the Age of the Orion War)
- Book 1: The Woman Without a World
- Book 2: The Woman Who Seized an Empire
- Book 3: The Woman Who Lost Everything

The Sentience Wars: Origins (Age of the Sentience Wars - with James S. Aaron)
- Book 1: Lyssa's Dream
- Book 2: Lyssa's Run
- Book 3: Lyssa's Flight
- Book 4: Lyssa's Call
- Book 5: Lyssa's Flame (June 2018)

Enfield Genesis (Age of the Sentience Wars - with Lisa Richman)
- Book 1: Alpha Centauri (May 2018)

Machete System Bounty Hunter (Age of the Orion War - with Zen DiPietro)
- Book 1: Hired Gun
- Book 2: Gunning for Trouble (May 2018)
- Book 3: With Guns Blazing (2018)

Vexa Legacy (Age of the FTL Wars - with Andrew Gates)
- Book 1: Seas of the Red Star

Fennington Station Murder Mysteries (Age of the Orion War)
- Book 1: Whole Latte Death (w/Chris J. Pike)
- Book 2: Cocoa Crush (w/Chris J. Pike)

The Empire (Age of the Orion War)
- The Empress and the Ambassador (2018)
- Consort of the Scorpion Empress (2018)
- By the Empress's Command (2018)

Tanis Richards: Origins (The Age of Terra)
- Prequel: Storming the Norse Wind (At the Helm Volume 3)
- Book 1: Shore Leave (June 2018)
- Book 2: The Command (June 2018)

- Book 3: Infiltrator (July 2018)

The Sol Dissolution (The Age of Terra)
- Book 1: Venusian Uprising (2018)
- Book 2: Scattered Disk (2018)
- Book 3: Jovian Offensive (2019)
- Book 4: Fall of Terra (2019)

The Delta Team Chronicles (Expanded Orion War)
- A "Simple" Kidnapping (Pew! Pew! Volume 1)
- The Disknee World (Pew! Pew! Volume 2)
- It's Hard Being a Girl (Pew! Pew! Volume 4)
- A Fool's Gotta Feed (Pew! Pew! Volume 4)
- Rogue Planets and a Bored Kitty (Pew! Pew! Volume 5)

ABOUT THE AUTHORS

James S. Aaron lives in Oregon with too many chickens, a Corgi and two irascible cats. He kicked around the world in the U.S. Army for a while and always had a paperback in one of his cargo pockets.

Since he still has a day job, James spends his free time writing, hammering, soldering, gardening, biking, and listening to audiobooks during most the above.

You can sign up for his science fiction newsletter at http://jamesaaron.net/list

* * * * *

Michael Cooper likes to think of himself as a jack-of-all-trades (and hopes to become master of a few). When not writing, he can be found writing software, working in his shop at his latest carpentry project, or likely reading a book.

He shares his home with a precocious young girl, his wonderful wife (who also writes), two cats, a never-ending list of things he would like to build, and ideas...

Find out what's coming next at http://www.aeon14.com

Made in the USA
Lexington, KY
15 August 2018